D and Buried

A Jack Mowgley Murder Mystery

George East

*For Sally and Richard, who waved the
wand that made the spell that bound
me to a magic land*

Dead and Buried
Published by La Puce Publications

© George East 2019

This paperback edition 2019

ISBN: 978-1-908747-62-4

Kindle edition: 978-1-908747-63-1

website: www.george-east.net

Typesetting and design Francesca Brooks

Jack Mowgley books

DeadlyTide
Death Duty
Dead Money
Death *á la Carte*

Fact

More buried treasure has been unearthed in Bulgaria than anywhere else on earth. Using metal detectors to loot the sites of Roman forts and ancient burial grounds is something of a national pastime, and it is conservatively estimated that a billion US dollars' worth of artefacts are smuggled out of the country every year. Searching for buried treasure in the proximity of protected archaeological sites and monuments is strictly forbidden, but somewhat curiously I could find no official list of protected archaeological sites and monuments in Bulgaria.

Fiction

The author would like to point out that all the characters and most of the places portrayed in this book are completely fictitious and not meant to relate to real people, locations or events anywhere at any time. This applies in particular to references to the activities and members of the alleged Bulgarian mafia - which of course does not exist.

Allegation

"The data coming to the *State Agency for National Security indicates the existence of a structure acting parallel to the state authority, which has serious opportunities, funds, and positions for influencing the executive and legislative authorities, and the political and social life in the country. This structure is aspiring to create sustainable forms of parallel authority within the state institutions and services, whose functioning would be guaranteed regardless of the changing of the ruling majority in the government and the Parliament.

There is categorical data that representatives of business, state institutions, media, and organized criminal groups in certain cases undertake synchronized actions for achieving their common interests."

An extract from an astonishing claim in an alleged report by the State Agency for National Security. The report was stolen before it could be made public. Allegedly.

*SANS is an autonomous organisation working regularly with the Directorate for Combatting Organised Crime.

The story so far

Once upon a time, John 'Jack' Mowgley was a Special Branch Inspector, charged with investigating all significant criminal activities in and around Portsmouth's continental ferry port. Detecting and detaining drug and people smugglers, fleeing or visiting murderers, terrorists and other undesirables all fell within his remit. Some of his critics were of the opinion that he and his unconventional methods would also bear investigation.

Mowgley was aided and abetted in his investigations and in coping with an often cruel world by the much brighter and cannier Sergeant Catherine McCarthy. She was a fiercely protective colleague, sometimes co-conspirator and always loyal friend, and Mowgley was the only man on earth allowed to call her by her canteen sobriquet of 'Melons'.

After being rumbled by a fast-track female superior with no love for his unorthodox methods (or gender), Mowgley took early retirement and moved across the Channel to Normandy. There he planned to restore and sell the ruined manor house which was the only relic of his failed marriage. Melons stayed on duty at the ferry port but kept in close touch.

After hindering and helping the local police with their enquiries in a series of grisly murders, Mowgley found a job with a private detective agency, while Sergeant McCarthy found love with a senior French police officer. We left our flawed and now fractured hero on the quayside as he was struck down by a speeding car...

The boy was very frightened. He'd been so absorbed with his mission to discover and conquer exotic foreign lands that he hadn't noticed how far he and his craft had drifted from the shore. The bustle of noise from the beach had faded to nothing. All he could hear now was the slap of the wavelets against the inflatable crocodile and his own panicked breathing.

Then he saw something in the water and felt a huge surge of relief. He shouted, then started paddling towards the figure. As he came closer he could see it was floating face down, but for a moment clung to irrational hope. The snout of the plastic crocodile nudged the shoulder of the figure, but there was no reaction. With terror rising in his throat, the boy began to back-paddle frantically. As he did so, the head rolled over and the dead face turned towards him.

The motion of the waves was causing the head to move up and down and the pallid face was set in a rictus of smile. It seemed to the boy that the corpse was nodding and smiling in a grim and silent greeting.

1

'Does it hurt?'

'Only when I try to tap dance. I keep falling in the sink.'

'Har de har. Will you have a limp?'

'A limp what?'

Detective Sergeant Catherine McCarthy tired of trying to get any sense out of her former boss, spat a grape seed into her hand and watched wistfully as Mowgley drew deeply on his odiferous cigarette.

He made his usual pitiful attempt at blowing a smoke ring, and she thought fleetingly about taking the *Gauloises* and showing him how it should be done. It would have been some sort of an excuse to fill her lungs with deliciously toxic smoke, but she resisted and reached for another grape.

'So what happened to the roll-ups?' she asked.

Mowgley paused for a coughing fit, then replied. 'I am making a personal protest.'

'What against - the cost of English baccy?'

'No – this stupid idea to ban *Gitanes* and *Gauloises*.'

Former Special Branch Detective Inspector John 'Jack' Mowgley waved a copy of *France Soir*. 'It says here they're going to ban the classic brands for being too 'cool'.

His former colleague frowned. 'How do you know that's what it says?'

'The nice nurse told me.'

'Ah'. Melons raised an eyebrow: 'But "too cool"? How can a fag be cool?'

'I remember ones that were as cool as a mountain stream according to the adverts, but let that pass. You've obviously never seen a classic film noir or Jean-Paul Belmondo lighting up in bed after a bit of how's-your-father.'

'Jean-Paul who?'

'Never mind.' Mowgley maliciously directed a plume of smoke in her direction. 'How was Nice? And don't say 'nice'

'Well it was.'

'That's nice. So when are you going to make it official with your Frog friend and come over here to live?'

'Why the concern? Do you miss me'?

'Yep.' Like a very unlikely snake charmer, Mowgley let smoke dribble seductively from his lip and, leaning forward, swung the bulky cigarette in a hypnotic arc under her nose.

Less than a year before, Catherine McCarthy had been Mowgley's aide, bag-carrier and constant bailer-out at Portsmouth's continental ferry port. Then he had been forced to jump before he was pushed and very possibly imprisoned, and had crossed the Channel to start a new life in Cherbourg. He had found a job with a private detective agency, tasked with investigating the misdemeanours and excesses of British expatriates.

Sergeant McCarthy had taken on a new boss, but had continued to prop Mowgley up by using her contacts and official and unofficial resources at the ferry port. In the course of a recent cross-Channel investigation she had fallen for a tall, distinguished and widowed Colonel in the national Gendarmerie, and had just returned from a stolen and, she suspected, very expensive week in Nice. Such was her commitment to the new man in her life that she had stopped smoking and cut back considerably on her drinking. As her former boss had it, she was now in danger of becoming respectable.

She cast another wistful look at his cigarette, then asked: 'How are they treating you here now you're a regular?'

They were sitting in the sunlit courtyard of the Louis Pasteur hospital. Built at the behest of Napoleon in 1860, it had been Mowgley's place of residence for almost two weeks. He had arrived with a badly broken upper left thighbone after being involved in a hit-and-run incident which seemed very unlikely to have been an accident. It was the private investigator's third visit for treatment in the past twelve months, so the staff were becoming used to his funny little and often alien ways.

Mowgley dropped his cigarette butt into the saucer of his coffee cup and tried to make himself more comfortable in the wheelchair. 'It's okay here, I suppose. But nobody speaks English... or they pretend not to, and the food's pretty crap- '

'By that you mean the food is French?'

'I suppose so.'

She shook her head in mock-disbelief. 'In a French hospital? How disgusting...'

Mowgley nodded absent-mindedly and scratched pointlessly at the plaster cast encasing his left leg.

Melons watched as he lit up another cigarette 'So when do they reckon it'll come off?'

'What, the leg?'

'Yawn, yawn.'

'Tomorrow, the nice nurse says. Did you know they call it plaster of Paris because the gypsum came from Montmartre?'

Melons watched Mowgley take a provocatively long and blissful drag on his *Gauloises*. 'You don't say?'

He nodded. 'I just did. But putting a cast round a broken bone goes back as far as the Ancient Egyptians.'

She licked her lips then bit into a ragged finger nail. 'I know you specialise in collecting mostly useless information, but where did you get that from? Nice Nurse again?'

Mowgley tried not to look smug. 'That's right. Suzi. She's teaching me French and I'm helping with her English. After I get out, we're going to have regular sessions.' He paused and gave her a concerned look: 'Are you okay? it looks as if you're sweating.'

'Bollocks.'

Melons reached out and grabbed his cigarette and inhaled a greedy lungful. She sat back and held on to the smoke for several seconds, then let it trickle decadently from her parted lips.

'Blimey,' said Mowgley, 'I thought you'd given up to keep

your bloke happy.'

'I have, she said, 'I give up after every bloody fag...'

~

'This is nice.'

It was the best part of an hour, two *Gitanes* and half a bottle of Merlot later. The sunny hospital courtyard was a pleasant place to be, the mutual mood was good and they had talked of times, people and cases past. Like the best of the old days, they were completely at ease within themselves and with each other.

For many years, ferry port speculation had it that Sergeant McCarthy either had a bloke salted away in Portsmouth, was more interested in arresting men than shagging them... or perhaps even batted for the other side. It was, went the argument, beyond credulity that she would be having any form of sexual congress with Inspector Mowgley. But it was also generally accepted that nobody in their right mind would have the nerve to ask her for details of her sexual orientation or preferences.

As Mowgley knew, there had been the odd dalliance with unsuitable men, but nothing that had threatened their relationship. It was a singular one, to say the least. Definitely not based on sexual attraction, nor as with brother and sister. They were, he thought, mates, and just liked each other and working together. Mowgley found Melons as close to a female friend as he could imagine. She could never be a bloke, but, apart from the tits and the occasionally girly relapse, came very close. In fact, he would concede when in generous mood or in his cups, she was better at some stuff than a bloke. Unsurprisingly, he had never asked himself what she saw in him.

'Bugger.' He had tried to offer her another *Gauloises* in the approved film-noir style by tapping the end of the soft packet, but had overdone it and ejected and scattered the remaining cigarettes on the floor.

She knelt to gather them up, and he relished being looked after again. He guessed she might guess that he had spilled the cigarettes deliberately, but didn't care much.

'So,' he asked as she lit two and passed him one, 'Has your bloke made any progress on my close encounter now you're back from swanning around down south?'

Melons made a wry face. 'Sort of, but not a lot.'

The incident had occurred shortly after Mowgley had been instrumental in helping Colonel René Degas clear up a major people-smuggling operation. Also cleared up in the process had been several murders, and a corrupt senior officer had been convicted. An Albanian mafia gang had been broken, and it had transpired that a dissident offshoot of the IRA had been getting in on the action. This meant that, if the incident on the quayside had been a determined attempt on Mowgley's life, there were a number of candidates.

'Anything new on the car?' he asked, looking as if in explanation at his plastered leg. 'Any luck with the Likely Lads?'

Melons shook her head. The car had hit Mowgley in the early hours and the only witnesses had been unreliable in their recollections. There were two rough sleepers finishing off a bottle who claimed to have seen the incident from their vantage point under an upturned dinghy on the quayside. One said Mowgley had been struck down by a white car driven by a black man. The other said the car was black and the driver white. When they heard there was no reward for information given, they both agreed they may have been somewhere else at the time.

The Likely Lads were two British youths on a booze cruise who'd missed their boat and been on a bar crawl around the docks area. Questioned immediately after the incident, they agreed they had seen the big man hit by a car (it had been they who raised the alarm), but disagreed on the gender of the driver. One said he thought a woman was in the passenger seat, but the other said his mate had forgotten they had the steering wheel on the wrong side in France and it was the woman who was driving. Melons had pulled strings and had a friend in the north speak to the lads at their Manchester homes a week later, but their memories were even foggier. The car had been found no more than a mile from the scene, but the only prints found were those of the owner, a schoolteacher who had reported his Renault missing earlier that evening. It was an ongoing enquiry, but one that appeared to be going

15

nowhere.

Mowgley shrugged philosophically. 'So, it's gone into your bloke's forever pending tray then?'

'No,' said Melons defensively. 'it's still live, but there's not a lot to go on. Perhaps,' she said brightly, 'whoever it was will have another go and we'll get some solid evidence.'

'Cheers,' said Mowgley. 'Any other news?'

Catherine McCarthy placed her glass carefully on the flagstone-slabbed floor and balanced her cigarette on the arm of her chair before reaching into her unfashionably voluminous handbag. From it she produced a phone and began punching buttons.

'Charming,' said Mowgley tetchily, 'can't you make your calls later? Where's your notepad?'

'This is my notepad, dummkopf. Things have moved on a bit since you were sucking your pencil and making up stuff to write down and use later in court.'

There was further button-punching, then: 'Do you want the bad news or the bad news first?

Mowgley frowned. 'Isn't there any good news then?'

Melons reached for her cigarette. 'Actually, there is; I was just teasing.'

Mowgley brightened. 'My ex-wife has snuffed it?'

'Not that good, but close. Looks like you've maybe got a buyer for your expensive, crumbling wreck.'

'Which one - the ex-wife or the house?'

'The house.'

'Blimey.'

It was a decade since Mowgley had been blackmailed by his wife into buying a rambling and near-ruined manor-house in Normandy. She had been so taken with the idea of being able to tell people who would never see it about her eight-bedroom château in France that she had threatened to leave him if he did not buy it for her. He had missed the opportunity but it had not turned out all bad as she had shortly afterwards run off with the man who had sold the property to them. After a messy divorce she had taken the family home in Portsmouth, and Mowgley had been left with the French ruin and the hefty mortgage on it. On leaving his post at Portsmouth ferry port he had moved over to the Cherbourg peninsula to work on making *La Cour* sellable while learning the ropes at being a private detective.

Mowgley re-filled his glass and topped Melons up. 'That's the best news I've heard since the cow said she was leaving me. When do I get the money?'

'Hang on,' Melons raised a cautioning finger, 'there's many a slip twixt offer and completion on any property - especially in France.'

'But me no buts,' replied Mowgley, savouring the aroma of the wine, 'How much has he, she or they offered, and is the offerer blind or just stupid?'

Melons studied her phone for a moment, then said: 'It's a bit complicated. He's an author and a poor one, he claims. He's a Brit and thinks *La Cour* would make an ideal venue for residential writing courses. The punters will pay to spend a fortnight in the glorious Normandy countryside while learning how to write a best-seller.'

Mowgley frowned. 'But if he's a poor writer in either or both senses of the word, how can he teach people to write best-sellers? And he'd have to spend a fortune to make *La Cour* habitable.'

'Ahah,' said his friend, 'according to the latest agent trying to flog your wreck, he has a cunning plan.'

'Do tell.'

'The idea is that, before the writing school is launched, he'll run some residential restoration courses.'

'Some whatters?'

'Courses for Brits who want to buy a place in Normandy and do it up. It's actually quite a good idea in theory. The students spend their mornings learning from local tradesmen how to plaster walls and lay bricks and plumb pipes in, then try their new skills out on the property in the afternoons. Your potential buyer reckons that after a few months the place will be at least habitable, and the customers will have paid to do it up'

'I see' said Mowgley, who clearly didn't. 'And who's going to pay the local tradesmen? And will they be happy to do themselves out of potential jobs?'

'That's the really cunning bit. Your buyer will tell the tradesmen that the Brits will be make such a mess of doing up their places that they'll have to call the professionals in. And one of the lecturers on the course will be an estate agent who will make sure the punters buy somewhere local.'

'I'm impressed, I think. So what's the catch?'

Melons reached out for the near-empty bottle. 'The buyer will pay the asking price...but wants you to lend him the deposit.'

'Ah. Sounds a bit like my wife.' Mowgley grabbed the bottle and emptied it into his glass. 'Any other news?'

Melons consulted her phone again, then said: 'Your landlady said she'd like some rent, and your boss wants to know when you can come back to work. I told him you'd be released in a week or so and I told Yvette that- '

She broke off, dropped and stubbed out her cigarette, then waved her hand in front of her mouth as if to try and dispel the smoke and smell. The guilty fanning action turned into a wave, and Mowgley shifted awkwardly in his wheel chair to look over his shoulder. Along the corridor leading to the courtyard from the wards strode a tall, distinguished-looking figure.

Colonel René Degas was carrying a man-bag in one hand, and a bottle in the other. As he pushed open the glazed door. Catherine McCarthy rose, kicked the cigarette butts at her feet towards where Mowgley was sitting, then moved to embrace her lover.

'Is that a bottle of good plonk I see before me?' asked Mowgley.

Degas gave a mock shudder. 'It is a Malbec from Cahors. Unpretentious as your wine 'experts' would say, but full of flavour and perfect for the colder weather. I heard you were mending yourself well, so brought it to mark the occasion.' He frowned slightly as he saw the empty bottle beside Mowgley's chair. 'But I see you have started without me. I will fetch another glass.'

As he turned to leave, he paused and looked at the cigarette butts littering the floor, then at his lover. 'I will also bring an ashtray. There is just one condition.'

'Don't worry,' said Mowgley, 'I know you're trying to quit. We - I - won't blow the smoke in your direction.'

'On the contrary,' said Colonel Degas, 'I was going to ask you to save one for me...'

~

Mowgley was alone again. It had been increasingly so since he had crossed the Channel and begun his new life.

The move had lost him his colleagues at the ferry port and all the people he knew from the regulars at the Ship Leopard to the staff and owners of at least four of the city's Bangladeshi restaurants. It was true that he could not claim them as friends and accepted that he was not liked by or did not like a good percentage of them. But like the local landmarks, smell and feel of the city and even the ubiquitous graffiti and dogshit on the pavements, they were all reassuringly familiar symbols of his belongingness. Here in Cherbourg there was at least as much dog shit on the pavements though the graffiti seemed markedly more artistic, but even just across the Channel he was indisputably in a very foreign land. After close to a year living and working in Cherbourg, he was getting to know the town and some of its people and even making tentative friendships, but he still felt alone and lonely most of the time. He spoke to Melons frequently and saw her at least once a month, but the sight of her leaving arm-in-arm with her lover reminded him she was no longer his in any sense of the word.

Mowgley was not given to self-pity, and it was a relief when his thoughts were interrupted by the tinny tones of 'Ring of Fire' issuing from beneath the blanket across his knees. He fumbled for his phone and, after two attempts, pressed the right button.

It was his former aide calling.

'Missing me already?' he asked.

'Of course - you've got the fags and booze. The thing is I just got a call from the ferry port office.'

'I'm all ears'

'I have to say they do stick out a bit since you've lost a bit of weight.'

'That's not being able to get a decent pasty or mutton vindaloo round here. But pray continue. How is the Fun Factory?'

'Like it always is. Fran said a lady was trying to get in touch with you and didn't know you'd left us. She left her number so I gave her a ring.'

Mowgley frowned as he scratched at the plaster cast. 'And?'

'And she said she was the wife of an old friend of yours.'

Mowgley frowned. 'Well, that narrows it down considerable.

Whose wife did she say she was?'

'Denny Cullan?'

She waited for a response, then said: 'Hello, are you still there?'

Mowgley ended the silence. 'Yeah.'

'So who was or is he? Someone from your dark past?'

Another silence, then: 'You could say that. I haven't seen or heard from him - or Jen - for yonks.'

'Yonks?'

'Catch up Sergeant. It means a long time, or used to when people spoke proper.'

'Of course, Stupid of me. So where do you know Mr Cullan from?'

We worked together for a while at Cannon Row SB many years ago. He was a Ghurkha.'

'Eh? I didn't know there were any in Special Branch, or anywhere else in the Met.'

'No, a Ghurkha was a copper who doesn't take any prisoners. Took a lot of bung, though, our Den. To his victims and his mates, he was always Dirty Den. Did Jen say what she wanted?'

'No but she sounded a bit…funny.'

'What, you mean? Was she a bit pissed? She liked a drink. And who could blame her when you think about who she was married to. Or should that be "to whom?"'

'Either would do, I reckon. But she sounded more panicky then pissed.'

'What was the problem?'

'Her husband.'

Mowgley frowned at the phone, 'Still? I thought he buggered off years ago. Why is he giving her grief?'

'She said he's gone missing.'

'Sounds like Den. He was always going walkabout when they were married. And she should care.'

'No, she says he's gone proper missing and she's got a very bad feeling about it.'

'Oh. Didn't you tell her I was out of the game and living over here?'

'Yep. But she said she wanted to talk to you.'

Mowgley's frown deepened. 'I don't know what she thinks I can do.'

'Well, you could give her a call. I've got the number.'

'Okay. Did she say if she's still in Kent? I could jump on the ferry.'

'Blimey, you're keen. Sounds like you could have been more than friends. I hope it was after her husband left.'

'I haven't see Jen for almost as many years as I haven't seen Den. And don't be jealous. You know my heart belongs to you.'

'Yeah right. Anyway, you'd have to jump on a plane if you want to see her in the flesh.'

'Why?'

'She's in Bulgaria.'

Down these mean streets a man must go who is not himself mean, who is neither tarnished nor afraid. He is the hero; he is everything.

He must be a complete man and a common man and yet an unusual man.

He must be, to use a rather weathered phrase, a man of honour—by instinct, by inevitability, without thought of it, and certainly without saying it.

He must be the best man in his world and a good enough man for any world.

He will take no man's money dishonestly and no man's insolence without a due and dispassionate revenge.

He is a lonely man and his pride is that you will treat him as a proud man or be very sorry you ever saw him.

The story is this man's adventure in search of a hidden truth, and it would be no adventure if it did not happen to a man fit for adventure.

If there were enough like him, the world would be a very safe place to live in, without becoming too dull to be worth living in.

Author Raymond Chandler on the qualities needed for the perfect fictional private investigator,

2

It should have been no more than a ten-minute stroll from the Louis Pasteur hospital to his office, but it took Mowgley a cautious hour.

He was hindered rather than helped by the walking stick presented to him by nice nurse Suzi, and found it necessary to stop for a rest at two bars on route. Crossing the road was the biggest challenge, as, being France, the signs of his disability seemed to goad rather than spark compassion in drivers.

He found Mimi sitting at his desk, holding and looking at a narrow-edged black frame. It held an extract from an essay by the creator of fictional private investigator Philip Marlowe, who was one of Mowgley's few heroes. The frame and its contents had been presented to Mowgley by Melons at his third and almost final farewell party at the Ship Leopard.

Mimi looked him up and down, then nodded at the frame. 'Did your friends give you this because they think you are like Philip Marlowe?'

'No. I think they gave it to me because they think I think I would like to be like Philip Marlowe.'

'And would you?'

'What man wouldn't?'

She gave a very French shrug as if to say that how men sometimes chose to think and act was beyond her. 'So you seek the hidden truth?'

'When it's not too well hidden. The older I get the more I wonder if there is such a thing.'

She looked at him for a moment to see if he was joking, then leaned forward and put the frame back on the desk. 'I think you may be becoming a little French.'

He tried not to look too obviously at the swell of her breasts above the halter neckline of her dress, then said: 'I'm doing my best.'

She laughed and stood up, smoothing the dress over her hips. 'I see you are back on your feet.'

Mowgley lifted the stick and balanced on his good leg: 'Well, more or less.'

'Does this mean you are coming back to work?'

'As you often observe Mimi, if I don't work, I don't get paid.'

She nodded. 'This is a truth for sure. And how is your French? I hear that you have been getting…lessons…from one of the nurses.'

'It's sort of coming on.'

'Ah bon. Vous voulez un café?'

'Vous etre tres gentile, Madame. Or may I say *'tu'*?

Mimi gave a wide-lipped smile. *'Mais oui. Je pense que ça irait bien'.*

Not knowing exactly what she'd said but feeling rather pleased with himself, Mowgley hung his walking stick on the side of the desk and eased himself into his chair. As it was fitted with castors this was never easy, and made more difficult because of his heavily-strapped thigh.

Sighing with relief as the chair took his weight, he watched Mimi sway her way to the store room and wondered how she had put all that effort into a short walk even though she obviously had not the slightest carnal interest in him.

It had not escaped Mowgley that as well as being very French, Mimi was intelligent, witty, sophisticated and extremely beautiful. She also appeared to have a natural instinct for making the most of her looks and body. Despite what most British women and some British men seemed to believe, he had observed that this apparently instinctive ability was not installed in every French woman. A visit to the checkout queue or clothing department of any provincial supermarket proved that.

Mowgley being on a paid-by-results contract, Mimi was the sole official employee of the Cherbourg branch of *Services d'Enquêtes Privés* Cornec. He suspected she might also be a sleeping partner of the boss. The young but thriving company was owned by Yannick Cornec, a tough Breton and former colleague of René Degas.

With an eye to expansion, Cornec had set up the new Cherbourg branch and invited Mowgley to become an associate. His specialty would be cases involving expatriate Britons. Given the history and activities of many expats it was a potentially fruitful market, and Mowgley's past and present connections made him a valuable asset.

Cristobel/Mimi arrived with his mug of instant coffee, carrying it disapprovingly away from her body and as gingerly as if it were an improvised explosive device. He nodded his thanks, took a swig, then regarded the collection of post-it notes, envelopes and official-looking documents she had also laid on his desk. He thought about making a start on them for at least several nano-seconds, then searched for his packet of *Gauloises*. In the process he found and pulled out a crumpled envelope.

Mowgley looked at it then handed it to Mimi and assumed the pretty-please-little-boy-lost face he had perfected by practicing on Melons: 'Could you phone this number for me?'

She frowned. 'I can, but are you in pain?'

'Only a bit, why?'

'Your face is all screwed up.'

'I'm okay,' he said mock-bravely, watching in appreciation as she sashayed across the office to her desk.

Picking up the phone, she looked at the scrap of paper then back up at him. 'It is an English mobile number, yes?'

He nodded, 'Yes, but she might be ...elsewhere.'

'Elsewhere? And where might 'elsewhere' be?'

'Erm, Bulgaria.'

'Bulgaria?'

'That's it. Is that a problem?'

Mimi arched an elegant eyebrow 'Not for me. But I think it may be for the people who have to live there...

~

A child of a different era, Mowgley still found himself mildly surprised at how easy it was to talk to people in distant lands and how clear and close they usually sounded.

After talking with his former friend and colleague's ex-wife he had needed to think about how he could and should respond. He liked to think he thought best with a drink to hand.

Consequently, he was sitting at a table on the pavement outside the bar next door to his office. The Bon Parle was also his home, so a true local. It was strange, he thought, how he'd always fancied the idea of living above a pub but had never imagined it would be in a foreign land.

The unintentionally retro bell at the top of the outer door rattled, and Mowgley's landlady in both senses of the word bustled out with a laden tray. She was so far one of the only two women in his life on this side of the Channel. They were, as it happened, very different.

Unlike Mimi, Madame Yvette was not in the least fashion-conscious, appeared to be almost as wide as she was tall and to roll rather than walk. Though a veteran and usually victim of a thousand hard-luck stories pitched across the zinc counter of her dockside bar, she'd somehow maintained her kind heart and had taken to Mowgley from the moment they met. He had also fallen for her. She spoke no more than a few words of English and his French was still infantile, but they understood each other perfectly.

Yvette smiled, blew him an extravagant air-kiss and placed the contents of the tray on his table. On it and in the French way there was a part-filled beer glass with the bottle beside it. Alongside was a branded ashtray, a packet of *Gauloises*, a disposable lighter and a small plastic saucer with a sliver of paper clipped to it. Rather than a bill for what was on the tray, Mowgley knew it would be what his landlady liked to call his *fiche d'évaluation*, or scorecard. It would be a hand-written update of his ongoing bar bill, and possibly the amount of back rent due. Without looking at the slip, he took out his wallet, removed a credit card and laid it on the saucer. His host and landlady smiled and repeated the air-kiss.

He did not need to follow her in to the bar as she was privy to the PIN number. She would take out a suitable amount, and return the card with the next round. This way there were no official receipts or bills or paperwork to bother with. The system involved more than a degree of trust on his part, but Mowgley quite enjoyed constructing what other people might call eccentric, risky or even stupid arrangements with who he thought of as suitable people.

With practiced ease he poured the rest of the beer into the glass till it threatened to spill over the rim, then opened the packet, extracted and lit a cigarette and filled his lungs. Then he sat back, exhaled lingeringly, sipped the top off his beer and surveyed the street-scene while he practiced dangling the plumptious *Gauloises* from his bottom lip.

Across the road a bored policeman was talking to a man sitting in a doorway in what looked like a puddle of his own making. Possibly it might have belonged to the spectacularly scabious old dog beside him.

A taxi pulled up and blocked Mowgley's line of view as the driver got out, leaving the door carelessly open as he hurried into the *tabac*. The dog barked as what must be the few surviving classic *Mobylette* mopeds buzzed by, and the aroma of what even Mowgley recognised as good cooking wafted across the street from the café specialising in workmen's lunches.

He took another pull on his beer and cigarette, stuck the latter back on his lower lip and smiled contentedly. It was all very different from a lunchtime visit to the Ship Leopard, but he was beginning to appreciate rather than resent the differences.

Mowgley was leaning down to retrieve the *Gauloises* from the pavement and place it more securely between his lips as a very old lady hobbled by. She was leaning on a walking frame and was accompanied by a middle-aged woman. The old lady looked resigned, and the younger one looked as if she was trying not to look as if she would rather be elsewhere. Perhaps, he thought, she was the daughter and loved the old lady and was filled with compassion and concern about what was to come. Or perhaps she wished the old lady would hurry up and die. Perhaps it would be a bit of each, which would guarantee a mixture of guilt and relief when the end came. As they passed, the old lady regarded him with dull, uninterested eyes; the younger woman looked faintly embarrassed, as if she suspected he knew what she was thinking.

Mowgley winced as he removed the cigarette and a sliver of skin from his lower lip and thought about the little epiphany. There would be specific and general truths about the couple and their relationship, but he could have read the situation completely askew. They could be unrelated and the younger woman a paid carer or a friend of the family or even a stranger who had offered help. Even with such an everyday and apparently obvious tableau, he could never know the truth about their situation and relationship. Possibly, he thought, neither would they.

He sighed and turned the glass around on the soggy beermat as he pondered on his search for inarguable truth, if there was such a thing. More than ever he found himself wondering about the existence of anything more than simple, certifiable facts. On show or not, the sun rose every morning. What people said and did and why they did what they did was another matter. It didn't help that most people would not admit - even to themselves - why they did what they did. He sighed lugubriously and returned his attention to the cigarette-drooping challenge. Perhaps, his growing absorption with the complexity of life was a result of his long years as a police officer or just be a sign of his age. Or, as Mimi had said, perhaps it could be an indication of his creeping Gallicization. If so, he was not sure if that would be a good or bad thing.

A shadow fell across the table. It was not a long one, but wide. He looked up and reflected that at least the shadow's owner was extremely uncomplicated. Generally, he had found that what you saw was what you got with Yann Cornec.

Though below average height even for a Breton, Cornec was an imposing figure and carried himself with the sort of assurance that would put most people off picking a quarrel or fight with him. In that they would be wise. Like Madame Yvette, he appeared to be almost as wide as he was tall, but his body was clearly an amalgam of very solid muscle, flesh and bone. His head looked small compared with the wide, sloping shoulders, and, like his face was completely hairless. This was in contrast to the rest of the visible bits of his body, and he had the hairiest knuckles Mowgley had ever seen on a human; and indeed, on some gorillas. Like a small gorilla, Cornec had small ears and wore them close to the sides of his head, while his nose had clearly been the focus of some malicious attention across the years. His face was unwrinkled except for the creases running from the corners of his small, bright eyes, and a thin scar ran from the left one to the corner of his full and oddly sensual lips. He looked like a man who was sure of what he wanted, and would disapprove strongly of any obstacles placed in his path.

Mowgley knew from René Degas that Yann Cornec had been an officer in the special investigative division of the national Gendarmerie. His work, Degas had also said, meant that Lieutenant Cornec made more enemies than friends in the upper echelons. Like Mowgley, he had been made an early retirement offer he could not sensibly refuse.

After setting up as a private investigator, Cornec had called in favours and used contacts and almost certainly greased the right palms. The Cherbourg branch of his company had yet to prove its worth, but the employment of Mowgley was integral to his game plan. Not only would a Special Branch officer at a continental ferry port particularly suited to the dealing with cases involving expatriate Britons, he would have much knowledge of and many contacts within the British law enforcement and administering network.

Mowgley's new boss took a seat, unzipping his expensive leather bomber jacket and hitching up the legs of his designer jeans. Mowgley marvelled to see that they had been ironed to produce the sharpest of creases.

Before Cornec was settled, Madame Yvette appeared and placed a bottle of beer and a glass on the table and a fresh bottle at Mowgley's elbow. Her new customer, however, was not treated to an air-kiss, wink or any form of acknowledgement. After so many years of a life behind bars, Madame Yvette was a woman of swift and constant judgement.

'It's not magic,' Cornec said, nodding at his beer bottles as their host retreated, 'Mimi phoned and said I was on my way...'

'Ah,' said Mowgley, 'Cheers, then.'

They drank, then Cornec reached for the cigarette packet. He took one without asking, lit up and then looked at the stick leaning against Mowgley's chair. 'You were,' he observed, 'in hospital a long time for a broken leg.'

Mowgley shrugged. 'I hit my head when I went down. They were keeping me under observation as they thought I was acting a bit funny.'

'You were telling jokes all the time?'

'No, I meant funny as in peculiar.'

Cornec gave a glimmer of a smile. 'I know. But then they found out that peculiar was normal for you?'

Mowgley accepted the dig. 'I reckon.'

They smoked in silence for a moment, then Cornec said: 'So when will you return to work? There are some things waiting.'

Another shrug of unconcern from Mowgley. 'Probably at the start of next week, but I need to do something first.'

Cornec nodded. 'Ah yes, Bulgaria. To see a lady.'

Mowgley didn't bother to ask how Cornec knew of his plans, but felt irrationally irritated at the way he had said 'lady.'

'Yes,' he said levelly, 'that's it.'

'And is she worth the trouble?'

'I think so. She's the wife - or was the wife - of a guy I used to work with.'

Cornec scratched his chin and then regarded his immaculately-kept fingernails. 'So you're fucking her?'

Mowgley looked levelly at his employer. 'Not at the moment, no.'

Cornec persisted: 'But you were? Before or after she became an ex-wife?'

By now, Mowgley would normally have made clear his dislike of the line of questioning, but supressed his natural instinct for two reasons. One was because the man on the other side of the table was his employer; the other because Mowgley would probably come off worst in any physical altercation as well as lose his job. He took his irritation out on the stub of his cigarette and swallowed a mouthful of beer. 'I'm going because she was married to an old friend who's gone missing.'

Cornec tilted his head in a 'so what' gesture? 'Why should she care? And why would she want to go to Bulgaria to see her ex?'

'She takes their teenage son to see his father a couple of times a year. He works there and never comes back to the UK.'

'So what's an old policeman doing in a shithole country like Bulgaria? No pension?

'He's a dealer.'

'In what? Tractors or drugs?'

Mowgley lit another cigarette and kept his voice level. 'Old gold mostly, I think she said. There's a lot of it about in Bulgaria.'

If Cornec had eyebrows they would have risen in mild interest. 'Ah. So how does Madame Jenny think you can help?'

Mowgley did not react but realised how closely Mimi must have been listening to the phone call.

'I don't know and nor does she. She sounded very upset and said she didn't know what to do. Den - her husband - and I were pretty close at one time. She's alone with her teenage son.'

'Did she ask you to go over and help her?'

'No. She said she had called because she just wanted to talk.'

Cornec smiled cynically and shook his hairless head. 'But you are riding to her rescue? Like a knight in shining armour?'

Mowgley took a deep breath, shifted in his seat, placed his cigarette carefully in the ashtray and said tightly: 'No. I'm going because she and her son are all alone in a fucking foreign country and his father's disappeared.'

Cornec held up his hands. 'Okay, okay, it's just a *plaisanterie*. I'm only joking.' He swivelled in his chair and rapped on the window, holding up two fingers.

Shortly afterwards the doorbell rattled and Madame Yvette appeared with two more beers. Cornec waited until she had gone then came as close to smiling as he probably could. 'As long as you're back in a few days,' he said, 'it's fine with me. Perhaps a change of scenery and some of that mountain air will do you good and put you in a better mood.'

3

As Mimi had discovered, anyone wishing to visit Bulgaria from the Cherbourg peninsula would have neither a cheap or easy passage.

The tariff for a return flight from Rennes or more distant Nantes averaged around a thousand euros. Caen offered a closer airport and direct flights, but at nearly twice the price. Bizarre as it might seem, the much cheaper option was to take a ferry to Portsmouth, then a train to Gatwick airport and from there to Bulgaria.

It was, she observed somewhat sniffily, common knowledge that flights from Britain could be almost laughably cheap, but French people understood that, in life, you generally get what you pay for. If he was prepared to spend nearly five hours in the company of the sort of people who overflowed their seats like melting candles, breathed through their mouths, ate disgusting things all the way, got drunk on board and thought tattoos were sexy, the cost would understandably be a much cheaper alternative to making the journey in comfort and peace with Air France.

There was, though, another option. Because they were on the right side of the English Channel he could get in a car and drive to the west coast resort of Varna. The drawback was that the journey would involve a distance of 2,700 kilometres and would take more than a day and a night non-stop even if he drove like a Frenchman and did not take a break in any of the eight countries through which he would pass. On the plus side he would avoid all the waiting at airports and mixing with all those people and could save money by sleeping in his car. Another bonus was that he would be able to bring back enough cheap tobacco and wine to last him for months. Having said that and given what she had seen of his driving skills and the condition of his ancient Citroën, he might well not make it to his destination or perhaps even out of France.

Whichever option and route he chose, Mimi concluded, he would have room for a small but rather expensive bottle of rose oil for her. It was, along with honey and yoghurt, she said, one of the few good things to come out of Bulgaria.

~

The plane was full and as noisy, messy and unsightly as Mimi had predicted.

After comparing costs and contemplating the marathon car journey, Mowgley had opted for the round-about flight option. He was not mean, as he explained to Mimi, just unused to paying for any form of travel with his own money. When you'd spent a working life claiming expenses for every journey, it came hard having to settle the bills yourself.

But it had been some consolation that he had managed to trim the costs further. As he had hoped, Melons had found an excuse to deliver him to Luton airport in good time for the evening flight. On the way she confessed she was meeting her French lover in London later that evening to take in a show and spend the night at a boutique hotel in Bayswater. He, or rather the French government would be footing the bill as René Degas would be attending a special conference on co-operation between Euro-zone and British law enforcement agencies after Brexit.

This news only served to make Mowgley more resentful of paying his own way, but, he had to admit, the flight was almost embarrassingly cheap. There was of course an inevitable price to pay for the cheapness.

Some hours after saying goodbye to Melons he had found himself entombed in the narrow fuselage of a plane that seemed much too overloaded to take off. Every seat was filled to overflowing and the overhead lockers were crammed with bags, rucksacks, clothing and even sustenance to see the travellers through the journey.

Looking around, it was clear that some passengers should have paid for two seats and, as Mimi had predicted, they were the sort of people who would be taking a budget flight to a very budget country. The travellers were mostly British and either holidaymakers or those curious to know how a house in Bulgaria could cost less than a second-hand car in Britain.

There was also a number of mainly young Bulgarians intent on visiting their families and friends while reminding themselves of what they were not missing at home. They were easily identifiable by their lack of tattoos and their general preference to eating with their mouths closed.

Mowgley flinched as small feet hammered on the back of his seat, groaned inwardly and tried not to look across the aisle at a woman picking her nose while she demolished a jumbo-sized chocolate bar. He did not think of himself as a snob, but did not relish five hours in the company of people with whom he would rather not share a lift.

Another downside was his fear of flying.

To be fair, it was not the time in the air that worried him, but the take-off and landing stages. The official term was aviophobia, which curiously also referred to a dread of fresh air. He could see that a sudden influx of fresh air on a plane in flight could be disconcerting, but objected to the term 'phobia'. According to most dictionaries, a phobia was an irrational fear. As there could be only one result of an aeroplane dropping unintentionally from the sky, he could not see how there was anything at all irrational in coming close to shitting oneself at the most dangerous moments of the journey.

In the absence of Melons he had held his own hand and tried not to groan too loudly, and stopped panting and sweating only when the plane had struggled into the air. Now all he had to do was survive the company and the landing.

Knowing the even more breath-taking price of in-flight food and drinks, he had reluctantly paid the price for a fancily wrapped egg and bacon sandwich and small bottle of water from a W H Smith outlet in the holding area. His cabin luggage – a smart and very expensive mini-suitcase on wheels that Mimi had bought for him, also contained his toilet bag, a couple of clean shirts and a change of underwear and socks. He had no intention of staying In Bulgaria for more than a day or two, but Mimi had refused to let him leave without them. Distributed about the ancient tweed jacket were two Curly-Wurly chocolate bars, his notepad, phone, cigarettes and a paperback copy of The Big Sleep. He had been told it would be warm on the Black Sea, but the coat had many pockets and there was no weight limit or restriction on how many layers of clothing passengers chose to wear.

~

An hour into the flight, and Mowgley had learned more about Bulgaria than he had accumulated in the previous half century. He had picked up a guide book at the airport, and now reckoned he would be able to hold his own in any pub quiz about one of the most recent additions to the European Union.

Primarily he had learned that Bulgaria had a lot of history, and most of it not at all happy. Having recovered from five hundred years of Turkish occupation, Bulgaria had opted to join the wrong side in both World Wars. Worse, those in charge had welcomed Communism in 1948 and watched insouciantly as the economy disintegrated.

On the face of it, joining the EU in 2007 had been a no-brainer, but as with Communism it seemed nobody in charge had considered the law of unintended consequences. On the upside was the billions of Euros in subsidies and grants, but most of it went into the wrong pockets. The real disaster came with millions of young people leaving home to live a much better life elsewhere in the Union. As a result, Bulgaria had the most rapidly declining population in Europe. If things carried on as they were, it would have the most rapidly declining population in the world.

~

Two hours on and the plane was flying over a seemingly endless chain of white-capped mountains. Probably the Alps, Mowgley thought, but then all mountains had a certain similarity when viewed from above.

The aircraft seemed to be behaving itself, but Mowgley was becoming increasingly irritated with what was happening inside it. It wasn't just the lusty Bulgarian babe-in-arms who had been sick on his shoulder, nor the enormous woman on the other side who kept offering him sweets and crisps. Even the members of the hen party dressed as cowgirls were causing no trouble. They had drunk too much too soon and were now sleeping the journey away.

The focus of Mowgley's growing annoyance was a man sitting in line with him across the aisle. He was tall and bulky in a flabby way, with short hair and most of his exposed flesh taken up by badly-done tattoos. The man had small, mean eyes, a snout-like nose and prominent ears, the lobes of which bore star-shaped tattoos. He could have been anywhere between thirty and forty, and looked like trouble. He was with another, shorter man of around the same age but with less of a tattoo fetish. From long experience Mowgley knew that the taller man would be the instigator of any problems, and that he would almost certainly cause some.

The pair had obviously been drinking before getting on the plane, and the cabin crew had made the mistake of serving them more. Rather than placating them, it had made Snouty more determined to enjoy himself by spoiling the journey for everyone else. It had started with obscene soccer chants and propositions to the prettier women passengers and the two stewardesses, then threats to the obviously terrified steward. Most of the passengers pretended not to notice, but there was apprehension and even fear on the faces of those nearest to the pair. The flight was barely half way to its destination, and all the crew and passengers could do was hope the lout would, like the members of the hen party, fall asleep. For now, the lack of response was provoking increasingly aggressive behaviour. If the cabin crew had followed official procedure, Snouty would have already been given a pre-written printed warning from the captain. Known as a red card by on-board staff, it would say that unless the bad behaviour ceased the plane would be diverted to the nearest airport and the perpetrator/s dumped there. They would also be billed for the cost of the diversion, which could run into tens of thousands of pounds. The problem with red cards was that they were an attempt to reason with drunk and very unreasonable people, so could actually inflame the situation.

Twenty years before, Mowgley would have already done something about the situation. Now he had an injured leg and was too old to get involved for the fun of it.

Things started to get really nasty when Snouty called for more beer and got no response. After the third bellow, he left his seat and lurched to the front of the plane. The small and slight steward appeared from the galley and tried to reason with him, but was contemptuously pushed back through the curtain. The big man then started hammering on the door to the flight deck, when a woman screamed and babies and small children started to cry. Getting no answer from the flight crew, the big man pushed his way into the galley and reappeared holding up two bottles as if they were trophies. Stumbling back along the aisle, he threw one to his mate, then saw Mowgley looking at him. He smiled in anticipation, got a grip on the back of a seat and bent down so their faces were level.

'What's up, you old cunt?' he asked, 'do you fucking want some?'

Mowgley said nothing and looked rigidly ahead as the man considered his options. Eventually he grunted in contempt, looked round for other possible confrontation, said 'fucking wanker,' then straightened up, unzipped his jean fly and made his stumbling way towards the back of the plane.

Mowgley remained looking ahead but was aware of the reaction of the women on either side of him. The young mother held her baby tighter and looked at Mowgley with a mixture of sympathy and concern for herself and her child. The sweets lady seemed disappointed, as if she had expected some other reaction.

The former Special Branch officer stayed where he was for a long moment, then sighed, unbuckled his seat belt and stood up. Leaving his walking stick behind he got up and limped toward the rear of the plane. Looking over his shoulder, he saw the sweets lady watching and the white face of the male steward peering out from the galley. Everyone else was making a point of minding their own business. Pushing through the curtained-off partition, Mowgley rapped briskly on the toilet door.

There was no response so he knocked again. This time he was given an invitation to fuck himself. Saying nothing, he knocked again, and then again, more urgently. As planned, his persistence was rewarded. He stepped back a pace and braced himself against the partition as, following a fumbling sound, the door was yanked open. Before it opened enough to reveal the occupant, Mowgley placed the sole of his right shoe on the approximate centre of the door and pushed it as quickly and as hard as he could. He had learned at the start of his career that, despite what happened on TV and in films, it was virtually impossible to shoulder-charge or kick the most modest of doors down; in this case the objective was to use it as a weapon.

There was a satisfyingly meaty thud and a muffled shout as the door made solid contact then swung back towards him. This time Mowgley kicked it, and was rewarded with the sound of further contact. Stepping forward, he squeezed into the restricted space, one hand already balled into a fist.

He found Snouty straddled over the toilet, his back against the partition. He appeared semi-conscious, and a trickle of blood ran from his brow to the top of his nose.

Deciding further action would not be necessary, Mowgley put his hand round the man's throat and lowered him on to the toilet seat. There was no resistance.

Backing out of the cubicle, Mowgley paused to rub his right thigh and smiled a dark smile. Then he said pleasantly 'So who's the old cunt, now, mater?'

Arriving at the galley Mowgley smiled blandly at the fraught-looking stewardess and said 'Just thought you should know someone has fallen asleep in the toilet at the back, Miss.'

4

Given their long history and after looking at a map of the Balkan peninsula, Mowgley could see that Bulgarians were entitled to feel a little defensive.

Like a wagon train under attack, the Republic was encircled by five other countries with the only relief a coastline on the Black Sea. Romania took up the whole of the northern border, Serbia and Macedonia shared the western boundary, while Greece and Turkey stopped the land of the Bulgars from falling into the Aegean Sea.

With time on his hands, Mowgley had also learned that if you were born and lived in Bulgaria you would probably die six years sooner and be fifty percent more likely to be murdered than if you lived in Britain.

Looking round the airport terminal, he was mildly surprised to see that the average Bulgarian looked no more or less unhappy than the average Briton. Some seemed positively eager to please. The pretty girl at the bar had given him a beaming smile, and he had returned it when he worked out how little his coffee and slice of cake had cost. Thanks also to his travel guide, Mowgley knew that the average wage in Bulgaria is a fifth of that in the UK.

He now also knew that Varna was the third biggest city in

Bulgaria and began life as a Thracian seaside settlement at least five centuries before work on the Great Pyramid of Giza had begun.

'Hello John.'

Mowgley looked up from the guide book and felt an almost-forgotten disturbance in his stomach as he saw her standing there and thought of what might have been.

He got up, not knowing whether to hold his hand out or embrace his former colleague's former wife. He settled for keeping his hands by his side.

'There really was no need for you to come over, you know. But I'm glad you did. How was the flight?'

'A bit crowded and noisy but okay.' Mowgley didn't think it necessary to go into the toilet incident, or that the still-dazed Snouty had been helped back to his seat by two male passengers and then bound to it with gaffer tape by the cabin crew. Or that he had been escorted off the plane by a couple of armed and unfriendly-looking Bulgarian policemen. He also thought it unnecessary to mention that although no reference was made to his part in the proceedings, a constant flow of complimentary drinks had arrived at his seat for the remainder of the journey.

'Would you like a drink or something?'

'I'm fine' she said. 'I'd like to get back to the hotel. John will be happy killing zombies by the cart-load in his room, but I don't like to leave him alone too long.'

'John?'

'My son.'

'Oh. I didn't know you had a son.'

There was a pause as she looked briefly away, then said:

'Well, we've not been in touch much over the years, have we?'

'True.' Mowgley bent over and occupied himself with the handle on his case. 'Okay.'

She watched as he struggled then said: 'You need to push the button to pull it out.'

He looked up at her and nodded. 'Of course. I've always been rubbish with technical things.'

He mastered the art of pulling the case after a few capsizes as they walked towards the exit.

'How old is your son now?' he asked.

'Coming up for thirteen,' she replied as she slipped her hand through his arm. 'He was born after Den left.'

~

The Black Sea coast takes up Bulgaria's entire eastern boundary and stretches for 378 kilometres north to south. A third of the coastline boasts sandy beaches, and before the collapse of Communism was known as the Red Riviera. Nowadays it is a popular destination for Europeans in search of a cheap holiday. Like all places where people like to take their ease and spend money, it is also a popular destination with those of criminal intent. Corrupt governmental figures and members of the Bulgarian and Russian mafias are said to be amongst honest developers who own or build luxury apartments in the choicer spots. By Bulgarian standards, property can be breathtakingly expensive and the asking price for a penthouse overlooking the sea might approach that of a studio flat in a fashionable area of London. Varna is the most northerly and largest resort on the black Sea coastline, and it was here that Jenny Cullan and her son were staying.

'How's your *shopska salata*?'

Mowgley looked dubiously at his heaped plate. 'It's a salad.'

She smiled and wagged a reproving finger. 'Don't let the locals hear you disrespecting their national dish. They're very proud of it.'

Mowgley cautiously prodded a chunk of red bell pepper. 'So what sort of country has a salad with some feta cheese on top as a national dish? Are they all vegetarians?'

She shook her head. 'Anything but. The story goes that it was invented by the Communists in the 1960s to show off the best of their national produce and attract visitors.'

He raised an eyebrow. 'Didn't work though, did it? A bit like Communism, really.'

'Quite. And by the way, feta is what the Greeks call that sort of cheese. Here, it's *sirene*.'

Mowgley shrugged. 'Does it matter?'

She reached over and helped herself to some of the white crumbly cheese. 'It does to most Bulgarians. Remember they're still getting over five hundred years of Turkish occupation. They need to have things they can call their own. Now finish your *shopska* like a good boy or there could be an international incident.'

They were at dinner on the terrace of the hotel in which Jenny and John Cullan were staying. As she explained in a resigned tone, her son was having a burger in his room while busy saving the universe on his gaming console.

Their waiter arrived to clear away the first course, and looked puzzled when she spoke to him in what Mowgley assumed was his native language. He was a short but very wide young man with no visible neck, a shaven head and fingers like sausages. He looked, Mowgley thought, much more suited to minding the door of a dodgy nightclub than waiting on tables.

The man picked up the plates clumsily, said in badly fractured English that he would be back soon, then ambled off with the odd, swinging gait that muscle-bound men often adopt.

Mowgley watched him go, then looked questioningly at her. 'I thought you said you could speak Bulgarian?'

She shrugged. 'I do. Don't forget I'm a language teacher and I've been coming here twice a year for a decade. It's not me who doesn't understand Bulgarian, it's him. There's a big shortage of hospitality industry staff here because the locals have buggered off to where the pay is much better. The operators have had to recruit from non-EU countries, and the adverts actually say there's no need to be able to speak Bulgarian, but English or Russian is essential. I think our man is probably from the Ukraine.'

'Ah. Well I hope he knows we're not Russian.'

'Of course he does. Why?'

'Given their recent history, if I were Russian I wouldn't want a bloke from the Ukraine having access to my soup before leaving the kitchen.'

She smiled. 'I suppose not. Are you okay? You look a bit anxious?'

'Just dying for a fag. Is it okay to smoke here?'

She looked around and nodded. 'Don't see why not. I do. We're outside and everyone else seems happy to light up. Anyway, I don't think Bulgaria has got used to the EU non-smoking rules yet. All the bars have 'no smoking' stickers on the doors, but they don't seem to work. Mind you, they also put 'no guns allowed' stickers on all the bar doors and nobody seems to take any notice.'

He looked to see if she were joking, then asked: 'What about you; do you mind if I smoke?'

'Not if you give me one.'

Mowgley reached for his packet of *Gauloises*, thought about trying the tap-the-bottom-of-the-packet routine but settled for teasing another cigarette from the hole in the top of the squashy packet.

She watched him and smiled. 'You really are adapting to your new life, aren't you?'

He nodded then held the packet up. 'The trick is to tear just enough from the top. The flash blokes tap the bottom and shoot one or two out, but I haven't managed that yet.'

She giggled and laid a hand on his. 'I do hope you never grow up. I think you are one of the funniest people I've ever met.'

As she bent forward for him to light her cigarette, he looked at the soft swell of her breasts beneath her lightweight summer dress and remembered their past and wondered why she had chosen not to tell him about her son.

~

Mowgley reached across the table to top up her glass, then sat back, looked up at the night sky and said: 'This is nice.'

It was, he realised, not one of the great after-dinner lines but the best he could do at the moment. Although she always sent a card at Christmas It had been several years since they spoke on the phone and fifteen since they had briefly been lovers. He was not sure of why he was here, or exactly what Jenny Cullan wanted from him, and he was not even sure that she knew. But it was not a bad way to take a break before returning to work.

Andriy the muscle-bound waiter had delivered their second bottle of wine and left more than well-rewarded for his clumsy if well-intentioned service. This was not because Mowgley was feeling especially benevolent, but because he hadn't realised that the handful of coins he'd dumped on the table as a tip added up to more than the average daily wage in Bulgaria.

Over dinner, they'd talked about the time Mowgley had

worked on attachment with Den Cullan in the Forgery Squad. Alike in some ways but not at all in others, the two detectives had got on well at work and play. Both had an appetite for getting results, but Cullan had an even more extreme approach to getting them. There were also dark rumours that he was too selective in which cases he pursued relentlessly and those on which he appeared to soft pedal. As Mowgley quickly learned, the Dirty Den sobriquet was not based on the then popular TV soap character or any shortcomings with regard to personal hygiene. In the best traditions of London-based policing in those days, Mowgley had turned a blind eye. It was also possible that part of the reason he took that approach was influenced by his growing attachment to his partner's wife. Unlike his own wife, he found Jenny Cullan gentle, understanding and tolerant. But however she might have found him, she was of course out of bounds.

The end of the partnership came suddenly when Den Cullan left the police force and his wife on the same day. It was possible that Mowgley had been the more surprised of the two. He did his best to support and comfort the abandoned wife, and it was almost inevitable that they had become lovers over one short but memorably hot summer. The only affair Mowgley had ever had ended by mutual if unspoken agreement. Jenny Cullan had got on with her life after Den, and Mowgley had tried to get on with his wife. One of the failed attempts at saving his teetering marriage was to agree to the purchase of an imposing but ruined manor-house in Normandy. His wife was not interested in the restoration of architecturally significant properties, but liked to casually mention their ten-bedroom château during weekly attendances at the gym and Waitrose.

After a few months his wife had left him for the French estate agent who had sold them the property, and Mowgley was still unsure who had had the best of the transaction. As a result of the settlement his wife had taken their home in Hampshire but graciously surrendered the wreck across the Channel.

Increasingly of late he had found himself wondering if the sequence of events ending in his becoming a tyro private detective in Normandy had been a whimsy of the Fates, pure chance or some form of subconscious self-determination.

'A *leva* for them…and may I have another drink?'

He looked up and saw she was holding a coin in one hand and her empty glass in the other.

'Oh sorry. Miles away.' He picked up the bottle, topped her glass up then looked at the indecipherable label. 'Blimey, I didn't know Russia made wine.'

She smiled. 'It's Bulgarian. The weird lettering is in the Cyrillic alphabet, invented by a monk and his brother more than a thousand years ago.'

'I won't ask why. Is it any good?'

'The Cyrillic alphabet or Bulgarian wine?'

'You know what I meant.'

She smiled again. 'I like it, and so do lots of people. Bulgaria is one of the biggest producers and exporters of wine in the world. And maybe the oldest. They will tell you the Romans learned about wine-making here.'

'Ah.' Mowgley filled his own glass, thought about making a toast to their reunion, then thought of why he was there. He reached for the *Gauloises* packet and said: 'So, do you want to tell me about it?'

'How long have you got? How far do you want me to go back? It's going to take at least another bottle of Bear's Blood...and probably another packet of *Gauloises*.'

He took the last two cigarettes from the pack, lit both and handed her one before crumpling the packet. 'That's the end of the French fags – we'll have to move on to a local brand. But there's no hurry if John's okay?'

'He's fine. I checked when I went to the loo. He told me he's still standing in his game, whatever that means, and I got room service to send up another monster burger and a gallon of fizzy drink.' She rooted around in her bag and then pulled out a phone and laid it on the table. 'He said he'd text me if he runs out of food and drink or too many lives in the game.'

Mowgley shrugged then took a pull on his cigarette and sat back. 'Okay then. Let's go.'

'Where shall I start?'

'How about why and how Den went, and ending with how we ended up having dinner in Bulgaria?'

'Okay' She took a deep pull on her cigarette then laid it carefully in the ashtray.

'As you know, our marriage was heading for the rocks for a while before Den buggered off. I had my job, but I found it a

45

real trial to try and keep things light on the rare occasions he deigned to come home. I know he worked long hours, but I saw enough blonde hairs and smelled enough expensive perfume on his shirts to know it was not all work.' She paused and looked directly at him.' For the last few months I felt depressed and lonely and, I suppose, neglected. I needed someone to show they thought something of me. And then there was you.'

Mowgley looked away and felt his cheeks colour. It was another unfamiliar experience. She saw his embarrassment, reached over and laid a hand on his and continued. 'Anyway, to cut to the chase I came home from work and found his wardrobe cleared. There was no note or even a text, but he phoned a week later to say he was working in Bulgaria. No apologies or reasons, just that he wanted to move on. But I have to say he tied up the loose ends and made sure I and John would be alright. He'd resigned from work and had the house and bank accounts put in my name, and I was the only one who didn't know what was going on. Unless you were in the dark as well?'

He shook his head. 'No, I didn't have a clue. My attachment to the forgery squad was coming to an end, and the last time I saw him was when we had a drink to, as he said, celebrate getting rid of me. Then you called.'

He picked up the bottle and waved it at Andriy, who was picking up the remains of a pile of plates he had been transporting from a table occupied by a noisy group of young women. Their waiter arrived sucking a cut thumb and put a fresh bottle on the table. He hung around a moment, but lumbered off when Mowgley showed no sign of putting another day's worth of wages on the table.

'But you kept in touch with Den?'

She raised a hand and shook it in a 'so-so' gesture. 'I thought it my duty to give John the chance to get to know his father as he got older. As far as I know Den hasn't been back in Britain since he buggered off to Bulgaria, so I've been coming over with John every year since he was four. It's a break for me and Den spoils John rotten while he's here. He takes him out on his flash boat and they go skiing together. John even has his own bank account here and there's a trust fund of some sort of shady set-up in his name with God knows how much money in it. Den says it's for the future, and that he can't send any money to the UK for obvious reasons.'

'And are they obvious?'

She nodded. 'Probably.'

'So what does Den do to earn so much money?'

She raised an eyebrow. 'I don't really know. It's something to do with trading in artefacts.'

'Arti-what?'

'It's a sort of portmanteau word covering anything made by human hands, but usually applied to ancient objects - particularly those of historical or cultural interest.'

'You mean like stone arrowheads and bone tools and stuff like that?'

She smiled. 'Well yes. But Den's customers are more interested in stuff made out of gold and silver.'

'Like buried treasure?'

'That's it. It never gets the credit, but this place bred one of the oldest civilisations in the world. Seven thousand years ago the Thracians were already renowned for their skills in making beautiful gold and silver ornaments and jewellery. More buried treasure has been found in Bulgaria than anywhere else on earth, and that's only the stuff that's known about.'

'So there's quite a bit of trading in loot the authorities don't know about?'

'You could say that. Not far from where we're sitting is the site of the oldest and one of the most valuable discoveries of precious artefacts. And just out there…' She waved her glass towards the sea, '…are hundreds of shipwrecks dating back thousands of years. The coastal waters are a graveyard for ancient shipping-and a lot of the ships would have been carrying very valuable cargoes.'

'Could that be why Den has a big yacht.?'

She frowned as if she had not thought of the link. 'I don't know if it's because of all that buried treasure or that he just likes having a flash boat to match his flash apartment.'

Mowgley used his glass to indicate the rows of luxury apartment blocks lining the shore. 'Like one of these?'

She smiled. 'Just like one of those. He's got a penthouse he shares with Magda.'

'Magda?'

'His current partner. All I know about her is that she's

Bulgarian and twenty years younger than Den and very attractive in a former pole-dancerish sort of way.' She paused and smiled. 'Miaow. I couldn't help that. To be fair, she's been with him for a long time - it's funny to think they may have been together longer than we were. I've never met her as Den is thoughtful enough to make sure she's not around when I arrive with John.'

'So you stay with him when you're here?'

She looked troubled. 'Usually. The routine is always the same. I phone him a few days before we arrive, confirm with an e-mail and he gets the guest rooms ready and sends Magda off somewhere.'

'And what happened this time?'

'His car was in the car park when we arrived three days ago, and it's still there.

I let us in to the foyer with the code and I've got a key for the penthouse lift. When we got up there, I pressed the intercom button but there was no answer. I tried the landline and could hear it ringing inside till it went to answerphone. It was the same with his mobile.'

'But you couldn't just let yourself in?'

'No. I didn't have a key or the code. He was funny like that. I suppose he would have seen it as letting me too far into his life.'

Mowgley frowned. 'What did you do next? Do you have Magda's number?'

She showed a flash of irritation. 'Of course not. I kept trying his number, then booked into this hotel. You have to remember that I know virtually nothing about his life here or his business or his friends.'

He held up a hand in apology. 'I'm sorry. What happened then?'

'I kept phoning and visiting the apartment and checking his car was there. Then yesterday I went to the police and reported him missing.'

'What did they say?'

'Nothing much. I think they thought I was some mad, bitter ex-wife trying to stir up trouble. They said there was no law against him not being at home when I arrived, and he'd probably gone off somewhere with his girlfriend; or on business. He was probably trying to tell me something by not answering my calls. If he didn't turn up in a week or so, I should let them know.'

Mowgley rubbed his jaw and fiddled with the empty cigarette packet, 'So then you called me?'

'Yes.' She looked contrite. 'I'm really sorry to have dragged you into this, but when I got no help from the police, I thought of you. I thought you would be still be at the ferry port and could have used your contacts like'- she threw her hands in the air and then ran her fingers through her hair- 'I don't know, Interpol or something to find out or make the police do something...'

He reached across the table and patted her hand. It was an unfamiliar gesture and he did it awkwardly. 'It's okay. I understand. I'll see if I can have a word with the local police tomorrow and make a few phone calls. I know people who know people here. At least we'll be doing something.'

He took his hand away and tried to look confidently reassuring. 'I'm sure it'll all work out. In the meantime, do you fancy a stroll along the prom in search of somewhere that sells French fags?'

~

'Blimey, has there been a bomb scare?'

'No, it's just a local tradition. People like to go for a stroll beside the sea at this time. It's what we used to do in Britain. A walk along the prom.'

They were sitting outside one of the bars lining a pedestrianised area leading to the seafront. They'd not found an outlet selling French cigarettes, so had settled for a Bulgarian brand.

'It's a funny name to call a cigarette,' Mowgley observed, looking at the packet on the table.

'What, 'Victory?' Do you think so?' Jen Cullan smiled. 'Unlike, say, 'Park Drive'... 'Diplomats' or 'Passing Cloud'? And what about 'Player's Weights'? Cigarettes are always called silly names, aren't they?'

'Touché.' He took a draw, coughed and reached for his glass of beer as he watched the river of humanity streaming by. 'Not bad. But who are all these people and where are they going?'

'A lot of them will be locals. You can tell the holidaymakers by their chronic sunburn and funny clothes. The residents will be on their way to the seafront for a walk along the prom or in the Sea Gardens. The visitors will be looking for a lively bar or somewhere to eat. The younger ones will be looking for action. The older folk like us like to gather here on the *silvinitza.*'

A group of rowdy, young and obviously British men passed by, one staggering against their table. They were dressed as vicars and waving bottles of beer and were noisy but did not look dangerous. As they passed like a noisy flock of crows, Mowgley thought how their boisterous behaviour was more noticeable because of the general orderliness of the crowd. He also wondered what natives of cheap sunspots around the world made of the flower of British youth.

He watched her watching the passers-by, then asked. 'Do you like coming here, or is it just for John to see his dad?'

She put her head on one side as if it was not something she had given much consideration to. 'I think it started as a duty, but over the years I've come to be very fond of the country...and the people. I don't know what it is about Bulgaria, but to me as an outsider it looks like a beautiful land of great promise that was never fulfilled. The people only got rid of the Communists thirty years ago and they left the country in a terrible state. Then Bulgaria joined the EU and the young blood has been draining away. It's incredible to think that there are more Bulgarians working abroad than the entire work force here. That would be like twenty million Britons working elsewhere in the world. It can be really hard for those who are left behind, but they get on with their lives. I know you could be in Benidorm or Rhodes here, but you shouldn't judge a country by its seaside resorts. What would happen if foreigners thought Blackpool summed up what the rest of Britain was like?'

'Good point, though now you mention it...'

'You know what I mean.' She reached over and flicked his arm in mock reproof. He winced and recoiled dramatically and thought how quickly they had returned to the easy familiarity. He had always found it difficult to relax in female company, especially, when he thought about it, his wife's. It was different with Melons, of course, but there were no sexual strings attached to the relationship.

He made as if to stand up and she put a hand on his arm.

'Where are you going? Is your leg holding up?'

He raised his shoulders and hands in a no-problem gesture and said 'It's fine, just a bit stiff. Walking is good for it, and anyway, I need a pee. I'll keep an eye open for any drunk drivers.' When she'd asked, he had told her that he had got in the way of a mad and bad French driver, which could be to some extent the truth.

After his visit to the cramped but clean toilet he stood at the bar and pointed in her direction, miming a drinking action. She nodded and smiled and he set about a further mime for the barman's benefit.

Hopeful he'd made the right order he returned to their table, trying to make his limp less obvious. It made him feel vulnerable and he could see why they said a wounded animal was at its most dangerous. Perhaps, he thought, that's why he had reacted as he did on the plane. Or perhaps not. Although he was not generally known for his sensitivity, he did not like bullies or those who made other people unhappy. And it was good to take retribution on behalf of others now and then.

As he arrived she lifted her glass. '"*Nazdrave*." It means "cheers"'.

He took a run at it as he sat down and liked the way it came out. "*Nazdrave*". It sounds very…Russian,'

'You know,' she said, 'I am really grateful you came over. I felt so alone and helpless and now I feel much better and more confident about Den showing up.'

'It's probably more to do with the wine than me. I'm sure he'll turn up soon. He wouldn't want to miss seeing you and John.'

She frowned. 'Not me, but certainly John. That's what worried me about him not being here when we arrived. He's always been an unreliable bastard, but he's always literally been there for John.' She nodded her thanks to the waiter, picked up the glass and said: 'When Den does appear, I'll be more or less on my own for a fortnight. I don't suppose you'll be able to stay on for a bit? I could show you how beautiful it is when you get away from the coast. There's a story about when God was making all the countries and handing them out. As usual the Bulgarians turned up late. God had run out of land by then, so he had to give them a piece of Heaven.'

Mowgley thought about the idea for all of a few seconds, then raised his glass. 'Sounds good to me.'

'Of course I'll settle your hotel bill and the cost of the flight, so you'll actually be here on business as my private investigator.' She reached for a cigarette, put it in her mouth and leaned towards him so he could light it. Before he did, she looked up and said with mock coyness: 'And I promise to try not to try and take advantage of you in other ways...'

~

'I can't believe it's nearly two in the morning.'

'Is it? Crikey. Will the boy be okay?'

Jenny Cullan laughed. 'You've obviously never had a teenage son. He's on holiday so I've got no excuse for confiscating his games console and tablet and trying to get him to go to bed and sleep. Anyway, he's in a really good mood. When I called, he'd moved on from saving the world to saving the universe.'

They were walking back to the hotel and the streets were still busy with a mixture of late diners returning home and party animals still on the go. Mowgley thought about putting a protective arm round her, but his nerve failed him in spite of the best part of two bottles of Bear's Blood wine.

Although obviously a strong and usually confident woman, she seemed to be more concerned than he would have expected about Den's absence. As she said, after eight years of marriage she knew how unreliable he could be, but she also said how he had always been there to meet them on previous visits.

'Mmmm,' she said, solving Mowgley's dilemma by taking his arm, 'that's better. A man's strong arm to rely on. I do believe I'm a bit tipsy. Thank you for a lovely evening. It's been such a treat to be escorted round and not have to do everything myself. I can't believe it's nearly ten years since we last met. Where did it go?'

To him it seemed there was more than a tinge of regret in her voice, though he could not tell if it were regret at not seeing him, or the way the years had slipped by.

But he was encouraged by her tone and words and the warmth of her arm through his. He stopped to light a couple of cigarettes, then asked: 'And are you not... seeing anyone at the moment?'

She pretended not to notice his awkwardness. 'Nope. I had a couple of dates after... you and me, and made the mistake of starting something with a colleague at the school. But nothing worked. I suppose you get selfish when you're on your own when you've got so much going on. There was John, of course, and work, and after Den I couldn't see me sharing my life with anyone and opening myself up to all that aggro and pain. 'It's alright for you men, you can love 'em and leave 'em or set aside a day a week for a regular bonk and be quite content. We gals like to have something a little more permanent. Though,' she said smiling through a haze of cigarette smoke, 'I wouldn't be against a holiday-type romance if one came along...'

~

At the hotel they were met by an elderly man in an apron who was obviously doubling-up as cleaner and receptionist. He was, Mowgley assumed, a local who was too old to want to join the exodus to other promised lands.

As they arrived at the desk the man took off his apron and slipped on a red-and-gold-striped waistcoat to signify his change of role. Jen told him their room numbers and he reached into the appropriate pigeon-holes and laid their keys on the scratched imitation leather surface between them. Next to the key with Jen's room number on the oversized tag he carefully placed a folded piece of paper. She looked quizzically at it and him, then asked him something as she picked it up. He responded with a shrug and a downturning of his withered old lips.

She looked at the piece of paper and then at Mowgley, then unfolded it. It seemed to him she did so reluctantly.

Almost immediately, she looked up and spoke in a dead, flat tone.

'It's from the police. They've found Den.'

5

Given their function, Mowgley had assumed that mortuaries would be much alike. He had visited more than most and they had all looked and smelled the same, at least on the inside. But, he thought, he would take a small bet that the setting for the one in which he now stood was probably unique.

In the heart of the town, the Varna mortuary was housed in a very grand building festooned with domes and spires and surmounted with a giant cross. It had clearly been built for the living to give thanks for life. Now it was a temporary home for those who had quit theirs.

The purpose and function of any mortuary is quite simple. It is to store corpses awaiting identification or autopsy. As refrigerators are used to keep food fresh, storage lockers in mortuaries are used to delay the process of corruption. A temperature of between two and four degrees Celsius will allow a body to be kept in reasonable condition for up to a fortnight.

The coldly functional white-tiled room in which they were standing contrasted oddly with the lofty domed ceiling, which was supported by massive curved beams and painted with saintly, bearded and often haloed figures. It was possible, Mowgley thought, that a preservation order or religious diktat had prevented the ceiling being covered over or brought in line with the clinical theme below. Or perhaps the authorities thought the Heavenly scenes would act as a suitable reminder to visitors of what hopefully lay in wait for the customers. They, of course, would be past caring.

Den Cullan's body lay on a stainless steel trolley in the centre of the room, entirely covered by a green cotton sheet. Mowgley thought it a thoughtful touch that the attendant, knowing there was to be a viewing, had pulled the sheet over the feet and the name tag which would be tied to a big toe.

Immediately above the trolley was a large and obviously very powerful lamp on an articulated arm. The floor was tiled and sloped slightly downwards to a drain from which radiated a star shaped pattern of runnels. Mowgley knew they were there to channel the blood and other liquid matter which escaped in the course of an autopsy.

Alongside the trolley was a smaller one and it too was covered by a green sheet. Beneath would lie the various pointed, bladed and bone-crunching and flesh-clamping tools which allowed the pathologist to gain access to the inner parts of the guest of honour at the autopsy ceremony.

Despite the solemnity of the occasion, Mowgley could not help reflecting on the surreal nature of his situation and surroundings. A couple of days ago he had been concentrating on getting back to what was now his normal routine in an office in northern France. Now he was standing in a very foreign country, looking at the remains of a past friend and colleague. He also had his arm around the dead man's ex-wife, who had been his lover for a brief, mad summer.

Amongst the living members of the tableau were two other figures. One was a mortuary attendant, a small, slight middle-aged man with pointy Slavic features and what looked like a painful boil on one side of his nose. He looked a kindly man and one who had seen much of life as well as death.

Next to him and standing at the head of the trolley was the man who had brought them here. Mowgley did not know what plain-clothes Bulgarian police officers looked like, but this one was unlikely to be a fair example. Passing him in the street, Mowgley would have taken him for some sort of old-style academic who preferred to live in the past.

He was of around Mowgley's age, of medium height and

comfortably overweight. A large corporation, small shoulders and feet added to the impression of his body being of biconic proportions, or two truncated cones joined at the base.

In contrast to the narrow shoulders, the head was larger than the norm, and made to look more so by a flyaway shock or wiry and probably uncontrollable hair. Though still mainly dark in colour, it was shot through with veins of grey, as were his protuberant and carefully groomed eyebrows and imposing walrus moustache. Mowgley was irrationally pleased to note that the lower regions of the moustache were heavily stained by nicotine. The nose above the moustache was bulbous and the mouth below it oddly delicate and rose-hued. The eyes were deep set and small, but sparkled with intelligence.

Their host appeared to have about the same level of fashion consciousness and concern as Mowgley. He was wearing a rumpled shirt with a badly-knotted and stained kipper tie which failed to conceal the missing buttons. Over it was a tweedy jacket which had probably fitted when it and the owner were much younger. The man's trousers were of the same material as the jacket, only even more careworn. They hung in baggy ridges from the thighs down, reminding Mowgley of the back legs of an elderly elephant.

Overall and in the unlikely event of being asked to nominate an actor to portray the Bulgarian detective, Mowgley would have plumped unhesitatingly for Peter Ustinov in his role as supersleuth Hercule Poirot in *Murder on the Orient Express*.

The biconic man had arrived at their hotel within an hour of Jen Cullan calling the number on the slip of paper, and had introduced himself as Inspector (First Grade) Georgi Georgiev of the National Police Service. He had apologised profusely for the clumsy means of contact, brought about by understaffing. After checking Mowgley's relationship with Jen Cullan, he had ushered them into an empty side room and explained the reason she had not been able to contact her husband.

Two days before, a small boy paddling unwisely out to sea in an inflatable crocodile had seen something floating in the water. He had approached it to find it was the body of a man. The man had unfortunately been identified as her former husband. Although they knew who he was, it was a necessary formality for the body to be identified. In the absence of Mr Cullan's current partner and knowing from the guardian at the apartment block that she was in Varna, he would have to ask her if she would be willing to come to the mortuary and confirm what the police already knew.

~

'Stupid question, but how are you feeling?'

They were sitting in the bar nearest to the mortuary. Inspector Georgiev had offered them a lift back to the hotel, but Jen Cullan had said she would rather walk.

Mowgley had been present at or broken the news of a husband or lover's sudden death to many women across the years, and had found there was no predictable or uniform response. There would always be some display of grief, from obvious pretence to genuine devastation, but when Inspector Georgiev had told her of the drowning, Jen had seemed strangely calm. Perhaps it was the shock or perhaps a sign of her inner strength. She had flinched, taken a sharp breath and stepped back a pace, but had shown no other outward sign of emotion.

She had been silent and still in the back of the car on the way to the mortuary, but searched out and held Mowgley's hand. Most noticeably there had been no breakdown or even a tear when the attendant had gently drawn back the green shroud to expose her former husband's face.

In death, Den Cullan looked more composed and relaxed than Mowgley could remember seeing him in life. The animation and whatever else it was that gave his features life had gone, and Mowgley had thought again how unoccupied dead bodies appeared. It was, he thought, true what they said about the remains being no more than a shell and the spirit having gone wherever spirits go.

It was no surprise to see that his friend looked older than when they had last met, but even in death he looked better than Mowgley did in life. Though a pallid, marble-like white, his face was unlined and the features had hardly coarsened. His raven-black hair had more than probably had help to retain its colour, but was enviably thick. There were no signs of damage to the head and face, and none of any cosmetic assistance to hold back the evidence of the passing years. Since coming to

Bulgaria to live and work, he had obviously looked after himself as well as prospered in business. In all, Den Cullan looked as well as any dead man Mowgley had seen, and appeared, quite literally at peace with the world.

~

'Can I have another drink? It was brandy wasn't it?'

Mowgley nodded and signalled to the man behind the bar, then lit her another cigarette. As the barman arrived with a bottle on a tray, he looked at Jen's cigarette and then the no-smoking symbol on the wall beside their table. He opened his mouth as if to say something, then met Mowgley's eye and closed it. Mowgley nodded and smiled affably and put a twenty *leva* note on the tray.

Jen Cullan watched the barman walk away before responding. 'I really don't know how I feel. Just sort of empty and sad and shocked at what's happened and, perhaps, what might have been. I don't mean I thought we might have got back together, but I suppose what might have been if he hadn't buggered off. But he did. We've been living apart for eleven years and I only see - saw- him twice a year. I stopped loving him well before he walked out on us, and still can't forgive him for doing that. Not to me, but to a two-year-old boy. But I loved the bastard once.'

She sighed heavily, lifted her glass and her features softened. 'But I suppose he did try and make up for it, and I think he grew to love or at least be really fond of John as he got older. That's why I made sure we came over so regularly.'

She looked around the empty bar as if it might help her gather and understand her thoughts better. 'Of course, it's what it's going to do to John that worries me. He only saw his father twice a year and obviously loved being indulged with all the goodies and money-no-object activities. As you've seen, my son is not exactly demonstrative or communicative, but that's no different from any other thirteen-year-old. I think, somewhere in that teenage mind he loves his dad.

'So will you tell him when we get back to the hotel?'

She shook her head almost vehemently and her voice cracked. 'I don't know. I don't know. I don't really want to think about it yet.'

They sat in silence for a while, then she ran her fingers through her hair, sighed again and said: 'I still can't believe it.'

Mowgley laid a hand on hers. 'It's bound to be a shock...'

'No, I mean I can't believe that Den would just fall off his boat and drown. He was a strong swimmer and such a determined character and loved being in the water. The policeman said the bloody boat was not that far from shore. If he couldn't get back on it, why didn't he just swim back to the beach?'

Mowgley set his features in neutral and shrugged in sympathetic agreement.

In a vacant office and after the formal identification of the body, Inspector Georgiev had given them a detailed explanation of the circumstances surrounding Den's death. It appeared, he said, that it had been a tragic accident. Mr Cullan's boat had been kept at the exclusive Varna Yacht Club, of which he was a long-time member. After the body had been found, the Treasure Seeker had been located about four kilometres from the coast. It was at anchor, with nobody on board. The keys had been in the ignition but the engines at rest. In the main cabin the investigators had found a near-empty bottle of vodka and one glass on the table.

There had been no dinghy on or attached to the boat, the inspector had further explained. It was too early to say, but it looked as if Mr Cullan had taken too much to drink, gone on deck and fallen overboard. The deck would have been too high to reach up to and there was no fixed ladder. Inspector Georgiev had concluded by giving them each a card with his contact details on it and pledging he would keep Mrs Cullan informed as to progress as the investigation developed, and give her any help she needed to go through the formalities. There was a British Consulate in Varna and he was sure the Counsul would be able to help with the arrangements and the repatriation of the remains if that was what she decided to do with her husband's remains. Finally, if it was decided there were no suspicious circumstances a Death Certificate would be issued.

Before they had parted at the entrance to the mortuary, Jen had asked if Magda Abadjiev had been informed of Den's death. The inspector had said that they knew of Mr Cullan's current partner, but not where she might be. Attempts were being made to contact her.

'Another one?' Mowgley nodded at her empty glass and prepared to summon the barman.

She sat back, looked absently at her watch and ruffled her short blonde hair again. 'No thanks. I must get back to the hotel.'

'Are you going to tell John now?'

'I don't know. I can't think what's best. I need to take some time. How do you tell a thirteen-year-old boy that his dad is dead?'

~

The phone in his room rang an hour later.

'Hello', he said woozily.

'I'm sorry, did I wake you up?'

'No,' he lied. 'How is John? How did he take it?'

A brief silence, then: 'He's fine.' Another pause and then she said: 'I haven't told him. I couldn't.'

Mowgley winced. 'I can understand that. Would you like me to be there when you do?'

'No, but thanks.' More silence and then she said quickly: 'I'm not going to tell him.'

'What?'

'I mean not now.'

He winced again. 'But when? He'll have to be told soon.'

Her eyes caught fire for just a second and her voice became harsh. 'Don't you think I know that?'

Another pause and then her voice softened. 'I'm sorry. It's just that I can't bring myself to tell him now. He'll know soon enough, but what good will it do to tell him straight away?' As she continued, her voice gradually hardened again. 'I'll have to stay on for at least a couple of weeks to look after all the formal stuff. Can you imagine what it would be like for a 13-year-old to have to trail round with me as I arrange for his dad's body to be shipped back to England or buried or burned here?'

'I understand, but-'

She cut in again. 'I've already phoned my sister and she's catching the early morning plane tomorrow. I'm sorry that you won't meet him, but what can I do? She'll take John home and look after him till I get back. I'm going to tell him that his dad is held up in Sofia and won't be back for a week or so. I'll say I have to stay on to sign some papers to do with John's trust fund and he'd be bored rigid hanging around with me. I know it's weak, but this way I can keep the news of his dad's death from him for a little while longer. Or maybe a good while longer.'

Mowgley thought carefully about his next comment before making it. 'Look Jen, I know you're trying to protect him, but how do you think he'll feel when he learns you kept the truth from him?'

A sigh of exasperation, then: 'Don't you get it? I know you've got no children, but I'm his mother, for Christ's sake. If I can keep it from him for even a few weeks I will. I'll worry about how he feels about me lying to him when it comes to it.'

Mowgley thought it best to say no more, and after a moment she spoke in a much softer tone: 'I really am sorry, but you must know how I'm feeling. I know it's a real cheek, but are you able to stay on for a while? I'm pretty good at looking after myself and know how things are done here, but it would be so good to have you with me.'

6

In his time in France, Mowgley had learned how hard it could be to find your way in a country when you speak little of the language. Now he was finding how much harder it was when the language is a complete mystery and the signs do not use the alphabet with which you are familiar.

The taxi ordered by the hotel had dropped him off in the middle of what looked like a sprawling industrial estate ringed by drab, high-rise apartment blocks. Abandoned on a pavement it was some time before he found a passer-by who understood a little English, or his impression of a Bulgarian policeman.

His guide book had informed him that, as befits the second-largest city in the country, Varna boasted four police stations. Standing at the gate to the yard he hoped the others were more impressive

In contrast to the town's mortuary, the police headquarters was housed in a most unremarkable setting. The bleak concrete single-storey square building typified the lack of Communist-era architectural aspirations, and the grimness was unrelieved by a wide and inexplicable stripe of girlie pink running around the top.

If the Varna police HQ was utilitarian and functional, the

office of Inspector (First Grade) Georgi Georgiev could have provided no greater contrast.

In the rest of the building the theme was gloss-painted walls, plastic-tiled floors and functional office furniture laden with the usual clutter of a place where people worked long hours on paper-intensive projects. The office to which Mowgley had been escorted was an evocation of a time when comfort and aesthetics trumped utility.

Three of the walls were lined with books, while a richly-hued oriental rug did its best to nullify the scuffed vinyl floor. Familiar Impressionist works hung on either side of the window overlooking the yard, and dominating the room was a sumptuous and heavily carved wooden desk which would have taken four men to shift. On it stood what to Mowgley's untutored eye looked like a Tiffany table lamp.

In its soft glow sat Inspector Georgiev, pipe in his mouth and toying idly with a small and battered golden tube. As Mowgley was ushered in he looked up and smiled with what seemed to be genuine pleasure.

Georgiev took the pipe from his mouth, stood up and gestured to a delicate-looking period dining chair in front of the desk: 'Please, Inspector, take a seat.'

As Mowgley had observed at their earlier meeting, Georgiev's voice was deeply mellifluous, his English precise and formally correct in the way it can be with those to whom it is a foreign tongue. If anything, the clarity and richness was enhanced by the faint influence and timbre of his Slavic accent.

'It's plain mister nowadays, I'm afraid,' said Mowgley, knowing that Georgiev had used his former rank to let him know he had been doing his homework.

'Ah yes, of course. I had forgotten. Can I offer you tea, or coffee or a drink?'

Mowgley lowered himself carefully onto the spindly chair.

'Tea would be nice. White, two sugars, please.'

His host nodded as if a wise choice had been made and spoke rapidly to Mowgley's escort. The tall young man nodded respectfully and left. He did not exit backwards, but his manner demonstrated his opinion of the inspector's status as well as the seniority of his rank.

Mowgley watched as Georgiev picked up his pipe and took a small penknife from his shirt pocket. He patted his pockets. 'Is it okay if I smoke?'

'Of course, but it is not compulsory.' Opening the knife, the inspector worked on removing the dottle from the bowl of his pipe before reaching towards an intricately filigreed cylindrical wooden container. Mowgley opened his cigarette packet and drew one out as the Inspector began filling the pipe and gently tamping the tobacco down.

The ritual complete and the pipe going, Georgiev sat back and watched as Mowgley lit up. 'What do you think of our cigarettes?' he asked. 'They are not so well-known in Europe, I think, but very popular in the Middle East.'

'Very good', said Mowgley. Then he nodded at the lamp and said, 'Is that the real thing?'

Georgiev looked at it and smiled. 'I wish it were. Excluding us, most of the objects in this room are fakes.' Almost apologetically he added: 'One of my hobbies is collecting them.'

'When you say 'fakes', you don't mean copies?'

The inspector pursed his lips. 'No. I would not want to be thought a pedant, but in my assessment - and that of my department - a copy is not pretending to be anything but a copy. A fake, like a forgery, is different. It purports to be the real thing but is not. A fake Rolex watch is a good example at the lower end of the scale'. He turned in his chair and nodded at one of the paintings. 'At the top end would be a Monet purporting to be the real thing.'

Georgiev laid down his pipe and picked up the small metal cylinder with which he had been fiddling when Mowgley arrived. 'This is a good example. If it were real, it would be almost priceless.'

'I see,' said Mowgley, although he did not. 'What is it?'

Georgiev slipped the tube on his little finger and held it up in the light from the table lamp. 'It purports to be a Thracian penis sheath.'

'A what?'

The inspector smiled, removed the cylinder and passed it across the deck. It was heavier than Mowgley had expected and had the dull sheen of old gold.

Georgiev picked up his pipe, re-lit it from a box of matches in a holder by the lamp.

'Forgive me if I indulge myself with the explanation, but it is in a way how I came to be here, doing what I do.'

The inspector took a sustaining pull at his pipe and cleared his throat. 'In 1972 a tractor driver named Raicho Marinov was making a trench on the outskirts of Varna. He noticed some small squares of shiny metal in the soil he had dug up, and took them to the foreman. Investigation revealed that Comrade Marinov had discovered the oldest and greatest treasure trove in the world.'

A knock at the door gave Georgiev the chance to pause and re-ignite his pipe as the respectful young man returned. He was carrying a tray, which he set down on the table before another bow and an almost courtly departure. On the tray was a very small cup, half-filled with what looked to Mowgley like black treacle. Alongside it was a larger, handle-less bowl filled with an insipid-looking but sweetly aromatic liquid.

Georgiev reached for his coffee and looked at Mowgley looking dubiously at the remaining cup. 'I'm afraid we have no Indian tea. Or milk. This is a typical herbal *chai*, which in this case is, I think, a mixture of lemon balm, marjoram and bilberry.' He smiled reassuringly. 'I will not be offended if you do not want to try it.' He took another puff on the pipe. 'Are you becoming bored with my lecture, or shall I continue?'

'Please carry on.'

Georgiev nodded. 'The tractor had unearthed a selection of gold and copper artefacts, so work was stopped and an archaeological investigation was launched immediately. It transpired that the driver had stumbled on a massive burial site, dating back more than six thousand years. The site contained the earliest and most gold artefacts ever found. There were more than 300 graves in the necropolis, and in them more than 22,000 artefacts. Then, in grave 43, Varna Man was discovered.'

Georgiev paused as if for effect, then carried on. 'The body was of a young and obviously high-status male, surrounded by precious items. They included a sceptre, and a penis sheath of solid gold. As you will understand, fertility was of vital importance in those early civilisations.'

Mowgley handed back the cylinder 'And this is a copy?'

Georgiev held his finger up and shook his head. 'No, as I said, it is not a copy; it is a very good forgery. It was modelled on the Varna sheath and touted round as having been looted from the same site. It is made of gold like the original, and as a copy would have been worth perhaps a thousand dollars. Because it was purporting to be the real thing, the asking price was half a million.'

Mowgley pursed his lips and, if he could, would have whistled. 'So there's a market for these sort of things?'

Georgiev smiled indulgently. 'You could say that. About a billion dollars' worth of ancient artefacts are smuggled out of Bulgaria every year. The illegal trade comes a close third to drugs and prostitution.'

'But apart from museums, who would want things like that? They could hardly show them off at dinner parties.'

The inspector picked up his coffee cup, which was made to look even smaller and more fragile by his sausage-like fingers.

'Some may be 'legalised' by false documentation, but there is always a huge demand for illegal artefacts. The customers are the same sort of very wealthy collectors who buy stolen art masterpieces. Sometimes they are the same people. They know they can never boast of their acquisition beyond a very small circle, but they know the right people will know, and that they have something completely unique. To them it is the owning of a Rembrandt or Vermeer that matters, not its beauty and what it might say about humanity and human achievement.'

The Inspector slipped the sheath on his little finger again and held it up. 'The difference between fake works of art and artefacts like this is that the collector cannot claim to himself or anyone else that he owns the original Mona Lisa. As long as it sits in the Louvre, everything else must be a copy - or a fake. Because there would or could have been more than one, this could be an original, undiscovered artefact.'

'It was made to order, then?'

'It was made to sell for a thousand times what it cost to make.' Inspector Georgiev drained the cup, wiped his moustache with an index finger, and looked thoughtfully at the penis-sheath. 'Part of what I do is to find those who make these things. 'He took the sheath off his finger and laid it carefully on the desk. 'I was of course a boy when the Varna necropolis was discovered, but it fired a lifelong interest. We have, as you may know, more buried treasures than anywhere else on earth. It makes us an obvious target for home-grown and foreign criminal organisations.'

Mowgley picked up his cup of *chai*, looked at it and then returned it to its saucer. 'But you chose to become a policeman instead of an archaeologist?'

The inspector shrugged. 'I am also fascinated by crime and in that aspect of humanity; why some people choose to turn to crime and some people like us choose to pursue them. I suspect you and I share that interest?'

Mowgley gave a slight nod. 'So, your job is to investigate gold and precious artefact smuggling?'

'Yes. The department of which I am head has a co-ordinating role between the anti-corruption agencies. I and my small team follow leads, make investigations, accumulate information and hopefully help to gain convictions.'

'And is that why you and not an ordinary policeman are investigating the death of Den Cullan?'

The inspector said nothing but nodded in recognition of Mowgley's observation.

'And you're based here?'

Georgiev nodded again, then turned to gesture at the window through which Mowgley saw a very fat man in straining overalls washing a blue-and white squad car in a desultory manner. 'Where better to be based than Varna for me?' Georgiev smiled. 'And those I want to do business with, of course. This ugly modern town sits on the site of a port which was a phenomenally successful trading hub trade for thousands of years. As well as all the treasures found at the necropolis and all those yet to be discovered, just off the coast is a vast shipping cemetery. Who knows how many of those dead and buried ships still contain virtually priceless treasures?'

'And that's why you have a special interest in the death of Den Cullan? Because you think he was a trader in looted artefacts?'

'Exactly. He has - had – a very luxurious lifestyle for an honest trader in legal antiquities. And where better could he be based?'

'And you have an interest in me and asked me to come here because I worked with him and was a friend?'

Georgiev smiled and tapped the bowl of his pipe on an ashtray. 'Again, exactly, but let me assure I do not think you are or have been complicit in his activities. But you may know things about Mr- and Mrs- Cullan that could help me with my work. And if I may say so, I also find you an interesting person. I know you have had a distinguished if unorthodox career and, like me, like to solve puzzles.' He looked at his watch, then said: 'I see I have been talking too much and for too long as usual and it is past my time to eat. Perhaps you will join me?'

'That would be good', said Mowgley, 'as long as I can have a beer rather than herbal tea.'

~

There was silence as the two men ate enthusiastically and Georgiev nodded his approval as Mowgley cleared his plate and wiped it clean with a chunk of bread.

As they finished and pushed their plates away a car raced by, leaving tyre marks on the road as it skidded almost out of control, straightened up and lurched through the crossing gates.

Georgiev smiled and pointed across the road. 'That's why we have so many places selling spare pieces of cars and recycled tyres. And why we have the highest death rate on the roads in all Europe.'

Mowgley watched as the skinny mongrel limped from the tyre compound and unconcernedly crossed the road and arrived at their table. It waited patiently as the inspector tore a chunk of bread in two and threw the pieces on to the floor. At a nearby table, a man picked up a piece of sausage and tossed it to the dog. 'It is a town dog,' said Georgiev. 'The law is that stray dogs may not be killed, and are the responsibility of the town. They live on the streets and are usually well looked after. Sometimes I think we look after dogs better than other nations. But I think that is the same in England...'

The waiter appeared to clear the table and Georgiev nodded at Mowgley and said something. As the young man replied and left, the inspector explained. 'I asked him to tell the cook that you liked her food. It is his mother and she will be pleased. I also ordered another carafe of wine and the owner asks that we take a glass of his father's special *rakia*.'

'That sounds interesting.'

Georgiev shrugged. 'Every country has its own home-made spirit. Where you live in France it is brandy made from apples, and in Russia it is vodka made from potatoes. Here we have *rakia*, which is made from any sort of fruit to hand. It is very strong and every village believes theirs to be the best. I find it quite tasteless but good for clearing the palate.'

The inspector tapped his pockets and said something in Bulgarian which was obviously a curse. 'I have left my pipe in the office.' He nodded at the cigarette packet at Mowgley's elbow. 'With your permission?'

'Of course.'

'So', asked Georgiev as two small glasses of innocent-looking clear liquid arrived, 'how do you find Bulgaria so far?'

Mowgley thought how best to frame his reply. 'It is a very... interesting country. I've been reading about Bulgaria since I knew I was coming here, but I still know very little.'

Georgiev puffed out his cheeks. 'You are not alone. I think all that the rest of Europe knows about Bulgaria is that it is in the east and very poor, and most of its young people don't want to live there. That is true, and, I think, very sad. The towns may be ugly and we may be as poor as dirt compared with the rest of Europe because of what the Communists did, but nature has made it such a beautiful land. I hope you will stay long enough to see that.'

Mowgley moved awkwardly in his seat. 'I would like that, but it depends on what happens and how long it all takes.'

Georgiev nodded. 'Now that her son has been sent home, I think Mrs Cullan will need to be here for at least a week to arrange what happens with her husband's body.'

Mowgley did not ask how the inspector knew that Jen's son had gone, and suspected that Georgiev had wanted him to know that he knew. 'Yes,' he said, 'so when do you think the body be released for burial or repatriation?'

'When it is decided the death was an accident.'

'And who decides that?'

'Me.'

And if you think there are suspicious circumstances?'

Georgiev reached for his glass. 'I would have to inform the office of the Public Prosecutor. That would mean the body would remain unburied and another autopsy would be undertaken and the investigation could take months.'

'But as you told Mrs Cullan, you believe Den's death was an accident?'

'Oh no, my friend,' said Inspector Georgiev before lifting the glass to his lips. 'I believe it was murder.'

7

The little man with the big wheel was taking his ease as a graffiti-daubed train of three carriages shuffled over the level crossing. It was travelling at little more than walking pace and Mowgley could see few passengers at the windows.

The queue of vehicles at the gates was made up of mostly elderly and sometimes spectacularly distressed vans and cars. Some were in such a state they looked as if they might have a problem getting going when the gates re-opened. Mowgley had read that the average car age in Euroland was a decade, but double that in Bulgaria. Going by the selection making up the queue, he would have thought the average age even higher.

Amongst all the decrepitude the gleaming black Mercedes saloon looked even more magnificent. It sat on the potholed road like a panther ready to pounce, and Mowgley saw that the windows were an opaque tint of black. He wondered if sitting behind them might be a high-level government official, a top sportsman, celebrity or even a genuine gangster. As he watched, the driver's window slid down to reveal the head and shoulders of a man who would have been a shoo-in for the role of Menacing Minder in any Hollywood movie. His head was shaven and he appeared to have no neck. He was wearing dark glasses, and a cigarette hung from the corner of his mouth.

It was probably coincidence, but it seemed to Mowgley that, after the driver lowered his window, the little man then began to crank his handle much faster.

Before they were fully open, the Mercedes pulled out of line and shot through the gates, narrowly missing a tractor waiting on the other side of the line. No horns sounded in protest and Mowgley wondered if that was because Bulgarian drivers were more benign than elsewhere, or because they knew who was likely to be in such a vehicle.

'A perfect epiphany of the privileges of wealth and power, was it not?'

Mowgley looked up to where Inspector Georgiev stood, a bottle in hand. The policeman placed it on the table and said in explanation: 'The waiter has gone to work.'

'Oh? I thought this was work for him.'

Geogiev smiled. 'You foreigners are spoiled. It is not uncommon for people here to have two or even three jobs. Iliya serves tables at lunchtimes and evenings, and works as a labourer in between. At harvest time he will pick vegetables from the fields and grapes from the vine. Many people have multiple occupations, and few have the luxury of not working. Benefits in Bulgaria are not very...beneficial.'

He pushed the bottle across the table, nodded at their empty glasses and said something in his own language.

'Beg pardon?

Georgiev smiled. 'I said 'Pass the *rakia*.' It is what Bulgarians say when there is a problem that needs solving.'

Mowgley unscrewed the cap and poured the colourless liquid into the glasses, lifted his and said '*Nazdrave*'.

Georgiev returned his toast. 'Very good.' And may I ask what you think of my country so far?'

'It's too early to say, but the people I've met have been friendly enough - especially the policemen.'

'Ah. Of course; you are also a detective and naturally of a suspicious nature. You are wondering why I should be so...affable?'

Mowgley nodded and took a cautious sip. 'It has passed my mind.'

The inspector patted his pocket then gave an exasperated

sigh as he remembered he had forgotten to bring his pipe. He accepted Mowgley's offer of a cigarette, then said 'You want me to be honest?'

'I find that people who ask that usually mean they are not going to be, but yes, that would be good.'

The inspector gave a wry smile. 'I find that, too. About the people who say they intend being honest. But what I will tell you will be the truth. You will decide whether to believe me.' The Inspector drew deeply on his cigarette and looked at Mowgley through a cloud of smoke before he spoke. 'As I said earlier I have become quite obsessed with your former friend and colleague. He is - or was - a remarkable man.'

'In what way remarkable?'

'He has been making a great deal of money here for more than ten years and had not - until recently- put a foot wrong. That is quite an achievement for a foreigner in Bulgaria unless he has some very good business contacts. Or is paying for help from the right people.'

Mowgley looked at his glass and, against his better judgement, drained it. 'You mean it is not Den you were primarily interested in? You think he was in bed with some corrupt officials?

Georgiev smiled. '"In bed with". I like that expression. But you know what usually happens when people get in bed together?'

'Yes; one of them usually gets fucked. I've heard that one. So who do you think Den was getting help from? Earning a good living and owning a flash apartment and a boat wouldn't make him an arch criminal, would it?'

Georgiev smiled wryly. 'No, but owning all the other apartments in the building as well as other properties and having an interest in other businesses as well as a Swiss bank account should have raised a few eyebrows.'

'And were they not raised?'

'Apparently not. As far as I know I am the only one who had Mr Cullan under scrutiny. I know our different departments and arms of government are not famed for co-ordinating and sharing intelligence, but even so...'

'And he was making all this money by trading in looted treasure?'

The inspector patted his coat pockets again, remembered he had forgotten his pipe and picked up the cigarette smouldering in the ashtray.

'I am sure that is what his business contacts and helpers thought, but I think there was more to it.'

Mowgley frowned. 'What do you mean more to it?'

'I think he found a way of trading in buried treasure without having to dig it up. But I will tell you more later, if our relationship blossoms.'

Georgiev topped up their glasses. Mowgley mumbled a *Nasdrave*, then said: 'And he would have had help from people in authority?'

'Of course. And from people with much unofficial power. He would not have prospered without sharing the fruits of his success.'

'So if he was paying people off, why kill the cash cow?'

Georgiev looked puzzled, then shrugged. 'He obviously upset someone or some organisation. Or perhaps I was responsible.'

'You?'

'Yes. Perhaps he died because I was paying too much attention to him. If I had arrested him, he might have revealed who he was paying off. Or who he was involved with.'

'Okay, I get that. But why are you so sure he was murdered? People do get pissed and fall off their boats.'

'That is true, but, taken together, there are too many coincidences.'

'For example?'

'To begin with, the boat left the marina after dark with no lights on. This meant nobody could see who was at the wheel or if there was anyone else on board. If it was only Mr Cullan, he left no information about his intended journey.'

'Okay, so perhaps he fancied a bit of night cruising. I don't know about Bulgaria, but in Britain it is not a legal requirement to notify anyone of your intended destination. And from what I do know, it's sometimes easier to manoeuvre in the dark with no lights on. But go on.'

Georgiev nodded. 'I will. For no apparent reason he moored just out of sight of the shore and decided to get very drunk on his own. He was not a heavy drinker, but we are supposed to believe he drank nearly a bottle of vodka, staggered up on deck and fell or jumped into the sea.'

Mowgley shrugged. 'As I said, it happens. I suppose people do leave ladders up or forget they haven't got a dinghy floating at the back. Especially if they're drunk.' Mowgley looked across the road to where the little man was going into action with the wheel again. 'Perhaps he was actually up to no good and there was some reason he moored there. Perhaps it was a rendezvous and whoever he was meeting turned up, found nobody on board and buggered off.'

The inspector held a finger up. 'What you have to know is that there was no ladder. The boat had what is called a swim platform on the back. It is there precisely so that people can get easily back on board when they have been in the water.'

'So you're wondering why he didn't use it?'

'He couldn't use it. A few days before, the man who looks after the boat backed it clumsily into its mooring place and damaged the platform so badly that it had to be taken off for repairing or replacing.'

'And have you spoken to the clumsy crewman?'

The inspector shook his head. 'I can't. He is nowhere to be found.'

'Ah. Okay' Mowgley held his hands up in mock surrender. 'As you say, that's perhaps too many coincidences. Can I ask one more question? Or rather, two?'

Georgiev unscrewed the top of the rakia bottle. 'Shoot, as Philip Marlowe might say.'

'You're a fan of Raymond Chandler, then?'

'Just because I am a foreigner does not mean I cannot read and admire the work of a great writer. But what is your question?'

Mowgley held his glass out. 'Why are you telling me all this? Despite what you said earlier, do you really think I'm involved?'

'With Mrs Cullan, or with the murder? No to either. I am telling you these things because, as I said earlier, you are a one-time friend and colleague of Mr Cullan, and a good detective. You would want to know if his death was an accident or not.' He looked over Mowgley's shoulder and shook his head. 'I am very much alone with this case, and cannot share my thoughts with anyone at any level in the police service. You can help me by asking the questions that a friend of the family would ask.'

He looked into his glass and then back up at Mowgley. 'You can imagine that it is not good to be working alone and not to be able to trust your own colleagues. It is possible that your friend was paying blind-eye money to someone at a senior level. For now, I shall continue as if I believe it was an accident. Not because I think that it was, but because I think it will be safer for us all.'

~

As if wearied by a long day on duty, the sun was having an early night.

As Mowgley had learned, the briefest of dusks was common practice in this part of the world. An hour before and the beaches at Varna had been awash. By eight the sun-lovers had gone and lights already twinkled along the promenade. All that was left of the day was a blood-red reminder on the horizon. Mowgley and Jen Cullan were sitting on the terrace of their hotel, looking at the menu and making the smallest of talk.

'Cheers.'

'Cheers.' She clinked glass with his and put her face towards the breeze from an inshore wind, then looked up. I see it's a gibbous moon.'

'A what?'

'A gibbous moon. It's any phase when more than half the circle is illuminated. It may be on the wax or wane.'

'I see.'

She laughed. 'I thought you'd find that interesting.' She put her glass down, leaned back and looked at the night sky through an imaginary telescope. 'I wonder if there's anyone up there, looking at us looking at them.'

'Not on the moon, I reckon, unless we left someone behind on the last visit.'

She shook her head and smiled. 'You do like to pretend to be thick and get the wrong end of the stick, don't you? I think you hope it will irritate people.' She looked at him with almost maternal fondness. 'You're still such a little boy in some ways. When do you think you'll grow up?'

Mowgley looked like he was considering the prospect. 'Never, I hope. I've seen what happens to people when they grow up.'

He lit two cigarettes, passed one across the table and judged it was time to ask about her day. 'You seem fine, or are you just being brave? How was it at the airport?'

She looked into her glass and then out to sea. 'Alright, sort of. At least it was not as bad as I thought it would be'.

'Do you think John knows something bad has happened?'

'I really don't know. He was unhappy not to have seen his dad, but he's at that age when you just don't know what's going through his mind. As I said, I told him that Den had called and said he was stuck in Sofia for a fortnight closing a big deal and wouldn't be able to see us even if we went there. I promised we'd come back later in the year and in term time. That cheered him up. And I gave him some money to buy a new game, and my sister told him on the quiet they'll pig out on takeaways and forget veg until I come back.'

'So, when will you tell him?'

'I don't know. I'll have to think about it.'

He persisted. 'And what about Den's mother and father? They'll have to be told.'

Her face darkened. 'I can't – I haven't got a bloody Ouija board!' The storm passed quickly and she reached over and touched his arm. 'Sorry, I'm a bit tetchy. Den's mum and dad died years ago, and he was an only child.' She smiled without affection. 'I think that's part of what made him who he was. Selfish, I mean.'

She ground her cigarette out in the vast ashtray, then said brightly: 'But how about you, what did you do today?'

'I just had a wander along the prom and a look round the Sea Gardens.'

'What about the zoo?'

'I looked in. Lots of birds but no bears.'

'Good. Bears should be free.'

Mowgley nodded. 'I read that there are still wolves and bears in some forests.'

'Perhaps. Forests can be dangerous places.'

They sat in silence looking out across the dark sea, then she said 'I'm going to see the Consul tomorrow. Could you come with me?'

'Of course.'

She nodded her thanks. 'And how long do you think you can stay? Have you got to rush back?'

'No, not rush. But I'll have to go back to work sometime soon.'

She toyed with her glass. 'So how would you feel about staying on for a week or two-in a professional capacity?'

'What, you mean as a minder – or a gigolo?'

She smiled. 'Maybe a sort of mix 'n' match. It would be really good to have you on hand to help with things and just be…around.'

He lifted the wine bottle, held it to the light and then shared what was left between the two glasses. 'To help with what?'

She picked up her glass. 'Just…things. Don't take this wrong, but if it helps persuade you to stay I really could employ you.'

'So you are after a gigolo. I don't think you'd get your money's worth.'

She ignored the joke. 'It makes sense. I was going to insist I cover what it cost you to come dashing over. I could pay you to stay on for a while longer if you're free. After all, you charge by the day as a private detective, don't you?'

He held his hands up. 'I can hang on for a few days while you sort things out, but not for a fee. Anyway, what would you need a private detective for?'

She ran her fingers through her hair, shrugged and then said: 'I don't know. I've looked after myself pretty well since Den left. I like to think I'm a strong sort of person, but I am all alone in a foreign land and my husband's laying under a sheet in the local mortuary. I need someone to just…be there.' She looked straight at him. 'And we do go back a long way.'

'Yes,' agreed Mowgley, 'we do.'

~

An hour had flown. On the table between them was a fresh bottle of Bear's Blood and a new packet of Victory cigarettes.

'Alright then,' Mowgley said. 'What's my first assignment to be? Which mean streets do you want me to walk down? How can I help you feel better?'

'Let's talk about that later.' She gave him an almost arch look over the rim of her glass and giggled. It was not her style, he thought. But in the circumstances she was entitled to a drink, for sure. She was what people used to call tipsy and on the road to being pissed, but not got there yet.

'I suppose,' she said, 'you could start by looking for Madame

- or Ms - Magda.'

'Why do you want to find her? Do you think she might have been in some way involved in what happened to Den?'

'No. Perhaps. I dunno.' She pouted and pushed her empty glass towards him. 'I'd just like to know where she is and why she's not around. And she should be told about Den. For all I know they might have got married. I don't know how they feel about having two wives at the same time here, but it could be that there are now two grieving widows.'

Mowgley sat up straight. 'I thought you were divorced years ago?'

She shook her head. 'In the end we just didn't bother. He'd said he'd done his bit by signing the house and his pension over to me, and couldn't be arsed about a divorce. At first I thought he might want to come back. Time went by and as I had no intention of getting married again, I let it lie.'

'Crikey.'

'What do you mean, "crikey"?'

'Well, I don't know how it works here, but whether or not Den did marry Magda, you might have first claim to his assets - or a good lump of them.'

Her eyebrows rose and her eyes grew round. 'Then it is a case of "crikey". I never thought of that. The penthouse would make a lovely holiday home, but this being Bulgaria and Magda being Bulgarian, I reckon I know what the courts would decide.'

She held out her hand for a cigarette and giggled again. 'Mind you, if she doesn't show up soon the policeman with the big moustache might suspect I knocked her off and buried her somewhere to get my hands on all Den's dosh. That's a good enough reason for me to employ a private detective to find her, isn't it?'

Mowgley drew on the cigarette, leaned over and placed it between her lips. 'Yes,' he said, 'I suppose it is.'

8

In the event of a sudden death in Bulgaria the body is transported to the nearest mortuary facility and examined by a forensic doctor. He or she will issue a Notice of Death. If the death is judged to be natural, a Death Certificate will follow within 48 hours. All deaths of foreign nationals must be reported to the police, who in suspicious circumstances may require an autopsy and inquest. The Death Certificate will not be issued until any police enquiry is completed.

This and other relevant information had been explained clearly and fairly concisely to Jen Cullan and Mowgley earlier that morning. It had come directly from Varna's Honorary Counsul.

Mihail Mikov was a short, rotund and helpful Bulgarian with a very bushy beard. From what Mowgley had seen, beards seemed unusual in Bulgaria, and he toyed with the thought that Mr Mikov had grown one to somehow identify with Britons who came to see him in times of trouble. Perhaps also relevant was that the beard of Mr Mikov was as large and imaginative as those favoured by Victorian emissaries in foreign parts in Colonial days. Or, he concluded, perhaps and more probably it was a compensatory beard. The Honorary Consul's scalp was totally hairless and, at first glance, it had looked to Mowgley as if his head had been put on upside down.

~

Jen Cullan's business with Mr Mikov done, they were sitting outside a bar in a square near to the Consulate.

'What do you think?' she asked as she held up her glass.

'It's very nice,' Mowgley conceded. 'It just seems wrong.'

'I could see you were looking nervous at the idea of coffee with ice in it.' She nodded at the pastry on his plate. 'And I suppose you think it's wrong to eat cheese for breakfast?'

Mowgley picked the pastry up, looked at it and took a bite. 'No, it's good. What is it?'

'It's a *banitsa*, which is filo pastry with whisked eggs and cheese or sometimes spinach in between. They put lucky charms or good-luck messages in them on New Year's Eve, sort of like Chinese Fortune cookies. The rest of the year you have them for breakfast.'

'Ah. I see.' He took another bite of the pastry, sucked coffee noisily through the straw and then said: 'Well, what did you think?'

'About what?'

'About Mr Thingy, the Honorary Counsul'

'Mr Mikov? She said. 'A very nice man, I thought. What about you?'

The slurping magnified in intensity as his straw sucked up the last of the liquid. 'Excuse me,' said Mowgley. 'Yes, nice bloke. I thought he had his head on upside down for a moment, though.'

'Head on..? Ah, you mean all beard at the bottom and nothing on top. I wonder if people do that to make up for a lack of hair. Grow a beard I mean.'

'Better than wearing a wig, I guess.'

He waited a moment, then asked: 'Have you thought about what you want to do - with Den, I mean? Will you take him home, or…'

She held her hand up to shield her eyes from the morning sun, and looked at him for a moment before replying. 'All things considered, I think it would be best for him to stay here. I don't think John would feel any better at having a box of ashes on the mantlepiece to look at, or a grave to have to visit in England. What with the trust fund and all the connections to his dad here, I reckon he'll be visiting Bulgaria a lot. Anyway, without being sentimental, it seems sort of more fitting that Den should stay in the country he chose to live in.'

'Was he fond of Bulgaria?' Mowgley asked.

'I think so. I don't know what makes expats like or hate living in a foreign country, but I think Den was pretty much as happy as he could be. He certainly made plenty of money out of living here.'

'Do you think you'll have him buried, or-'

'Cremated?' She shuddered. No, I hate the idea of disposing of someone like that. I'll take a look at the cemeteries on the list Mr Mikov gave us. Perhaps they'll be somewhere on a hill, looking out to sea. He'd like that.' She smiled wryly. 'Listen to me. People say things like that at times like these, but of course he won't give a buggery what happens to him now - or what the bloody view is like.'

She looked on the verge of tears and Mowgley thought about and rejected the idea of giving her a hug. Instead he said: And what about John?'

She looked at him quizzically. 'What about him?'

'Do you think he ought to be given the choice of coming over?'

As on the previous evening, he saw the flare of anger in her eyes. 'No,' she said, sharply, 'I don't. Why would I drag him 1600 miles to see his dad disappearing into a hole with only me and him and you at the graveside?'

The fire died as quickly as it had flared and she made the signal for him to make her a cigarette. 'I'm sorry; you're right to bring it up. I just think he needs to be protected for as long as I can keep it from him.'

She reached out, took the lit cigarette and drew on it and It seemed to him her hand lingered on his.

'I'll tell him when it's all over and I can bring him out here to see the grave when it's got a nice stone on it. We might even stay in the apartment if Magda doesn't get it.'

Mowgley nodded as if he agreed with her thoughts, then looked at a sleek limo with blacked-out windows gliding by. For a moment he wondered if it could be the same one he saw at the level crossing, but then thought how there would probably be at least a dozen cruising around Varna at any time. In a town like this, there could be any number of business tycoons, senior government officials and the odd gangster who liked to draw attention to themselves by pretending they did not want to be looked at.

'Talking of Magda,' he said, 'Do you still want me to try and find her?'

She nodded. 'Yes please. Perhaps she went away for a break while I was here and doesn't know what happened. Or perhaps she does know and has chosen not to come back.'

Mowgley frowned. 'You really think so? Surely, if she knew she'd have been in touch - with the police if not you?'

Jen Cullan took another long draw on her cigarette and gave him a cool look. 'Not if she had anything to do with Den's death, I reckon.'

~

The Royal Bulgarian Sailing Club is, the website claims, the first and only one of its kind in the country. Although the monarchy was abolished and Tsar Simeon Saxe-Coburg-Gotha exiled in 1946 as a result of a national referendum, the regal designation was chosen to encourage co-operation with other clubs around the world that have royal connections. Cynics might wonder if the regal title might also encourage investment in the ongoing development of luxury properties in the hills overlooking the marina.

The Club offers 600 moorings and what it called 'all imaginable facilities' to members and visitors, and with the help of other owners and crew, Mowgley eventually found Den Cullan's boat amongst the forest of masts and avenues of sleek superstructures. The vessels came in all styles, types, shapes and sizes, but shared the obviously common factor of very wealthy owners.

To those in the know, the Treasure Seeker was a most desirable Grand Banks 46 Europa. To Mowgley, it was a big, workmanlike and probably eye-wateringly expensive boat.

Had he been able to ask someone in the know, he would have learned that the Europa is rated in boating circles as a reliable, safe and serious cruiser. It has a top speed of 20 knots and, most relevantly, a high freeboard. In landlubberly terms that means it is a long way from the deck to the water level, and why so many are fitted with a swim platform.

The Treasure Seeker was moored stern-to against the pontoon, and he could see there was some damage to the transom. Obviously, this was where the platform had been fixed.

Mowgley stood and looked at the boat and tried to imagine what it would have been like for Den Cullan trying to get back on board, with fingers scrabbling against the sleek and shiny perfection of the hull and a growing awareness that he was going to die. That was, of course, if Den had been conscious when he fell or was put into the sea.

He shivered, then picked his way carefully along the swaying pontoon to the marina buildings, trying to look like the sort of person who could afford to keep a boat in such an exclusive parking lot.

~

Mowgley was not a habitué of marina bars, and this one reminded him why. The posher ones he had visited always seemed more like hotel reception areas than somewhere to relax. They also seemed to be striving too hard to impress and could be as garish and even vulgar as the craft their customers owned. This one was certainly a strange fusion of styles and themes.

The long, arched ceiling was lined with varnished wooden planking which made it look uncomfortably reminiscent of the inside of the hull of an overturned yacht. The walls were clad with shiny metal sheeting, hung with varnished wooden display cases containing examples of long-redundant nautical knots. The bar was sheathed in the same metal sheeting as the walls, and behind it was a rolling backdrop of digitalised paintings of windjammers leaning into the wind on turbulent seas. Scattered around were vast glass-topped coffee tables with chrome legs and uncomfortable-looking tubular armchairs.

Mowgley felt slightly queasy as he crossed the black tiled floor towards where the procession of old and ultra-modern ships wallowed or sped across the screen. The opulence also made him unusually conscious of the scuffed sandals, oversized shorts and Hawaiian-print shirt he'd picked up the day before in a second-hand clothing store for the equivalent of just over three pounds.

His appearance was also giving someone else concern. As he approached the bar, the man behind it regarded him with a mixture of hostility and uncertainty. Because of the nature of marinas, this big, ugly, scruffy and probably dirty man might be a valued crew member on a two million leva yacht. He might even be an eccentric and super-rich owner. Some liked to dress like tramps to show that, with all their money they didn't have to try to impress anyone. The man might, of course, just be the vagrant he appeared. Boran Andronov decided it would be best to take a neutral approach, and asked politely if he could help. He spoke in English because that was the mutual language of most marinas around the world.

'Good afternoon,' said the visitor. 'I'm trying to find Yosif...' He pulled a scrap of paper from his shorts pocket, unfolded it and decided to take a run at it. '... Boyadasa...shev?'

The barman looked as if he had felt a sudden stabbing pain to his temples, then silently held his hand out. Mowgley smiled apologetically and gave him the slip of paper on which Inspector Georgiev had written the name of Den's occasional crew member.

He looked at it with a frown, then shook his head. 'I do not know this man.'

A voice came from behind. 'I think he may be looking for Meyka.'

Mowgley turned to where a man was sitting at a table with a glass of beer and an empty plate on it. His accent and diction made it obvious that English was his first language. He was dressed as casually as Mowgley, but his ensemble could have cost a hundred-fold more. To an informed observer a further indicator of his financial status was the Rolex Yachtmaster 40MM on his tanned wrist and the Dita Mach One sunglasses on the top of his well-groomed head.

Mowgley nodded to the barman, then walked over to the table. 'Am I?' he asked, 'looking for Meyka, I mean?'

The man gestured towards the chair opposite his and raised a finger. 'Another beer, Boran,' he said to the barman, then 'How about you?' to Mowgley.

'Beer sounds good,' said Mowgley, lowering himself with care into the spindly chair.

The man took the piece of paper and looked at it. 'Yeah, I think that's Meyka's name. He told me it means 'bear' or 'hulk', either of which is a pretty good description.'

The barman arrived and put two beer bottles and glasses on the table and proffered the tray to Mowgley's host. The man scribbled on a slip of paper before giving a dismissive wave and inviting the barman to have a drink or the money instead. Boran nodded his unsmiling thanks and returned to the bar. Mowgley wondered what the Bulgar actually thought of the rich and often vulgar people he had to serve every day. And how much he got away with when taking his revenge.

'Cheers.' The man lifted his glass and Mowgley responded, and they both drank.

'So,' said the man, 'What do you want to see Meyka about?' He had a south London accent and together with his choice of dress and expensive accessories would have been, Mowgley thought, more at home in Southern Spain than eastern Bulgaria.

Mowgley took his time before answering, taking a slow pull on his beer as he regarded the figure opposite him. He must have been pushing seventy but from a distance and in a good light would have looked much younger. The impression would have been helped by a full head of curly and suspiciously lustrous black hair. His mahogany-hued face emphasised the cornflower blue eyes and perfect set of the whitest of white teeth. He vaguely reminded Mowgley of someone famous, and he realised it was the actor Ian McShane.

'Sorry,' he said, putting the glass down and holding his hand out. 'Jack Mowgley.'

'Ah,' said the man, taking Mowgley's hand limply but neglecting to give his own name.

'I've got a friend with a boat here,' said Mowgley. 'Someone told me that this…Meyka…crewed for him now and then.'

'Ah,' said the man again, 'So who's your mate?'

'Den Cullan.'

The man reached up and fiddled with a medallion hanging from a fine gold chain around his neck. Mowgley saw that it looked like a misshapen yellow emoji with a benevolent expression. Then he realised it was a facsimile of the mask professor Kirov had been holding aloft in the video.

'Okay,' said the man, looking at Mowgley thoughtfully. 'And do you know about Den?'

'Yes,' said Mowgley. 'I came over with his ex-wife a couple of days ago.'

The man nodded. 'I heard about her. How's she taking it?'

'Upset but alright, I suppose,' said Mowgley, becoming faintly irritated and trying not to show it. 'It's been a long time since they split up.'

The man nodded. 'Yeah. I think Den had been with Magda for ever. 'Have you seen her?'

'Not yet,' said Mowgley. 'Have you?'

'No. So what was it you wanted to see Meyko about?'

'I just wanted to check the boat out for Jen - Mrs Cullan - and find out if this Meyko will be looking after it. And I need to find out about mooring fees and stuff, you know.'

The man smiled knowingly. 'You mean in case the Treasure Seeker comes to your lady friend, you mean.'

Mowgley's irritation grew and he frowned to show it. 'She's got a lot on her plate at the moment. I'm just helping with the details and tying stuff up.'

'That's good of you.' The man smiled a don't-take-me-for-a-pratt smile, then said: There's a lot of 'stuff' to be tied up, I reckon. The boat's worth half a million and then there's the penthouse and whatever Den had tucked away. If the missus or you can find it.'

Mowgley emptied his glass and looked at the man for a moment before speaking. 'So, have you seen the crewman?'

The man shook his head. 'He wasn't really Den's crewman, just a guy who helped out when needed. He does all sorts and likes to travel around. I expect he'll show up, and if you leave your number and a few quid with Boran, I reckon he'll give you a call when he does.'

Mowgley put his glass down and heaved himself out of the chair. 'Thanks for your help.'

'No problem.'

As Mowgley began to walk away, the man called out. 'Give my regards to Mrs Cullan-as-was, and good luck with helping her get her hands on the stuff. Of course, the lovely Magda might have something to say about who gets it.'

Mowgley stopped and looked back down at him. 'Of course. But like Mr Bear, she ain't around, is she?'

9

When asked, more than half of all Bulgarians claim to be Eastern Orthodox Christians.

One of the main tenets of that religion is that the soul remains earthbound for forty days after death, and during this time the shade may visit familiar places or continue daily routines to allow it to adjust to the transition from life to death. Throughout their loved one's last days on earth, devout families will set a place and a meal at table and even converse with the dearly departed so he or she will not feel neglected.

Funerals traditionally take place within days of the death. Traditionally and when practical, close relatives will walk with the hearse to the church carrying flowers and a cross. The body will be on show in an open casket and the hearse followed by mourners playing drums, cymbals or horns. Because of the forty-day transition period, food or drink to sustain the deceased may have been placed in the coffin.

Varna has been the setting for funerals for at least five millennia, and the Necropolis is recognised as a key archaeological site in world pre-history. Other necropoles from later Greek and Roman periods are dotted around the ancient city.

The modern-day cemetery is approached through a wide

arch with a cross at its highest point. This leads to a quiet place of wide pathways overlooked by marble figures and angels and sometimes more exotic creatures. Box-like family vaults line routes through the older parts of the cemetery, and they put Mowgley in mind of rows of very stylised beach huts.

If there could be such a thing, it was a good day for a funeral. Den Cullan was to be buried in a quiet corner, away from traffic noise and in the shadow of a neat, red-tiled and white-painted church. Mowgley stood close by the widow, and thought how funerals were somehow sadder when far from home. It was, he knew, a common saying amongst British expats that nobody likes to be ill in a foreign country. It would be even less fun to be buried in one, Mowgley thought. If given the choice and regardless of how settled he was here, he suspected Don Cullan would have preferred to be laid to rest in the earth of his native country.

Being careful not to move his head he stole a glance at Jen Cullan's profile, then slipped his arm around her waist as the coffin was lowered into the grave. He had considered how she might react, but was still surprised there were no tears or show of emotion. She had so far watched the proceedings almost as if she was attending the funeral of someone she had not known too well. Perhaps, he thought, that was what she was thinking.

The coffin came to rest with a scraping, crunching sound and she stepped forward and took a metal scoop from one of the gravediggers. After sprinkling earth on the casket, she turned and handed the trowel to Mowgley. He looked at it and her awkwardly, then followed her example. This part of the funeral rites with the hollow sound of clods of earth and stones hitting the top of the casket always struck him as very final, which was perhaps why it had come about. Each of the mourners was helping to cover the body and separate it from the world of the living.

As they moved away and the short queue shuffled forward, Jen Cullan's body sagged momentarily and she made a soft keening sound in her throat. Mowgley replaced his arm around her waist and held her tightly. 'You okay?'

She put a hand over his and patted it and gave a watery smile. 'I'm okay, but God I could do with a fag. Seriously, I'm really glad you're here. All these people are strangers and you're my only link with where I come from and my life with Den. And before you ask, yes, I'm glad I haven't told John yet - and that he's not here.'

Mowgley gave her another supportive hug. 'What do you want to do afterwards? There's nothing planned, is there?'

She smiled. 'I think we should have a very private wake - just the two of us, and get very drunk. I think Den would approve.'

The queue shuffled on towards the grave and Mowgley wondered who they were and why they had come. Then the only woman in the line arrived at the graveside. She was of middle age and very attractive and followed the sprinkling of earth by dropping a single white rose into the grave.

'Is that -?' Mowgley asked.

'Magda?' said Jen Cullan. 'No, Magda Abadjiev is younger and even prettier in the same sort of Slavic way.'

'So who is she?'

Jen Cullan shrugged. 'Don't know. I bet Mr Big Moustache does, though.' She nodded to where, on the other side of the grave, Inspector Georgiev was fiddling with his pipe as he stood in a group of three other men. One was very big, taller and broader than Mowgley. He was in late middle-age and had a full head of iron - grey hair and a matching moustache. It was not as extravagant as Georgiev's, but very Bulgarian. Next to him was a much shorter and slighter and younger clean- shaven man. Both wore sober suits and ties, and looked as if they wore them for a living. The fourth man was of middle height and stocky and Mowgley would have made a bet against him being a suit-wearer by inclination or profession. He had obviously not dressed for the occasion and wore a rumpled white linen jacket and baggy off-white trousers. At his side he carried a battered straw hat. Above the open-necked denim shirt was a square, hard-looking Slavic face and features which somehow blended high intelligence and low cunning. With the rimless glasses on the end of his nose and grizzled grey beard and hair cropped close to the skull, he looked to Mowgley a curious mix of academic and eastern European thug.

Georgiev seemed to sense them watching and looked over and nodded gravely. Turning back he said something, at which the big man looked their way. He then spoke to Georgiev and waved brusquely to indicate that the inspector should lead the way. The bearded man glanced in their direction, swiftly shook hands with the other three and walked off in the direction of the cemetery gates.

As the trio arrived, Inspector Georgiev reached out and took Jen's hand. 'Mrs Cullan, once again my sincere condolences.' Still holding her hand he half-turned towards the smaller man and said: 'Mrs Cullan, may I introduce Varna's Public Prosecutor? This is Andrey Andreev.' The man stepped forward and gave a stiff half-bow and muttered something about it being a sad day. Georgiev then turned towards the big man and said: 'And this is Commissar Boris Dragov of the Directorate for Combatting Organised Crime. He is my boss's boss.'

'Madame Cullan. I am sincerely sorry for your loss.' Dragov looked at Mowgley and then expectantly at Georgiev. 'Ah,' said the inspector. This is Mr Mowgley, a friend of Mrs Cullan.'

Mowgley shook the small man's proffered hand, then the huge paw of the giant policeman. Having given the briefest of nods to acknowledge Mowgley's presence, Dragov turned back to Jen Cullan: 'Will you be staying long?'

'Another week or so, I think,' she said. 'Just until everything is settled.'

He gave a slight bow. 'I hope that this tragedy will not stop you returning to Bulgaria.'

'I hope so too. It is a beautiful country and everyone has been so kind.'

'As you saw today,' said Commissar Dragov, 'your husband was much respected and a valued member of the business community. We will miss him.'

'Yes,' said Jen Cullan, 'so will I.'

~

'You certainly know how to give a girl a good time. A pub crawl and a kebab takeaway. Reminds me of my early days with Den.'

'But that's what you said you wanted to do,' said Mowgley defensively.

She licked a finger and nodded. 'True. After today I really didn't fancy a formal dinner. This is much nicer, and we certainly covered some territory. But it's weird that after all that booze I feel dead sober.'

'Me too,' said Mowgley through a mouthful of pitta bread.

It was after midnight and they were sitting on a plinth below a statue of a man astride a horse, his sword raised high above his head.

She saw him looking up and said: 'Tsar Kaloyan is a bit of a local as well as a national hero. He led an uprising against the Byzantines at the end of the 12th century and held them off in the siege of Varna.'

Mowgley cleared his mouth. 'Gosh, professor, is there anything you don't know?'

'Lots and lots, but you might be surprised how much you can learn in a decade sitting with a book in planes and trains and hotel rooms. Besides, I really believe you enjoy visiting a country much more if you know something about its culture and history. And I'm a schoolteacher, remember. Anyway, you're just the same as me in a different way.'

'What do you mean?

'I can tell you like learning about people and places and how things work in foreign places. Knowledge is power as the man said. And I saw you watching Georgiev and his cronies.'

Mowgley saw off the last of his *kebapche* and wiped his mouth with the paper serviette. She watched him expectantly, then said 'So, what did you think of them?'

'Very nice but I would have liked the sauce to be a bit hotter. Apart from that- '

She leaned over and aimed a mock blow at his arm. 'You know what I mean.'

'Oh, you mean Little and Large? I don't know but I wouldn't like to meet the big one in a dark alley. Little looked like he's tougher than he looks, and what about the bloke in the dirty white outfit. Do you know him?'

She shook her head. 'The face looked sort of familiar. Perhaps he was a business contact of Den's.'

'And the lady with the rose?'

She shrugged. 'Pass. Could have been a rival of Magda's, or perhaps she worked for Den.'

Having finished their takeaway, Mowgley conducted the now-familiar double cigarette ceremony. As they sat and smoked, an elderly lady with a tiny dog on a short lead walked slowly by. She said something, and Jen Cullan looked up at the night sky and then replied.

When the old lady and her old dog had passed by, Mowgley looked around for a waste bin and asked what she had said.

'She said God had made another beautiful night, and we must make the most of it while we are young, and I agreed. I guess she thought we were lovers.'

'Ah.' The old lady reached the entrance to a tower block and stood watching fondly as her dog defecated on the pavement.

'You really do feel at home here, don't you?'

She considered his question, then said. 'Yes I do. What about you?'

'I like the food for sure. Except the salad'

She smiled. 'And could you see yourself living here?'

He frowned. 'Don't know about that, but I can see the appeal to Brits on a tight budget. Everything seems so cheap.'

'Not to Bulgarians.'

'I suppose not. So when are you thinking of going home?'

'Not sure yet. I want to get back to John but there's some more legal stuff that the nice man at the consulate is helping with. I don't need to be here for the reading of the will, if that's what happens here.'

'But you know there is a will?'

She hesitated then said: 'I think there is. The consul gave me the number of Den's lawyer. I called and he said Den had made one.'

'Aren't you interested what's in it?

She dabbed at her mouth with the serviette. 'Not really. Den did his duty to John with the trust fund, and the *advokat* said that's safe. I guess Mr Apostolov will let me know if Den left me anything or I'm entitled to a widow's share or something.' She took a reflective draw on her cigarette. 'I am curious about Magda though.'

Mowgley put his arm round her shoulder. 'I'll check with Georgiev tomorrow if there's any news.' He looked round for a litter bin, then crumpled the box and paper napkin and put them in a pocket. 'Will you come back to Bulgaria?'

'Of course. John will want to visit his dad - I hope - and, like I said, I like it here.'

Mowgley too his arm from her shoulders, stood and looked up at the statue. 'You never know. It's quite possible you'll be a rich woman when the will is sorted.'

She laughed. 'Think so? Not if Magda has anything to say about it, I reckon.'

'What if she doesn't turn up?'

She stood up and slid an arm through his. 'What makes you say that?'

'Well, it's strange she wasn't around for the funeral and nobody's seen her.'

They started to walk along the wide, silent boulevard and she said: 'Like I said before, perhaps she hasn't heard about Den. Perhaps she had a row with him and didn't intend coming back. I'm sure the police would know if something had happened to her.'

Mowgley frowned. 'Hmm, not likely she wouldn't come back with all that money slushing around, I reckon. Oh bugger!'

She stopped and turned towards him. 'What's the matter. Are you okay?'

'I'm fine.' He ran a forefinger down the lapel of his newly acquired second-hand suit jacket and held it up. 'It's just that I've got hot sauce on my new coat…'

Jen Cullan took a handkerchief from her bag, spat on it and started dabbing at the stain. 'Never mind. I don't suppose you'll have any more funerals to attend in Bulgaria. And as the suit cost less than a fiver it's no big deal. As they say, worst things happen at sea.'

'Yes,' Mowgley said thoughtfully as he licked his finger. 'they do, don't they?'

10

'Did you not see that donkey cart?'

Mowgley was a nervous and consequently bad driver and an even more nervous passenger. Inspector Georgiev was an atrocious driver but obviously unaware of or unconcerned by the level of his incompetence. He also liked to wave his arms a lot and fiddle with, fill and maintain his pipe while at the wheel. It seemed to Mowgley that his only redeeming feature was how slowly he drove.

'It was a pony, not a donkey,' Georgiev said cheerfully. 'Peasants have donkeys to pull their carts, Roma gypsies have ponies. Don't ask me why.'

'Okay, I won't.' Mowgley concentrated on the road ahead and wished his driver also would.

At Georgiev's request he had caught a taxi to a railway station on the outskirts of Varna where the Inspector had picked him up in an unmarked car.

Opening his eyes after another near-miss, Mowgley saw the dark skyline ahead and asked. 'Am I allowed to ask where we're going, and why? That looks like some big hills ahead.'

'Those hills are what we like to call the Balkans, Mr Mowgley.' Georgiev waved his pipe majestically and continued: 'People talk about the Balkan peninsula and include all the countries

95

on it as if they had a share in our mountains. In fact, the Balkan range is completely contained within Bulgaria and is all ours. Even the Turks cannot steal our mountains.'

'Got it', said Mowgley. 'and why are we heading for them?'

'I thought you would enjoy seeing how beautiful the countryside is and have lunch at a nice little restaurant in a small village in the foothills. And as I said before, it is best we are not seen together now the case on Dennis Cullan is officially closed.'

'You mean you're not closing it but you want certain people to think you have?'

'Exactly.'

'And are you going to tell me who these people are?'

The inspector transferred his pipe to the hand on the wheel and began rummaging about in his pocket. 'Of course, but first we must get something important settled.'

'I'm all ears.'

Georgiev cast a curious look at his passenger, then said: 'We are still on very formal terms of address, and I do not like having to call you Mr Mowgley all the time. May I call you John?'

Mowgley winced as what looked like a pre-World War II lorry laden with logs roared by, showering the car with branches. 'Of course, though most of my friends call me Jack.'

Georgiev pulled a tobacco pouch from an inside pocket and tried to open it by pulling at the zipper tag with his teeth. 'Oh? I thought your given name was John?'

'Can I help with that?' Mowgley relieved Georgiev of the pouch and pipe. 'It is, but Johns are often called Jack by their close friends.'

Georgiev watched as Mowgley teased out and lightly packed tobacco into his pipe and nodded his approval. 'What a strange custom,' he said, 'and am I close enough to call you Jack?'

'Help yourself.' Mowgley handed the pipe over, lit and held out his lighter as Georgiev chose to ignore a red light and a flashing warning light on a railway crossing at the same time. The inspector took a few puffs and nodded his thanks. 'Then you must call me Gosho or Gogo They are diminutives of Georgi.'

'Which do you prefer?'

Georgiev pondered for a moment then said: 'In your language Gosho is a term of surprise, and Gogo is what lady dancers do, I believe? Perhaps to call me Gosho would be best?'

'It's a deal, Gosho.'

~

'Did you enjoy the mish mash?' Inspector Georgiev asked solicitously. 'I thought you would prefer it to our national salad starter.'

Mowgley pushed his empty plate away and sighed contentedly.' Lovely. What was it?'

'It is an omelette, usually made with cheese, peppers, garlic and paprika and other spices and herbs. Or there could be mushrooms or sausage. In Italy it would be a *frittata*, in Spain a tortilla Espanola. Here it is a mish mash.'

They were sitting at a table on the decking outside a bar overlooking what passed as the village square. Children played some sort of game in the dust, and the occasional donkey cart rattled slowly by. Now and then a car would drive noisily past, its rarity making it seem an almost alien vehicle.

'So, Gosho,' said Mowgley, 'what's next?'

Georgiev emptied his tumbler of red wine and stroked his lush moustache. 'If you have room I thought we would try the musaka - it is a speciality here and a national dish. It's also something else the Turks stole from us and then ruined by adding aubergine. Then perhaps we could try the *mekitzi*, which are dough balls made with yoghurt and fried. As an aid to digestion, we could finish with coffee and a glass of rakia.'

'I'm game,' said Mowgley, 'but what I actually meant was what you're going to do next about Den's murder...or what you think was a murder?'

Georgiev puffed reflectively on his pipe, blew out a small cloud of smoke and said: 'So you are not of my opinion?'

Mowgley shrugged. 'The missing swim platform could have been an accident. The man who crewed the Treasure Seeker is a drifter and could have gone off to work somewhere else. It is possible Den had too much to drink and fell off his boat.'

'And Magda?'

Mowgley nodded assent. 'Yes, that is a bit of a puzzler. Do

you think she is somehow involved, or another victim?'

'I don't know. Either is possible. That is why I need you to help find her.'

'Me? Mowgley frowned. 'I know I'm a detective but I don't speak a word of Bulgarian - and I wouldn't know where to start.'

Georgiev smiled. 'No, but Mrs Cullan speaks excellent Bulgarian - for a foreigner. She also knows what Magda looks like, and I believe she would like to know where she is and if she knows about the death - and what she plans to do.'

'But like me, she won't have a clue where to start looking.'

Inspector Georgiev pointed with his pipe to a road leading from the square. 'You could start at the next village. It is where the parents of Magda Abadjiev live.'

'How do you know that?'

'Remember I have been investigating and trying to catch Mr Cullan out for two years. Magda was an important part of the investigation and I still think she may be a key witness.'

'And you think she could be there - at her parents' home?'

Georgiev waited while the bar owner delivered two heaped plates of moussaka and another carafe of wine. 'Perhaps. We know she visits her parents regularly and has a room there.'

Mowgley picked up a fork. 'So why don't you send someone you trust to find out if she's there...or where she may be? Anyway, don't you have a duty to inform Magda of her lover's death?'

The inspector raised a bushy eyebrow. 'It is not as easy as that. I cannot send a policeman who I believe to be honest as that would show I am still pursuing the case. Even if I did, the parents would not want to speak to him. They are simple villagers and would be frightened and worried. Perhaps they will know of Mrs Cullan and Magda's relationship with her husband. In any case, Mrs Cullan could tell them of her husband's death and say that their daughter should get in touch with me - and only me.'

'Okay, I get all that, but what about me? Why would I be there?'

'You are, of course, Mrs Cullan's friend and are helping her in her time of grief. Why would you not be there?

Mowgley loaded his fork. 'Fair enough. I'll talk to Jen. Now what about your mates at the funeral?'

'My mates?'

'Little and Large and the dodgy-looking bloke dressed like a character from Our Man in Havana?'

Inspector Georgiev gave him a puzzled look but did not ask for clarification. 'Andrey Andreev is young to be a Regional Public Prosecutor. He is ambitious and has made his stand against corruption very plain. That of course may be the truth, or as you might say, a convenient smoke screen.'

'And the man mountain?'

Georgiev smiled. 'Ah, our Commissar Dragov is an interesting character. Before we were released from the yoke of Communism, he was an enthusiastic and influential member of the Party. When the dictator Zhivkov was ousted in 1989, Mr Dragov suddenly became an equally enthusiastic and influential democrat and capitalist.'

'So what was a high-up officer in a body formed to fight organised crime doing at Den's funeral?

The inspector shrugged. 'Perhaps he wanted to see who would turn up at the funeral. Or perhaps he had another reason.'

'Okay. And what about the mystery blonde lady who threw the flower into Den's grave?'.

'She was a...friend of Mr. Cullan.'

'Ah. And did Magda know about her?'

'I don't know. The lady lives in Sofia and they only met when he was there, which was often.'

'Do you know if she had anything to do with what he did?'

Georgiev pursed his lips. 'I don't think so. She is very wealthy and is the widow of a quite prominent member of the Bulgarian Mafia.'

'Are you kidding me?'

'No, I am serious.'

'Then there's another possible reason Den was murdered, if he was?'

'Perhaps, but I think not.'

'So there is an actual Bulgarian Mafia?'

'Certainly, though here they are known as the *Mutri*. Whatever you call them, hundreds of loosely-related organised crime groups operate almost with impunity here. Not a single gang member has been punished, there are regular assassinations and they have influence everywhere.'

'And do you suspect the Commissar of corruption?'

Georgiev expelled a puff of air. 'I suspect all high-ranking government-appointed officials. Especially if they wear suits which would take three months of an honest working man's wage to pay for. And if they live in a house worth more than a working man could earn in a lifetime.'

The inspector clenched his teeth around the stem of his pipe so fiercely that Mowgley feared it would break. 'I get the picture,' he said. 'But how does he get away with it? Why has nobody spilled the beans?'

Georgiev looked down at his plate and prodded his moussaka with a fork. 'Perhaps they have. If so, it could be they who would lose their job, or even disappear. Under Communism it was privileges for the few and poverty for the masses. Now it is dog eat dog and corruption is endemic. According to a report from the Centre for the Study of Democracy, corruption in Bulgaria is three times that in other European countries. The CSD estimated that 15,000 bribes are made every month at every level. It may be a judge being bribed to ensure a favourable verdict, or a big company seeking permission for a very inappropriate land development. Or it might just be a simple matter of getting to the head of the queue to see a doctor or dentist. In your country it is a scandal if a politician uses public money to pay for a house for a duck; in Bulgaria, corruption is the norm, and it has become worse since the country was admitted into the European Union in 2007. Add the organised crime gangs into the equation and you have, as it has been said, a melting pot of crime, greed and corruption.'

'And is nothing being done about it?'

The inspector shrugged. 'The government say they are intent on defeating corruption, but those are just words and it can be a very dangerous thing to speak out too loudly. Just last week the body of a woman was found in a park in the town of Ruse. She had been raped and badly beaten. Viktoria Marinova was a journalist and the host of a new television programme called Detector. Its aim was to report and expose corruption at the highest levels. When asked for their reaction, the Minister of the Interior said he believed the murder was about rape and theft as the woman's car keys and phone were missing. Our Prime Minister is said to share that view. The Prosecutor

General has already said it was unlikely that the murder was connected to Miss Marinova's work.'

'And that's why you are being so careful with your investigation into Den Cullan's murder?'

'Of course.'

Their moussaka had grown cold while Georgiev talked and Mowgley listened. The inspector looked at his plate and sighed. 'I am sorry, but I seem to have lost my appetite. I think it may be time to pass the rakia?'

~

Even by YouTube standards, the clip was poorly filmed and more than amateurishly presented. If it were seriously claiming to represent one of the most significant moments in Bulgarian archaeology, it also looked very bogus.

A stocky man had his back to the camera as he knelt amongst a heap of rubble. He was stripped to the waist and wore a pair striped swim shorts. On his head was the sort of pith helmet usually seen only in old movies about colonial jungle adventures.

Around him a bevy of attractive young women were cooing and chattering excitedly. Some of them held unsullied paint brushes. scrapers and small trowels, and were holding them in a way that suggested they were not familiar with what they were for. At first Mowgley had thought it might be the introduction to a low-budget porn movie, then the central figure straightened and held up a gold-coloured, dish-shaped object. It was roughly round and had been worked into a representation of a misshapen face with extraordinarily large ears, a beaky nose and downturned mouth. To Mowgley its expression suggested it were indignant at being disturbed and made to feature in such a vulgar an obviously contrived scene.

Inspector Georgiev leaned forward and hit the pause button, freeze framing a close-up of the strange mask-like object, then looked at Mowgley to gauge his reaction.

They were sitting in the inspector's car alongside a bridge over a shallow, slow-moving river. It was a pastoral scene and the noise of the main road to Varna was no more than a drone. In a field next to the lay-by three sheep, a donkey and two goats regarded them incuriously. They were being watched over by an elderly man sitting on a grassy knoll. On his head was a broad-brimmed hat which had obviously seen the passing of many seasons. He was leaning on a staff, and despite the weather wore a buttoned-up heavy overcoat. Further along the river, a much younger man in a camouflage jacket was kneeling on the bank. He seemed absorbed in his work, which was scooping water into a shallow dish, examining the contents and then emptying the bowl before repeating the process. Like people who do repetitive work in factories, the sequence seemed to be happening automatically and perhaps while his mind was elsewhere.

'He is looking for gold,' explained Georgiev. 'It is legal to do so in Bulgaria.'

'What's his chances of finding any?'

The inspector shrugged. 'This is a land rich in gold, which is why there is so much buried treasure here. He may find a few lev's worth, and a little extra is always welcome in such a poor country. And like the lottery, there is always the chance of a really big win.'

He pointed at the laptop screen. 'So, what did you think of that?'

Mowgley frowned. 'Well, it's our man from the cemetery, but what was he up to and is it really supposed to be real?'

Georgiev smiled. 'That is the acclaimed archaeologist Professor Kiril Kirov. He came to fame in 2004 when he was excavating in the Valley of the Thracian Kings.'

'Is that like the Valley of the Kings in Egypt?'

'Yes. It was the professor who coined the name. He is very good at attracting publicity as well as finding buried treasures.' Georgiev closed the lid of the laptop and tossed it carelessly on the back seat. 'After the first discovery in the valley in 1944, a growing number of burial mounds and tombs have been located and excavated. In 2004 and after twenty years of searching, Professor Kirov discovered the gold mask. It is believed to be the likeness of Teres, a Thracian ruler in the fifth century before Christ. The discovery made his name and he went on to discover many more priceless artefacts. And is still finding them.'

Mowgley scratched his chin. 'And that crappy clip is supposed to be the moment of discovery of the mask?'

Georgiev smiled again. 'That's what the professor claims, but it certainly looks staged. He still spends his days there and regularly comes up with artefacts. It is fair to say that he is regarded with mixed views in academic circles.'

'In what way mixed?'

'Kirov is much admired by the media and has been honoured by the government, but is criticised in academic circles for his aggressive methods and, as you saw, love of the theatrical. He has been known to use heavy machinery to quickly get rid of top soil, can be secretive and unscientific and make extravagant claims, but he does make some remarkable finds.'

'And what happens to them?'

'All historical artefacts must be reported to the government for registration, research and cataloguing and then display in suitable museums. Or at least they are supposed to be.'

'You mean they don't all get reported?'

The Inspector scratched his cheek thoughtfully. 'No, of course not.'

'And there must sometimes be collusion between the smugglers and those who are supposed to stop them?'

'Exactly. Just last week a gang was arrested in a joint operation by the Directorate for Combatting Organised Crime and SANS - The State Agency for National Security. There were many bracelets and other jewellery, and the centrepiece was a crown of pure gold.

'A few bob's worth, then?'

'Very much so. Not all the hoard has been recovered, and the asking price for the crown alone was two million dollars. Significantly, one of the gang was a long-time officer in SANS.'

'And that's where your lot, the anti-corruption agency, come in?'

'That's correct.'

Mowgley watched the gold panner stand up and stretch his limbs. 'So why do you think the professor turned up at Den's funeral?'

'To simply pay his respects, perhaps. We know they did business together as Mr Cullan would often employ professor Kirov to comment on and validate items he was offering for sale. Or perhaps he thought the regional press and TV people would be there. As I said, he is a relentless self-publicist. We know they knew each other, but not what their connection was, if there was one.'

'But you think he's a dodgy character?'

The Inspector frowned. 'Dodgy?'

'Crooked, untrustworthy.'

Georgiev sucked at his pipe, then said: 'Perhaps. I do not like a mystery, and it is a mystery how Professor Kirov is so lucky when it comes to unearthing so many buried treasures.'

11

'How's your poorly leg?'

Mowgley shifted in the passenger seat of the hire car, then looked across at the driver. 'Fine, why?'

'You seem to be squirming about a bit,' said Jen Cullan. 'Is it my driving?'

'Of course not. Just a bit stiff, that's all.' He tried not to yelp and duck as a giant car transporter hurtled towards them, occupying most of their side of the road. 'Fancy a stop for coffee and a fag?'

They were retracing Mowgley's journey of the day before, on their way to the village where Magda Abadjiev's parents lived. Jen Cullan was a much better and more considerate driver than Georgiev, but Mowgley still felt ultra-nervous. It was not her driving skills and attitudes that concerned him, but the almost unimaginable insanity of the other road users. In France, drivers ranged from bad to mad; in Bulgaria they all seemed to cherish a death wish.

'Did you know,' she asked as if reading his thoughts, ' that Bulgaria has a higher road death date than anywhere else in the EU except Romania?'

Mowgley hunched his shoulders and shrank back into his seat as they were undertaken by a battered pick-up truck with a goat in the back. 'Yes, I did,' he muttered. 'Perhaps it's because they don't think they've got that much to live for.'

~

He had begun to breathe more easily, helped by his second cigarette in ten minutes.

They were sitting at a rusty garden table outside what appeared to be a combined bar and grocery store. It stood in a lay-by off the road westward from Varna to Denia, sandwiched between a mobile home which would certainly never be mobilised again and the inevitable car breakers yard. The shop had been cobbled together from old planks and plywood sheeting, and the awning under which they sat was an old, much-holed tarpaulin. Their treacly coffee had been brewed up on a camping stove and Mowgley's cup was missing a handle. Between the shack and the road were scattered an assortment of terminally distressed and mismatching chairs and tables, some with less than the usually agreed number of legs.

Directly fronting the road like a leguminous barrier stood a row of boxes and crates filled with vegetables that looked as if they had been harvested from a land of giants. Spring onions were the length and breadth of small leeks, radishes the size of golf balls and tomatoes like cricket balls seemed the norm.

Sitting next to the display and wearing a long, tattered dress, shawl and headscarf in spite of the heat was the proprietor. She looked as if she had once been pretty, but it was hard to tell her age. She could have been anywhere from forty to seventy. She was sitting on a stool next to the redoubt of boxes, and nearby a couple of dirty but obviously happy small children were playing ever more dangerously close to the busy road. Further along the lay-by, a short, fat man was sitting on a plastic chair beside an old Trabant P50 saloon, the roof, bonnet and boot of which were covered with all styles and sizes of footwear.

The owner was sitting very still and watching the passing traffic fixedly as if trying to will a potential customer to pull over and look at his wares.

'That's what I call a travelling salesman,' said Mowgley. 'I wonder if it's worth his while?'

'At least he's having a go,' said Jen Cullan. 'He probably has a daily route around villages and places like this. In some villages it's a social event and women turn up just to look at what he's got. I don't know why, but shoes are really expensive here. Some traders buy job lots at boot sales in the UK and bring them all the way here by road.' She pointed at the roof of the Trabant. 'That pair of Nike trainers could have belonged to a gym bunny in Rotherham who couldn't bear to be seen in last year's style and gave them to a charity shop.' She shook her head. 'You have to spend time here to understand how hard things are, and what people have to do to scrape a living.'

Mowgley waited until the roar of a passing petrol tanker had faded, then said: 'Or they could go bent and make a fortune out of looted treasure.'

She shrugged. 'That's the same rule all over the world. There are always the clever crooked ones and those who just get by. I think a lot of people in Britain who live comfortably off benefits and still moan should be made to come here and see just how tough life can be in other places not so far from home. And remember, Bulgaria is a member of the European Union. All those billions of Euros flooding in but so little of it trickling down to those in most need.' She leaned over and laid a hand on his arm. 'Sorry, I'll put the soapbox away.'

'Not on my account. At my age I'm beginning to understand and come to terms with the fact that life is not fair. Trouble is I can't see a way of fixing it'

They sat watching the traffic speed by, then she said: 'It's funny, isn't it?'

'What is?'

'How things turn out. That lady is trying to sell her vegetables and bring her kids up. The little man is trying to earn a living flogging other people's cast-off shoes. I'm a widow from the Home Counties who's just buried her husband, you're a private detective in France and we're both sitting beside a road in the poorest country in Europe. Kismet or happenstance or self-determination, do you reckon?'

Mowgley scratched his chin and reached for the cigarettes. 'Pass. I've been trying to work that out for a long time. But it was you who called me and set things going, remember.'

'True. Are you sorry you came?'

'No,' he said thoughtfully, 'I'm not. Fancy another coffee?'

'Not for me.' She looked into her cup, shuddered then looked questioningly at him.

'How about you?'

When he made a face and shook his head she got up and walked to where the woman was guarding her giant vegetables.

Mowgley stood by the hire car and finished his cigarette, watching as she paid the woman for the coffee with a note and waved away the change. Then she took some coins from her pocket and gave them to the children. Passing the shoe-covered Trabant she hesitated, then took a pair of badly scuffed, gold-coloured court shoes from the roof. The man got up and hurried across and money changed hands. Getting in the car, she threw the shoes on to the back seat, found her keys and started the engine.

'How do you know they'll fit you?' Mowgley asked as she waited for a gap in the traffic.

'I don't,' she said,' and I don't really care...'

~

'Crikey. I wonder what the kids do for fun around here?'

'There aren't any,' said Jen Cullan. 'They've all left town.'

After a long uphill climb they had arrived at the outskirts of the village where Magda Abadjiev had been born and her parents still lived.

Most of the squat, box-like houses dotted along the track looked abandoned, but there were some signs of human occupation. A line of washing flapped in a yard and the sound of an animated conversation came from an open window. Dogs barked and sheep bleated. The metalled road had come to its end and the baked earth track was scarred with tractor ruts and sometimes gaping fissures caused by alternating hot summers and wet and cold winters. A tethered goat was grazing on the verge, and looked up as they passed. It had probably not seen such a shiny new car, Mowgley thought, or perhaps even one that moved.

They bumped on past a wheel-less Lada, and a trio of hens fluttered out of their improvised coop to see what the fuss was about. Further along and round a bend, they found their way blocked by a shaggy dog the size of a Shetland pony. It lay in the middle of the track and was, Mowgley guessed, either dead or dozing in the midday sun. There would be not much danger of being run over on this little-used thoroughfare.

'Before you ask,' said Mowgley, 'I'm not getting out to tell it to move.'

'I could give a beep.'

'Better not; it might get angry and decide to eat the car.'

Their problem was solved by the arrival of a donkey cart piled high with freshly-cut grass. The driver was an elderly man in overalls, a collarless shirt and an I Love New York ballcap. As the cart stopped outside one of the less-ruined properties the giant dog got up, stretched and walked across to the verge. It was, Mowgley noted, almost as big as the donkey tethered to the cart.

The old man eased himself down from the seat and walked towards them. As he came closer, Mowgley saw that his face was disfigured by an angry-looking growth running from his top lip across a cheek bone and ending below his left eye. It gave his face a lopsided look and the affected eye an alarming squint.

The man stopped at the driver's window, and Jen Cullan lowered it and said something. The man replied, and she fired off a long sentence in which Mowgley thought he recognised Magda Abadjiev's name.

The villager shook his head vigorously and pointed along the track. Then he spoke for what seemed an inordinately long time, accompanied by hand gestures and more head-shaking. Eventually, he was done, and she smiled and nodded, said something which was probably a thank-you, then wound the window up and drove slowly on in the direction to which the man had pointed.

'He took a long time telling you he didn't know where Magda's parents lived,' Mowgley observed.

'Oh, he knows them alright,' she said, 'I guess people don't here get much chance to have a chat with strangers. He was telling me about Magda and how she was one of the last young people to leave the village. There isn't anyone under seventy living here now.'

'So what was all the head-shaking about?'

She smiled. 'In Bulgaria, shaking your head means 'yes' and nodding means 'no'. Don't ask me why and it's mostly the older people who stick to it.'

'But,' observed Mowgley, 'you nodded when you said goodbye.'

'Ah,' she said knowingly, 'that was a thank-you and farewell nod as against a 'no' nod.'

'And what's the difference?'

'Intent.'

'Gotcha.'

~

'Are they the Bulgarian equivalent of those pictures of Pit Bull terriers and Alsatians people put in their windows to frighten off burglars?'

She looked to where Mowgley was pointing and saw he meant a small poster fixed to one of the gates. There were many of them, and each bore a photograph of an elderly face. All the owners looked unhappy or even angry. For whatever reason, it was clear that they, unlike the more civilized parts of Europe, had not enjoyed posing in front of a camera.

'No,' she said, 'they're Death Notices. It's another very Bulgarian thing. You see them everywhere on gates and lampposts, even in towns.'

'So, all the houses with the dead people photos are empty?'

She nodded. 'That's why they call places like this ghost villages. The young people have gone to work and live in towns or abroad. As the old people die, their houses are locked up and left to rot. Nobody wants to buy them so they're virtually worthless.' She nodded to the endless swathes of undulating green stretching towards the distant, mist-shrouded mountain range. 'Ironic isn't it? Breathtaking scenery and unpolluted air and wonderful weather, but no-one wants to live here. If you did, you could probably buy the village and the fields and vineyards surrounding it for the price of a lock-up garage in Brixton.'

~

The vista became ever more striking as the track got worse, and the natural beauty of their surrounding emphasised the ugliness of the drab properties on either side of the track.

'Another reminder of the Communist years,' said Jen Cullan. 'To be fair you could say it was one of their better ideas. They built thousands of simple four-room buildings in the yards of the old mud cottages and supplied them with electricity and a water supply. They weren't very aesthetically pleasing and had no toilets or bathrooms, but the roofs didn't leak and they were an improvement on what people had had to live in before. Apart from that, life hasn't changed much in all these mountain villages.'

Mowgley looked to where an old lady was standing by the side of the track. She was swathed in layers of clothing and wore a heavily patterned headscarf with a trilby hat perched incongruously on top. She was supporting herself on two shoulder-high sticks and was surrounded by a melee of goats. As the car lurched by, the woman raised one of the sticks. Mowgley returned what he thought was her wave, then realised she had lifted the staff to belabour a recalcitrant goat.

Looking up and towards the distant peaks and vine-laden slopes, Mowgley watched an eagle soar overhead and wondered if the villagers appreciated the beauty of surroundings. Perhaps they did, or perhaps they just accepted them because they had always been there. He looked across to where Jen Cullan was concentrating on avoiding a fissure which would have swallowed the giant dog whole.

'Would you fancy living here?' he asked

She frowned. 'For sure John wouldn't.' Then she looked thoughtfully at him and said: 'But I do think, with the right person, you can live in most places and be happy.'

12

The parents of Magda Abadjiev lived beyond the village at the end of the track, overlooking a lush green valley. In more affluent parts of the European Union the view alone would have been worth the best part of a million Euros.

The couple's home was one of the original village dwellings, a single-storey cottage with whitewashed walls contrasting pleasingly with the rich red of the terracotta roof tiles. There was no chimney stack, but smoke rose from a voluminous black-painted stovepipe.

A thick, rope-like vine had been trained along the top of the chain-link fence, and from it hung dozens of bunches of plump and luscious-looking grapes. A flagstone pathway led from the gate to the house, and on either side stood regimentally straight lines of tomatoes, peppers, beans and sweetcorn. Beyond was an orchard, with plum, peach, nectarine and mulberry trees laden with fruit. Chickens scratched in the earth around a giant pile of neatly stacked logs, and on the edge of the sharp but unfenced drop into the valley stood a small wooden outhouse the size and shape of a sentry-box. The low-pitched roof was neatly tiled, and the planking door was pierced with a pattern of circular holes. They were there, Mowgley assumed, for ventilation rather than to let in light.

In its idyllic setting, the cottage was what many permanently stressed city-dwellers would conjure up when daydreaming about an ideal home in which to end their days. But, Mowgley wondered, how long it would be before they found life intolerable without central heating, broadband and a flushing toilet. It would also be a long and chilly trudge to the earth closet in the depths of winter.

The solid-looking door to the cottage opened before they got out of the car, and two figures emerged to stand under the sloping roof of the porch. The woman was short and round, the man tall and spare. They stood close together and looked as if they had been doing so for many years.

As they walked towards the gate with the man leading the way, Jen Cullan reached into the back of the car and pulled out a bunch of cut flowers and a bottle of wine. Mowgley did not know if it was a Bulgarian tradition or a device, but it seemed to do the trick. As she called out and held the flowers up, the looks of apprehension were replaced by smiles. The man stepped forward, opened the gate and gestured that they should enter.

'What did you say?' Mowgley asked as they followed the couple into the house.

'I said we were friends of Magda and her boss and we were from England, and she had said we should visit her parents and see where she had grown up.'

'Her boss?'

She looked askance at him. 'We don't know if they know their daughter is living in sin with Den. Or was.'

'Ah. Smart thinking, chief. You're good at inventing stories, aren't you?'

She shrugged. 'I had a good teacher in Den, didn't I?'

The inside of the cottage was not what Mowgley would have anticipated, but then he had never been in a house made of earth and animal shit which had not been ruthlessly and expensively updated.

Like the whitewashed walls, the floor of the main room was of earth, compacted over the centuries. It was mostly covered by a costly-looking carpet with an Oriental design and Mowgley wondered if it were a gift from the Abadjiev's daughter.

In one corner and beneath a small window was a wooden work surface with shelves beneath. Alongside were more shelves bearing rows of bottles and jars, and a large and deep porcelain sink of the type which were all the rage in middle-class kitchens in Britain.

Near the kitchen area was a massive wooden table and four delicate-looking bentwood chairs. A heavily stylised and obviously valuable oil lamp stood on the table, and from a beam overhead hung an ornate lighting cluster. More gifts from a fond daughter, Mowgley guessed.

Dominating and in the centre of the room was a large, square wood-burning stove with a pipe running from it at an angle up towards and through the heavily-beamed ceiling. Offshoots from the main pipe ran across the room to pierce the walls above three doors. The stove was alight and on top were two black pots with long handles. Whatever was in them was giving off a pleasant odour.

Their host gestured for them to take a seat, then pointed at the stove and then the table. When he had finished speaking, Jen Cullan translated: 'Mr Abadjiev says we must stay for dinner. It is not much, but all comes fresh from the garden. The chicken was walking around this morning, he said. In the meantime, would we like coffee or tea or a glass of their wine or rakia?'

'It would be rude to refuse,' said Mowgley,' but can you ask if, like the stove, it's alright to smoke in here?'

~

A little later and they had been given a tour of the house by Lazar Abadjiev while his wife prepared the meal.

The earth floors of two of the three bedrooms were covered with deep rugs, on which stood double beds of tubular metal with springy wire frames and thick mattresses. Both rooms were furnished with identical 1950s-vintage wardrobes and chests of drawers and also smaller versions of the stove in the main room. On the wall above each chest of drawers hung a small wooden cross, and a small window framed a view of the valley and distant mountains.

The walls of what was obviously the old couple's bedroom were covered with framed photographs of the family as the years passed. One showed a much younger Lazar and Lidiya

Abadjiev, bending over a little golden-haired girl sitting on a child's bicycle. Already she had learned how to engage the camera with a shy but also assured smile. Next to her was a boy who looked a couple of years older. He was standing with hands in his baggy shorts, scowling at the photographer. Other individual and group pictures showed the children growing up and their parents growing old.

The second bedroom had an unlived-in air, and felt as if it had remained unchanged for some time. A chair in one corner had a tee-shirt draped on its back, and on top of the chest of drawers was a hair brush with a comb stuck in it and an ashtray containing a number of cork-tipped cigarette butts. A pair of shoes peeked out from beneath the bed. A magazine lay open on the bed where it had apparently been tossed, and on one wall was a framed head-and-shoulders photograph of a man in his thirties. He was looking at the camera in the same unsmiling way as his younger self standing with his sister for the family tableau in his parents' bedroom. Along the top of the frame was a large black bow.

The third bedroom was the largest, and as their guide unnecessarily pointed out, where their daughter stayed when visiting. The combined cost of its contents, Mowgley guessed, would be more than the market value of the whole house.

The bed was a divan with golden sheets, duvet cover and matching pillow cases, sitting on a deep Oriental rug of the same design as the carpet in the living room. On the walls was a selection of abstract paintings, their frames continuing the golden theme. A wafer-thin plasma television sat in one corner, next to a tall chest of drawers and double wardrobe. Both were of ultra-modern design. On a leather-topped desk with tubular chrome legs sat a closed laptop bearing the Apple logo, and alongside Mowgley noticed a photograph in a gold-coloured frame. It showed three figures standing in a hole in the ground, surrounded by rubble and piles of earth. Looking closer, he saw a woman dressed in an expensive-looking and unsuitable two-piece outfit flanked by Den and the celebrated archaeologist Mowgley had seen at the funeral and in the YouTube clip. The men were smiling at the camera and Professor Kirov was holding a trowel in one hand and a mud-encrusted goblet in the other. The woman who Mowgley assumed to be Magda was very beautiful, with shiny blonde hair, big eyes, pert nose, high cheek bones and full lips set in an affectionate smile. Rather than at the camera, Mowgley noted, she was looking at Den Cullan.

~

The meal was over, the plates stacked in the sink and two empty bottles stood on the work surface. One was the visiting gift from Jan Cullan, the contents of the other made by their host.

As Lazar Abadjiev had explained, wine merchants did no business in the Bulgarian countryside. Every house would have its own grapevine, and most villages were surrounded by vineyards. Even in towns, people could buy grapes at market and making wine at home was a popular and money-saving hobby. Winters were long in this part of Bulgaria, he said, and strong wine helped keep out the cold and made the time pass quicker. Sometimes there would be a village co-operative, but most people preferred to make their own, individual batch. They also liked to drink it before it got too old, and would add lemonade to give more flavour and sweetness. That was fine by Mowgley, as the result reminded him of jugs of sangria taken on holiday in southern Spain.

The rakia was another story, said their host through the translating services of Jen Cullan. Every village claimed to make the best in Bulgaria, and every house thought theirs the best of the best. Mr Abadjiev's speciality was fruit-flavouring. In all modesty, his was well thought-of in the village and even beyond, especially the elderberry and peach versions. After trying several versions Mowgley had lost his sense of taste, but tried to remember to smile and shake rather than nod his head in enthusiasm after each glassful.

As they sat and drank and smoked and chewed on toasted sunflower seeds, Lazar Abadjiev told how he had been born in the village and Lidiya on the other side of the valley. Even in the days before the young people left, there had not been much of a choice of potential spouses. Then, people believed that love at first sight was a rare luxury. If you lived and worked and stood together against the hard times, love was sometimes a consequence. If not you just had to put up with each other.

In his case, said the old man fondly, pausing to reach over and pat his wife's hand, he had known as soon as he had set his eyes on Lidiya that they were meant to be together. Luckily for him, she had eventually agreed. Parents believed in traditional courtship in those far-off times, and he would walk the five miles to and from her village most days to sit with his intended under the unwavering gaze of her mother.

After a year he had followed tradition and sent a friend to ask Lidiya's father for his agreement and help. He had agreed, and keeping to tradition had asked his daughter three times on different occasions if she wished to spend the rest of her life with Lazar. Lidiya had shaken her head and smiled on each occasion, and so the engagement had begun.

A year on and on a fine June morning Lazar was being sprinkled with barley by family and friends for good luck. His male friends and hunting companions had also fired a volley of shots into the air to frighten off evil spirits. After asking his parents for their blessing, Lazar and the wedding guests had set off in procession to the best man's house, music and dancing setting the mood along the way. Eventually and after several stops for refreshments the procession arrived at the bride-to-be's home, where more wine was taken. After further rituals, the couple had been led outside, bound together at the wrists by a strip of cloth. The procession then made it way to the church, with the couple being sure to put their right foot over the threshold first, again as custom dictated. Rings were exchanged at the end of the ceremony, and it was time for the final rite to be enacted. This involved the couple trying to be the first to step on the other's feet. The winner, it was said, would be the dominant partner in the union. As Lazar said with another squeeze of his wife's hand, Lidiya had been the quickest, and the prediction had proved entirely accurate.

After persuading their guests to try a mulberry-flavoured variety of rakia, Lidiya Abadjiev had taken up their story. The first five years of their lives together were spent in a commune far from home, with the couple assigned to work in a pig processing factory. Then, a sympathetic and compassionate official had found them work on a collective farm outside the village and they had moved into this cottage, then the home of Lazar's parents. And here they had lived as the seasons came and went, and with them the inevitable times of joy and sadness. Joy when their daughter and son were born, sadness when their parents had passed on.

After Jen Cullan had explained to Mowgley what his wife had said, Lazar Abadjiev took up their story. Their daughter, he said, had been clever, quick and eager to learn about the outside world and what it might hold for her. Magda had gone to school in Varna and won a scholarship to college. She found a place in local government, then as their guests would know, she went to work for an Englishman who was very rich and successful. She had become ever more sophisticated and had an apartment near the sea at Varna, but never forgot her parents and where she came from. Over the years she had tried to persuade them to allow her to buy them a house in town so they would have a more comfortable old age. When they refused she had said she understood, and came to stay with them whenever she could. She brought expensive gifts and could never stay long, but that was the nature of her work. She had been to see them a few days ago, but had been suddenly called away.

Another pause as Lazar saw to the drinks, then the mood changed as Lidiya Abadjiev continued their story. Their guests, she said, would have seen the photograph of their son on the wall of his room. He had been a good boy, but, like Magda, wanted a life beyond the village. Unlike Magda, he had not been prepared to study and work for the future. He had left home and gone to live in Varna while still in his teens, and only came back to see them when Magda brought him. He would never tell them what he did to earn a living, and nor would their daughter. But he always came dressed in expensive clothes and carried a lot of money. After one visit, he had rushed off back to Varna and left a roll of money on the bedside table. It would have bought a whole herd of cows.

Lidiya Abadjiev paused and looked into the past with a sad smile, then continued. A little more than five years ago a police car had arrived at their gate. It had come from Varna. The officer said that their son was dead, killed in a shooting incident. Later they had learned that Boyko had been a member of a gang with links to the *mutri*.

As she finished the story, Lidiya Abadjiev crossed herself and looked at her husband as a single tear rolled down her face. It was, she said, God's will that they should lose their son. He was not a bad boy, just unhappy and unwilling to have an ordinary life. But they had their memories and, of course, their lovely daughter.

~

'Am I imagining it, or is that star jumping about a bit?'

'It's your imagination,' said Jen Cullan. 'As any schoolteacher should be able to tell you, stars don't really twinkle. It's an optical illusion. I reckon that's a couple of stars that appear to be near to each other, but are probably billions of miles apart. Their 'twinkling' sequences are so close it looks as if there's one star moving back and forward.'

'Ah,' Mowgley nodded to show he got it. '- a bit like the smoking dog, then.'

'The what?'

'When I was a kid in Portsmouth one of the big attractions in the season was the lights along the prom at Southsea. The ones marking out figures used to flash in sequence to give the appearance of movement, just like those stars do. There was a cowboy with a lasso and a man who doffed his hat, but my favourite was a dog that wagged its tail and smoked.'

She looked at him for a moment and then back up at the night sky. 'Not much I can say to that, is there?'

'I suppose not. On that note, have we got any fags left?'

They had come outside to take the air and use the earth closet, though Mowgley had opted for a bush a little way along the track from the Abadjiev's home. Now they were sitting on a donkey cart, taking in the utter stillness and serenity of their surroundings. Lazar Abadjiev had given Mowgley a torch to light their way to the bottom of the garden, but it was a full moon and almost light as day.

'What do you think, then?' Mowgley lit their last cigarette, took a deep draw and handed it over.

'About what?'

'About Magda. And her brother. Sounds like he was mixed up in some murky business in Varna.'

She took a draw on the cigarette, then said: 'Yes, but that doesn't mean to say she was.'

'What about the photo of her with Den and the dodgy

professor?'

'Doesn't mean she was, as you and Den would have said, complicit, does it? She could have just gone along with Den to visit the site and met the professor. Who knows?'

Mowgley reached for the cigarette. 'True. But if she's got nothing to hide, why the disappearing act?'

'We don't know she's disappeared. She's only been gone a few days as far as we know.'

'Well, we know she's not here.'

'True.'

'So what's next?'

'What do you mean, "what's next?" I suppose the Inspector Georgiev will keep looking until she shows up.'

'Whoah - don't do that!' Mowgley quickly reached out and caught her hand as she was about to throw the cigarette butt away. He delicately pinched the end between his fingers and took a last draw before dropping it to the ground. 'What I meant was hadn't we better start heading for home? It's a long drive back.'

'Ah,' she said, 'I meant to tell you about that. We've been invited to stay for the night. Our hosts say we've had too much to drink and anyway we'd never make it to the road.'

'Aren't they worried about one of us sleeping in the shrine to their son?'

'That's not the deal.' Jen Cullan examined the night sky for a moment, then said: 'We're sleeping in Magda's room.' She paused, then added: 'Don't look like that. It wasn't my idea.'

Mowgley stroked his chin. 'I believe you. Did you tell them we're married?

She grew irritated. 'Of course not - they just assumed we were. Anyway, if you feel so strongly about it you can sleep on the floor.'

'Mowgley looked up and pointed at a shooting star as it left a fleetingly glorious trail across the Heavens. Then he stood up, sighed as if committing himself to a chore, and said: 'I suppose I'm game if you are. But I have to tell you something.'

She held out a hand to be helped up from the cart. 'And what might that be?'

'I snore.'

She smiled and took his arm as they walked back towards the cottage, 'That's okay, so do I - or have you forgotten?'

13

They adorned her naked and unresisting body with gold as the sun fell from the sky.

Round her waist they fixed a golden belt and on her head a golden crown. Each of her remaining fingers was given an intricately worked golden ring, and around her body were strewn golden platters and cups as if to aid her journey to the next world.

She woke from her opiate-induced slumber as the first clods of earth hit the lid of the casket. Still drunk from the effects of the drug she tried to understand why she lay on her back in the total darkness. Then she explored the confines of the box till gradually it came to her who and where she was. And why.

She was the only one who could hear her attempts to scream, and soon they exhausted the air in her lungs and in the coffin.

Then came a final shuddering gasp, and she was troubled no more as she became one with the earth and the buried treasures surrounding her.

~

The sun was still low in the sky when the hire car bumped along the dirt track and away from the home of Lazar and Lidiya Abadjiev.

The elderly couple had stood at the gate to wave them off and had ensured their visitors would be taking more than memories away with them. On the back seat was a giant bunch of grapes, a box of ultra-fresh eggs which Jen Cullan had helped to collect, a netting sack stuffed with fruit and vegetables and a bottle of Lazar Abadjiev's blackberry-infused rakia.

Before leaving, the visitors had shared a simple breakfast with the kindly old couple and promised to return when Magda was there.

'What lovely people,' said Jen Cullan after a final wave before turning to concentrate on navigating around the hazards of the track. 'And they're so happy and contented with each other and their lot.'

'Or rather their little,' said Mowgley thoughtfully. 'Makes you feel guilty, doesn't it?'

'Not really. I can envy them their love and togetherness, but not their poverty, regardless of how photogenic it is.'

He pursed his lips. 'Fair enough, but I think the western world has proved that money and having things doesn't make you happy.'

'True, but I'd rather be comfortably unhappy, than uncomfortably unhappy, wouldn't you?'

Mowgley thought about it for a bit. 'I know what you're saying, but what about Montaigne?'

She snatched a look at him before returning her attention to the track. 'I don't think we've met.'

'I was talking about the sixteenth-century French philosopher.'

'I know you were. But what about him?'

'He said that all you needed for contentment was a roof over your head and a bit of land to grow food on. The Abadjievs have got that - and each other.'

She snorted. 'Remind me, was that the same Montaigne who inherited vast wealth, never did a day's real work in his life and spent his time having great thoughts at the top of a tower from where he could keep an eye on the army of peasants working on the family's vast estate?'

'Yeah, but…'

'I rest my case.'

Mowgley looked out at the rows of mostly deserted cottages.

'Okay. I get what you're saying. But I got the feeling from what you said they said that the Abadjievs were sort of nostalgic about Communism.'

'They did, but we all feel a bit nostalgic about the Good Old Days even if they weren't, don't we? Especially as we grow old. To be fair I suppose it can't have been all bad when you consider the alternatives. When I asked Lidiya what life had been like under Communism, she said it meant you had a roof over your head and food to eat, but no real freedoms. After Communism went away, people had freedom, but that included being free to be starve.'

They drove on in silence, then Mowgley said: 'Did you notice that big slab of marble in the living room? Do you think Magda has persuaded them to have a posh floor?'

She smiled. 'It's not for their floor; it's for their grave. I asked Lidiya about it when we were washing up. She said funeral companies won't come out to the isolated villages, and nobody can afford their prices anyway. When either he or she goes, they'll be a DIY funeral at the cemetery outside the village. The one who's left behind will have the slab inscribed by a quarry worker who lives in the next village. Apparently it's a sort of paid hobby and he's more and more in demand.'

'And what if they go together?'

'Lidiya said she's already left the wording and some money with the quarryman. It'll be cheaper if he does it in one go. And anyway, if Lazar leaves her first she's sure she'll be hard on his heels. She said they'll both want to be back together before too many days apart.'

~

'Was she practicing for her Death Notice poster, do you reckon?'

They had stopped at the village where Lidiya Abadjiev had been born to buy cigarettes in the shop next to the bar where Mowgley had lunched with Georgiev. The formidable-looking woman behind the counter was of indeterminate age, with a crash-helmet of rigid grey hair and a mouth set in an expression of permanent disapproval.

Jen Cullan shrugged. 'It can't be much fun with only yourself for company for most of the day,'

'I suppose not. Especially if you don't like the company.'

He picked up his cup and examined the contents. 'Do you know I think I could get used to this.'

'What, living in Bulgaria?'

'No, the coffee. It's a bit like alcohol and caviar and fags, I suppose.'

She gave him a concerned look. 'In what way?'

'When I was a kid my dad let me have a sip of his beer. I wondered why anyone would want to drink something that tasted so bad. I coughed my lungs up when I had my first cigarette, and now look at me.'

'What about the caviar?'

'No, I still think that tastes like shite.'

She smiled. 'I suppose it's what they call an acquired taste. Like some people.'

'Ha ha.'

She looked around the square and then at the door to the bar outside of which they were sitting. 'The patron here seems nice enough. Strange that he seemed to recognise you.'

'Yeah, he did, didn't he?' said Mowgley. 'Must have mistaken me for someone else. So where do you think Magda is?'

She lifted her shoulders in a 'who knows?' gesture. 'Perhaps she's gone on a cruise or run off with Den's liquid assets. But it is interesting that Inspector big-moustache seems to want to find her so badly. Don't forget it was his idea we come out here and see if Lazar and Lidiya know where she is.'

'But you would too?'

'I would too what?'

'Like to know where Magda is.'

She nodded. 'Well, yes, of course, but only because I'd like to know that she knows about what happened to Den,'

'Is that all?'

She pursed her lips and signalled for another cigarette, 'What else could it be?'

'Don't take this wrong,' said Mowgley, reaching for the packet, '...but don't forget that how deeply - if at all - Magda was involved in Den's dirty doings could greatly affect your financial status and wellbeing.'

'Mine? How do you work that out?'

He lit and handed her a cigarette. 'Well, for a start and as discussed, if Georgiev does get to the bottom of what Den was up to and if Magda was anything but an innocent bystander she could have gone on the run.'

She looked puzzled. 'From who, or do I mean whom?'

'Either from whoever killed Den - if he was killed - or Inspector Georgiev if he was closing in on the scam.'

She shrugged. 'What's that got to do with me and my financial wellbeing?'

'If she's done a disappearing act she can hardly come back to claim whatever Den has left her. And if she is found and was part of whatever the scam was, she could end up in clink.'

'And so..?'

'I don't know anything about Bulgarian law but you're still Den's wife, remember. Or rather his widow. That could mean that you'll get the lot. The apartment, the yacht and the car and anything else that was legally his.'

She nodded unconcernedly. 'True. Unless they have some law here about not profiting from ill-gotten gains.' She puffed smoke in the air. 'Anyway, would me being a slightly rich bitch make any difference to you and me?'

'Why would it make any difference?'

She let smoke trickle from her nostrils and did a bad impression of Mae West. 'It could do if you played your cards right, big boy.'

He raised his eyebrows. 'The gigolo thing? I'm too old for a new career.'

She smiled. 'You did alright last night.'

He tried not to show his pleasure. 'Please, you'll embarrass me.'

'Okay, let's talk about me being well-heeled if Magda doesn't show, then. Would you believe me if I told you I never even gave that possibility a thought? And, now I think of it, could it be that you and your inspector mate suspect me of having something to do with Den's death?'

'Don't be silly.'

She smiled without humour. 'Then why have you been meeting with Georgiev and not telling me? Before you make something up, I know you were here with him the other day.

The patron grassed you up.'

Mowgley spread out his hands, palms up. 'I've met Georgi a couple of times because he asked me to visit the boatyard and ask the questions he couldn't be seen to be asking. And I wanted to check out if anyone there had seen Magda or know where she was.'

Her eyebrows arched. 'Georgi? First name terms, eh? Okay, but why not tell me and why come all the way out here to talk business? It can't have been just for the food and the scenery.'

'Like I said, he didn't want to be seen with me. He wants people to think that he's closed the case on Den.'

She blew out a stream of smoke and licked her lips. 'People? In or outside of the police?'

He shrugged. 'Either...or both.'

'And what about me?'

'What about you?'

'Do you think I might have done away with my husband and his girlfriend?'

Mowgley raised his hands in the air. 'Not necessarily. But I don't think you've got it in you to be a psychotic killer - unless someone really pissed you off.'

'That's a relief.' She stubbed her cigarette out and stood up. 'Your turn to pay. And better treat me nice or I might knock you off too...'

~

Mowgley's phone rang as they got into the car. He patted his pockets then looked at her as if for explanation.

'It's your phone ringing,' she said. 'They do that when someone's trying to get in touch with you.'

'I know, but who could be calling me?'

She sighed. 'Why not answer it and find out?'

He frowned, then took the call after two attempts. Following a series of nods and grunts he scrabbled in a pocket, pulled out a piece of paper and made a writing motion in the air. She rummaged in her bag, took out a ball-point pen and handed it to him. Resting the piece of paper on the dashboard, he told the caller he was ready, then jotted something down.

As he said goodbye and put the phone away, she started the

engine and pulled away from outside the bar. 'Well,' she asked, 'who was it and what did they want? Not Magda saying she was sorry she missed us?'

'No,' he said. 'It was Georgiev. He wanted to know where we were.'

She leaned over to look at the piece of paper. 'And what's with the numbers? His insider tip for the State Lottery?'

'He said it was his Google co-ordinates, whatever that means. He said you'd know and he wants us to meet him there.'

She took the piece of paper and looked more closely at it. 'This is all a bit cloak and dagger isn't it? And didn't he ask whether Magda was at her parents' house?'

'No', said Mowgley. He said he knows where she is now.'

~

The co-ordinates led them through the outskirts of the city and then around Lake Varna. At the southern shore the GPS system on Jen Cullan's smartphone directed them up a steep and deeply wooded slope and finally into a large parking area. Inspector Georgiev was standing by the bonnet of his unmarked car at a viewpoint looking across the lake to the Black Sea.

Hearing their approach, he looked round and acknowledged their presence with a small flick of one hand and then returned to his observations. As they parked and walked across the otherwise empty car park, it was obvious that the inspector was not taking in the panorama, but leaning over the low wall to look directly downwards.

Joining him, Mowgley saw there was another clearing about a hundred feet below.

Two police cars were drawn up blocking the entrance, and between them stood a black van. Three policemen leaned against one of the cars, smoking as they watched two white-overalled figures kneeling beside a rectangular-shaped hole with a mound of earth beside it.

'So,' said Jen Cullan, 'what's going on, Inspector? Another discovery of buried treasure?'

Inspector Georgiev looked at her, sighed and shook his head.

'In a way, Madame' he said. 'We have found Magda Abadjiev.'

~

'What I don't get,' said Jack Mowgley, 'is why whoever did it would go to all that trouble.'

They were sitting in Inspector Georgiev's car. Mowgley and Jen Cullan were in the back seat, he with his arm around her shoulders and she crying softly into a paper tissue. The inspector was sitting in the driving seat, his head and shoulders turned towards them. He was smoking one of Mowgley's cigarettes and they were sharing the contents of a small, silver flask he had taken from the glove box.

'The killers clearly wanted the circumstances to be as dramatic as possible,' said Georgiev. 'And the location is very suitable. We are only a few miles from the necropolis where Varna Man was found. This will get full media attention around the world. I can already see the headlines about the finding of the Bride of Varna Man. It was clearly done to send out a message.'

'A message?'

'If it is the work of the *Mutri* - the mafia - they will want everyone to know that this is what happens to people with whom they are not pleased, or who have tried to cheat them. They also have a great sense of theatre. It is well known that the members like to watch The Godfather films. They will often quote a line from one of them to show who they are or to recognise each other.'

As Mowgley began to ask another question, they were alerted was a noise of a car turning in to the clearing. It was, for Bulgaria, a noticeably new and expensive saloon. As it pulled up by the low wall at the viewpoint, Mowgley saw that Georgiev had reached again for the glove box which had contained the flask of brandy. As they watched, both back doors flew open almost before the car stopped and there was an angry shout from the car.

Then as Georgiev fumbled with the catch on the glove box, two small children erupted from the open doors of the Lexus. The boy and girl were clad in expensive leisure clothes, and ran laughing and shouting towards the wall between them and the sheer drop.

The little girl stopped short of the wall, but the boy jumped up on to it and posed there, making as if he was about to dive into space. Another angry shout from the car, and this time it was enhanced by a female shriek. A man jumped out of the driver's door and wagged an admonishing finger at the boy, and a woman got out of the passenger's side and let out an angry tirade.

Though he did not get off the wall, the boy dropped his superhero pose and then noticed what was going on in the clearing below. He watched for a moment and then pointed and shouted and waved for the others to join him.

In the car, Georgiev closed the glove box and then turned on the ignition so he could shut the car windows.

They sat silently for a moment, and Mowgley thought how the two youngsters were at the start of their journey through life, and looking down unknowingly at where someone had ended hers long before her time. He reached for his cigarettes, gave Jen Cullan another squeeze. 'Are you okay?'

She nodded, wiped her eyes and blew her nose into the tissue. 'I'm sorry,' she said as Georgiev handed her another tissue from the box on the passenger seat. 'It's just so...horrible. Why did they need to kill her? Think what it will do to her parents. They were so happy last night...'

'I am sorry to be so...clinical...' said the inspector, 'but there are two possible reasons for what has happened. Either it was purely malicious and callous and a punishment for any connection Ms Abadjiev may have had with whatever your husband was involved with. Or they may have thought she knew something they needed to know.'

Jen Cullan gave a little gasp into her tissue. 'You mean they... tortured her?'

'Yes,' said Georgiev gravely, 'but that does not mean they wanted to find something out. It could have been part of the punishment, or, I am sorry to say, just for fun.'

She gave another gasp and buried her face in the tissue, then reached across to the door handle. 'I'm sorry, I need to get some air.'

Mowgley reached across her, pulled the handle and opened the door. 'Would you like me to come with you?' he asked.

She shook her head. 'No. Thank you. I just want to be on my own for a moment.'

They watched her walk slowly across the clearing towards a bench. Her shoulders were hunched and her face still buried in the tissue.

'She is clearly most upset,' said Inspector Georgiev.

'I don't suppose she gets involved in a couple of deaths every week of her average year,' Mowgley said heavily. 'She knew Magda slightly, of course, but I think she is most unhappy for the parents. This means they have lost both their children, and both murdered.'

'Yes,' said Georgiev, shaking his head. 'Sometimes I think it is a good idea not to bring children into such a terrible world. You do not have the pleasure of them, but neither do you have the pain. I could send a car to tell them, but I will go myself when we have spoken. It will do no good, but I want to tell them how sorry I am. I will not of course tell them how their daughter died.'

'And how did she die? Because of the torture?'

'No. If anything it was worse than that.' Georgiev looked through the windscreen to where the family were getting back into their car, then turned on the ignition to lower the windows again. He tossed his cigarette butt out of the driver's window then looked back across the head rest at Mowgley. 'Three of her fingers had been cut off. As I said, this might have been to force her to tell them what she knew, or simply for pleasure and to more horrify the public.'

Mowgley opened the cigarette packet and handed one to the inspector. 'So how did she die?'

'Probably suffocation, or perhaps sheer terror. Such would have been the horror her heart could have given up. It is too early to tell - you saw that the forensic people were working on the grave and the body will not yet have reached the mortuary for a full examination. As well as her fingers, her tongue had been torn out. Her eyes and her mouth were open as if she was screaming, and I have never seen such a look on a dead face.'

They were silent for a moment and Mowgley thought about what it could have been like to be in the dark, full of terror and despair and knowing what was going to happen as you took your last breaths.

'And what about the things you said were buried with her?'

'She was naked,' Georgiev continued, 'but wearing an amount of Thracian jewellery and the crown of a princess. There were also a number of artefacts in the coffin with her. Ironically, they were the sort of things that would have been put in the grave of a person of high birth and status to help her on her journey to the other world.'

Mowgley looked out of the window to where Jen was sitting. 'I understand about torturing her for information or fun and killing and leaving her like that to set an example to others. But who would leave a fortune in gold treasure to make the story more dramatic?'

'That is the whole point, I believe' said Georgiev. 'Even the *mutri* would not leave a fortune of ancient treasure to make a dramatic effect. I do not know yet, but my guess would be that the artefacts will prove to be fakes.'

'Fakes?'

'Yes. Like the penis sheath I showed you in my office when we first met.'

'But they would still be worth a small fortune, surely.'

Georgiev nodded. 'Quite. But I think whoever did this would have left them just so they would be revealed as fakes.'

Mowgley frowned. 'And why would they want that to happen?'

Georgiev shrugged. 'I don't know, Jack. That is what I have to find out.'

'And do you believe that Magda's brother was involved in all this before he was killed?'

'I do not know that, either. He was a minor gangster and liked to say he was a member of the mafia, but I don't know if that was the truth or just a boast that young men like him sometimes like to make.' He looked to where Jen Cullan was sitting on the bench. She was leaning forward, the tissue in one hand and a cigarette in the other, looking across at the low wall. 'It is something else I must investigate when you and Mrs Cullan are safely on the plane.'

'You think we are in danger?'

Inspector Georgiev shrugged. 'Of course. Mrs Cullan is a regular visitor, on good terms with and stayed at her husband's apartment when here. She knew Magda, and to the minds of the killers, could have been some sort of courier or fixer for what Denis Cullan was doing. If I were them and had not got what I wanted to know from Magda, Mrs Cullan would be next on my list.'

'What about you?'

'Me?'

'Do you think Jen is or was involved?'

Georgiev shook his head. 'No, not now.'

'And what about me?'

The inspector smiled a small smile. 'I think you are just a good man who came to help an old friend who was in distress. But if I were the people who did this, I might think you were involved. You are, they will believe, very close to his wife. The *mutri* have contacts far outside Bulgaria. They may even know you are an old colleague and friend of Mr Cullan who left under a cloud and now work as a private detective in France. This would be enough to make them suspicious, and you a target.'

'So, we should leave now?'

'As soon as possible. There is a flight to England in the morning, and I have had you and Mrs Cullan booked on it. Until then I will put a man to watch over you.'

Inspector Georgiev sighed and reached over to offer Mowgley his hand. 'I am sorry that we must part this way. I knew when we had met that you were an honest and decent man, and hoped that we could become friends. Now, and however this turns out, I do not think it would be wise for you to return. It is a beautiful country, but, as you can see, it can be a very dangerous one.'

14

The bars lining the walkway to the beach were busy, but they found a table outside the bar they had used at the end of his first day in Bulgaria.

'I can't believe it's less than a week since you arrived.'

'You're reading my thoughts.'

'Oh, am I? Sorry.'

Mowgley frowned. 'You must stop doing that.'

'What, reading your thoughts?'

'No. Saying "sorry." You haven't got anything to apologise for.'

She smiled ruefully. 'Really?' You mean like dragging you out here and getting you involved in two murders, to say nothing of putting your life in danger.'

'Oh come on, we all have bad weeks.'

At last she smiled. 'I do like you.'

'Not lurve?'

'That can grow. No, I mean the way you make... light of things. It makes me feel better and somehow safer.'

He reached over and put his hand over hers. It felt the most natural of things to do. 'Better light than heavy, I reckon.' He nodded at her glass. 'Fancy another one? Drink or cigarette, I mean?'

She put her other hand on top of his as if to stop him taking it away. 'Both, please.'

After Georgiev had dropped them back to their hotel they had told the clerk they would be checking out early in the morning. He had asked if they would need a taxi, and Mowgley had said they had a lift arranged. He did not add that it would be in an unmarked police car. After looking at how little packing he had to do, he had phoned her room and proposed that they eat in the hotel restaurant. She had said she would rather go out as she didn't want to stay in on what could be her last night in Bulgaria.

'Do you think you'll come back?' Mowgley waved to a passing waiter and pointed at the empty bottle on the table between them.

'I don't know at the moment. I can't really think straight. I know Georgiev says we could be in danger, but he can't know that for sure. Unless he knows something he's not telling us.'

'You mean he's heard something specific?'

She shrugged. 'Perhaps. Or maybe he just wants us safely out of the way.'

'Well that's a good thing, isn't it? He's obviously concerned about your - and my- safety.'

'Or we're getting in the way.'

Mowgley nodded to the waiter, who poured wine into their glasses and put the bottle on the table.

Mowgley lifted his glass. 'Well, I suppose there could be a bit of that to it. If we can't help and he doesn't think you're involved, why would he want us on his plate? We'd be just another worry.'

'Or it could be he doesn't want you putting your policeman's head on. He knows how bright you are. And good at this sort of thing.'

Mowgley gave a grunt of amusement. 'You mean he's worried about me clearing up the case and taking the credit if I stay on?'

She shook her head. 'No, I didn't mean that.

He looked at her and his eyes widened. 'You don't think he's actually on the other side, do you? That he's involved in the whole banana, including Den and Magda's deaths?'

She ran a hand through her hair, then took a long pull on her cigarette. 'Why not? You know how utterly corrupt things can be here. Especially in high places.' She smiled without humour. 'You think he's some sort of eccentric and kindly avuncular sort of figure, don't you? It's not Agatha Christie land here, you know. How do you think he's survived and even prospered in this swamp of corruption?'

Mowgley put his glass down, sat back and looked at it. After a moment he said: 'Blimey. I honestly never gave it a thought.'

She reached over and patted the hand holding his cigarette.

'One thing I remember about you was how you always liked to think the best of people in spite of your experiences. You even liked Den and thought the best of him.'

Mowgley emptied his glass and screwed up his face. 'I wouldn't say that, but I can sort-of see what you mean.'

~

'What will you do when you get back?'

'I'll have to tell John when I get home, of course. That's not going to be easy...for him or me. Then I'll need to sort things out here from a distance, I guess. Or I'll come back on my own.'

'Do you think that's a good idea?'

She wrinkled her nose. 'Probably not, but I'm not going to be scared off by a bunch of thugs – or Inspector First Rate Georgiev. What about you?'

'What about me? I've got no reason to come back. Unless you want some company.'

'That would be good, but I meant what are you going to do with the rest of your life?'

Mowgley lifted his shoulders. 'Dunno. Keep carrying on carrying on, I suppose.'

'Being a private detective in France?' She regarded him closely. 'Do you really like doing that and being there?'

He lifted a shoulder. 'Poking my nose into other people's business is all I know. And I'm sort of getting used to France and the French and their funny little ways.

'What about doing what you do on the home side of the Channel? You said you'd sold your house in Normandy - or think you have.'

He smiled wryly. 'What I'll get from flogging my once-stately home wouldn't buy a flat above a fish shop even in the ropey old town I come from.' He looked thoughtfully around him. 'Though I guess it would buy a very nice place here. Bit difficult being an investigator in a place where you don't speak the language, though- as I found out when I moved to Cherbourg.'

'But you'd like to set up business in the Home Counties?'

'I hadn't thought about it. Are you offering me a loan, perchance? I don't think I'd be able to offer very good security.'

She smiled at him over the rim of her glass. 'I was thinking more of a partnership. I've got a good pension plan and no mortgage on the house. And there might be something coming from Den's will. Would you fancy having a sleeping partner?'

'Depends what sort of sleeping partner you mean.'

She smiled again. 'How about both?'

~

Lights were coming on along the walkway. In the distant velvety darkness, rich men's toys were moored in the bay and lit like Christmas trees.

'Would you like a yacht?'

He saw her watching him looking out to sea and shook his head. 'Not me. I've enough trouble looking after a car. And I'm not a boaty person.'

'I don't think Den was, really, but he liked to show off.'

Mowgley nodded. 'And maybe his boat was useful for other things.'

She seemed not to pick up on his implication, and said: 'Yes, he liked to dive. He had all the gear and was quite good at it. He always took John out to dive on wrecks when we were over.' She lit a cigarette, then said: 'Apparently there are lots of sunken ships out there. Last month they found the oldest shipwreck ever discovered. It's a mile down somewhere off the coast out there.' She waved an encompassing arm towards the sea. 'For some reason they're not disclosing exactly where it is.'

'So there are treasure looters at sea as well as on land?'

'Of course.'

Mowgley picked up and looked at the empty bottle and its label. 'I like the idea of drinking bear's blood.' He stood up, smiled at the young couple on the next table, then looked at his watch. 'I'm off for a comfort break. 'Do you want me to order some food?'

'She shook her head. 'Not for me, or not yet. I'm enjoying this. We could do another monster kebab takeaway later and walk hand-in-hand like young lovers back to our room.'

He paused in mid-turn and looked down at her. 'Don't you mean rooms plural?'

She leaned back in her chair and aimed a plume of smoke in his direction. 'I know what I said and what I mean.'

~

After noting the shortage of paper towels in the dispenser, Mowgely ran his hands though his hair to dry them and was checking he'd zipped up when chaos erupted outside.

First came the scream of tyres, then a cacophony of shouting and screaming and crashing, interspersed with three sharp cracks. There was no mistaking what they were. He had heard people claim that a car backfiring could sound like a pistol shot but had never noticed any great similarity.

It seemed to take a long while to get to the outer door of the bar, and outside it was as if things were happening in slow motion. This was something he had found to be not uncommon in times of crisis. The first thing he noticed was a white van splayed across the cobbles, its back doors open.

Then he saw that the table at which they had been sitting was on its side, pieces of smashed bottle and glasses beside it. A man in a floral shirt and chinos lay on his side, blood spreading into a pool alongside his chest. Other customers were sitting as if frozen as they watched Jen Cullan being dragged towards the van. Much of the screaming was coming from her.

In a long couple of seconds, Mowgley realised that the man and woman dragging her were the couple who had been sitting at the next table. He supressed the natural instinct to shout pointlessly at them, then lurched forward on his stiff leg, picking up the tubular black metal chair on which he had been sitting. By the time he had crossed the space between them, the couple had reached the open back doors. Someone inside was reaching out and had grabbed hold of Jen's hair, while the man and the woman were attempting to bundle her in.

Most civilians would have thrown or swung the chair at the couple; Mowgley held it out horizontally with one hand on the back rest and the other on a leg. Over many a close bar encounter he had found a chair or stool could be used much more effectively that way.

Now he went into shout mode, bellowing out a string of curses. This caused the man to look round at the source of the noise and just in time for the end of the chair leg to be driven into his right eye. Even amongst the screaming and yelling and his own shouting, Mowgley clearly heard the squelching sound and kept pushing. The man gave an agonised and strangely high-pitched scream, released his hold on Jen Cullan and fell to the floor.

Now Mowgley turned his attention towards the woman. Reaching out he grasped the front of her blouse and pulled her towards him. She was screaming and spitting, but was hampered by keeping her hold on Jen. As she pulled away from him and the front of her blouse ripped open, Mowgley threw himself forward and smashed the top of his head into her face. Her nose split open and blood spurted down and on to the cleavage revealed by her torn blouse. Her head snapped back and hit one of the van doors, but she clung doggedly on to her target.

Mowgley pulled his fist back and for a split second his eyes met those of Jen Cullan. Then, a hand appeared from the darkened interior of the van. It was holding a pistol, the muzzle pointing directly at him. He knew what was coming but had no time to react beyond instinctively shutting his eyes.

The flare of intense light burned through his closed eyelids as a great booming sound shut out all other noise, and his face was engulfed by a searing pain. Then he knew no more.

15

The light was too bright.

He found it hard to think, but knew he was in a strange place, laying on his back and that the side of his face felt as if it was on fire.

He raised a hand and shaded his eyes from the overhead bulb, then realised he could not see out of his left eye. Exploring with his fingers, he found the side of his face was covered in a sort of bandage poultice, held in place by wide strips of adhesive tape.

His throat was dry and his call for help came out as a croak. He tried to sit up, but could not, so croaked again.

Eventually a blurred face appeared in his line of vision. It slowly came into focus, and he saw it was a woman of late middle age. She was wearing a white cap pinned to her grey, piled-up hair. She laid a hand gently on his shoulder and said something he knew he would not have understood had he been able to hear above the ringing in his left ear.

She saw that he did not understand, raised a finger as if asking him to wait, then disappeared from view.

He slept again, then woke and became aware of another face looking down at him. It belonged to a young man and was of classic Slav appearance. High cheekbones, low brows, full lips and a thin, straight, pointed nose with narrow nostrils. Small ears lay close to the head, which was barely covered by a military-style buzz cut. The strong jawline emphasised the look of hardness, but there was humour in the eyes. Whoever he was, he looked like someone a sensible man would not pick an argument with.

The lips opened, revealing strong white teeth as the stranger spoke. Because of the ringing in his ear he could not make out the words, but thought the language might be English. The man saw that he was not getting through and turned away and lifted a phone to his ear. After speaking for a moment, he looked back down and gave a wintry smile, repeated the unnecessary 'wait there' signal the woman had made and left Mowgley to wonder where he was and what had happened to him.

~

'If it is not too predictable and irritating a question, how are you feeling?'

It was the next day and Mowgley was more alert. The dosage of pain-killing drugs had been reduced but he was still plagued by the constant ringing in his left ear. He was feeling better but no happier and had only a patchy and jumbled recollection of the sequence of events which had led to his present situation.

He looked up at the figure standing beside the bed and scowled. 'If you're asking how I'm feeling,' he growled, 'how the fuck do you think I'm feeling with this bloody noise in my ear. And speak up, will you?'

Georgiev raised an apologetic hand, leaned closer and repeated his enquiry at a louder level.

Mowgley waved the question aside. 'Never mind about me, what about Jen? Where is she? Is she okay?'

Georgiev looked down and tugged at his moustache. 'I'm afraid we do not know yet'

Mowgley struggled to sit up higher against the stack of pillows. 'How the fuck can you not know? Is she okay or not?'

The inspector reached into his pocket and took out his pipe.

'Do you remember what happened to you?' he asked mildly.

Mowgley shook his head as if it might ease the relentless

buzzing. 'I remember a gun and then hearing the shot, but nothing after that. 'Did they get away, and is Jen hurt?'

The inspector put the empty pipe in his mouth, took it out and tugged at his moustache again

'We are doing all we can, I promise you.'

Mowgley shook his head in despair and groaned aloud in frustration. 'Will you just tell me how Jen is?'

'We cannot know. She was...taken.'

'Taken?'

'Yes.'

Mowgley stared dumbly at Georgiev, then the memories returned. Without speaking, he threw the blanket and sheets aside and began to swing his legs out.

Georgiev leaned forward and placed a hand on Mowgley's chest, pushing him back onto the pillows. He was, Mowgley thought fleetingly, stronger than he looked.

As they struggled, Georgiev called out and a figure appeared from beyond the curtain surrounding the bed. It was the man who Mowgley had seen the day before. He was not tall, but broad and wide-shouldered and obviously heavily-muscled under the close-fitting polo shirt. He pushed past the inspector, took hold of Mowgley's arms at the biceps and squeezed. Both arms immediately went numb, and Mowgley groaned and gave up the struggle. As he did so, the man smiled as if at a recalcitrant child, showing the near-perfect set of teeth Mowgley had noticed at their first meeting.

'I am sorry,' said Inspector Georgiev. 'I thought this would be your reaction and was delaying having to tell you.'

He patted a pocket and pulled out his tobacco pouch, and watched as the man gently released Mowgley's arms and stepped back.

Mowgley massaged an arm but made no attempt to get out of the bed. 'What are you doing about Jen? Can I help? Have you no idea who took her?'

'No, not yet, but we are talking with people who may know.'

'What do you mean?'

Georgiev took out his pipe. 'Like any police force, we have informants. Those who work within the *mutri* do not usually last long, but some survive and are very useful. They are also very well-paid. Sometimes, though and when they want us to know or believe something, the information comes from the mafia

141

themselves. The trick is to ask the right questions of the right people.

'And have you asked why they've taken her? And what they want from her?'

Georgiev tugged at his moustache again. 'I do not know. If they had wanted her dead it would have been much easier to kill her on the spot, not take her away. I cannot think it is for ransom, but perhaps they think she knows something that they need to know.'

'But how could she know anything She's a schoolteacher from Essex who comes over here a few times a year for her son to see his father, for Christ's' sake. What could she know about all this?'

'Yes, Jack,' said Georgiev thoughtfully, 'what indeed?'

~

'So, when can I get out of this place and what's wrong with me?'

An hour had passed. A man in a white coat had been to look at Mowgley and question him through Georgiev. Now the detective was sitting beside the bed and smoking his pipe. Mowgley was drawing hungrily on his first cigarette for a night and a day and a morning. The nurse with the grey hair had appeared to admonish them, but Georgiev had waved her away with a few obviously polite but firm words. The man with the buzz cut was sitting languidly on a chair on the other side of the bed. He was watching them and obviously interested in their exchanges. Now and then he put a hand up to scratch or rub his bristly skull, and Mowgley had noticed a small tattoo in the hollow between his thumb and forefinger. They were, he had also noticed, large and capable-looking hands.

'There is very little wrong with you,' said Georgiev. 'though I am sure it feels as if there is.' Georgiev looked up and paused as the elderly nurse arrived with a carafe of water and a plastic tumbler. She filled the tumbler and Mowgley took and emptied it in a single swallow.

'You are a lucky man,' continued the inspector. 'Apart from the loss of hearing and noise in your ear-which the doctors think will be temporary-you merely have some powder sprinkle burns on your cheek as a result of the pistol being fired within inches of your face. It will feel much worse than it is' He looked thoughtfully at the bandages. 'It is very unusual, but I am told it can happen, and the shorter the barrel and wider the muzzle, the wider the pattern of powder distribution. I asked my colleagues in the Forensic Division and they said it could have been a very old gun, or something like a wide-barrel Glock. It was so close that the powder specks would still have been burning when they hit your face. I am told there will be little scarring when the bandages come off, but for a while you will look like a man who has fallen asleep in the sun.'

'Thank you doctor. Did I see a man on the floor, bleeding?'

'Yes, you did. It was the officer assigned to protect you. He was not able to do much as he was shot as soon as the van pulled up. He stood and pulled out his sidearm, but had no time to get off a shot. He is in the intensive care ward, but no vital organs were hit and he should make a complete recovery. He has been lucky, but as I said, you have been luckier.'

Mowgley put a hand up and touched the swathe of bandaging. 'If you say so. But how did he miss? Nobody is that bad a shot.'

Georgiev shrugged. 'Normally, I would agree. The more observant witnesses say the van lurched off across the cobbles just before the shot was fired. You fell down and hit your head on the door. The man with the pistol jumped out and helped the man you hurt into the van. Then he and the woman dragged Mrs Cullan in and it raced off, leaving you lying on the ground.'

'And there's no clue to who they were?'

'No. The van was stolen shortly before the event and looked as if it were delivering to one of the bars. As always when things happen so quickly, the witnesses disagree on the appearance of the attackers' looks - and even the clothes they were wearing. They do agree that the man you hit with the chair will have been badly damaged to the eye, but there are no reports of anyone visiting any hospital in the area with such an injury.'

Mowgley took a final draw on his cigarette, then dropped it into the glass on the bedside table. 'So when can I leave?'

'The hospital or the country?' Georgiev sucked at his now-empty pipe. 'It is your choice. They can do no more for you here. I think you should leave Bulgaria as soon as possible, but I do not suppose you will agree.'

Mowgley made no comment, so Georgiev continued: 'If you are to stay, you will need to be moved to somewhere less...public than your hotel. And you will need someone to look after you.' He waved a hand across the bed. 'This is Ivo. He will take you back to your hotel to collect your things, then on to a safe place.'

Mowgley nodded at the man who gave another lazy smile and returned the acknowledgement. 'I hope he speaks good English.'

'So do I' said Georgiev dryly. 'I spent a lot of money on his education. Ivo, say hello to Mr Mowgley. Jack, say hello to Ivo. He is my son.'

~

In the hotel foyer, Mowgley looked dubiously at the full-length mirror opposite the entry doors. He saw a big, dishevelled man with a lopsided haircut where a large patch had been shaved above his left ear. He stepped closer and saw that the side of his face was bright red and pocked with small black dots. As Inspector Georgiev had said, it did look as if he had gone to sleep in the sun with his head on one side.

In the mirror he saw that his bodyguard was standing by the door, regarding him impassively.

'Do you want to get a drink in the bar or something? Mowgley asked. 'I won't be long.'

'It's okay,' said Ivo Georgiev. His father's investment had paid off and his English was very good, though with a Slavic twang to some words.

Mowgley nodded. 'Right, I won't be long.'

He left Ivo sitting in the reception area and noticed he took a seat facing the entry doors.

The old man was on duty, pottering around behind the desk. He looked up as Mowgley approached, turned round and took a key from a pigeon hole. Mowgley nodded his thanks, then pointed to the hole in which the key to Jen Cullan's room sat. Then he pointed to the vestibule and the toilet area and mimed a woman slapping make-up on her face. The old man gave a gummy smile and handed him the key, watching as Mowgley walked up the stairs.

~

The room was dark, and Mowgley wondered who had closed the curtains and why they had not been opened by the cleaner that morning. He felt for and flicked the light switch and looked around. There was no visual sign of occupation, but Jen's presence was there in the echo of the perfume she favoured.

Starting by the window, he began to work the room. At the wardrobe he checked the gap beneath it and felt along the top and looked into the scuffed but expensive suitcase. Then he went through the garments hanging in the wardrobe. Finding nothing in or on them, he ignored the three pairs of shoes but picked up the boots, inverted and shook them.

He moved on, and in the chest of drawers found some neatly arranged blouses and a selection of underwear. Beside the bed was a small table with a paperback book on it. It was open and lying face down, and he picked it up and flicked through the pages. It was A Happy Death by Albert Camus and in the original French.

In the bathroom a toilet bag sat on the hand basin and a dressing gown hung from the back of the door. Having checked behind and in the cistern, he was going through the pockets of the dressing gown when he heard a phone ringing.

He found it underneath a cushion on the sofa he had not yet checked. He picked the phone up and looked at the illuminated screen. It read KIR. Pressing the green button, he grunted in what he hoped was a generally and gender-neutral tone.

There was a silence, then a man's voice responded. It was high-pitched and strained and, though he could not understand what was said, he could tell the speaker was full of fear. He tried the grunting technique again, but after a silence the phone went dead.

Mowgley looked at the phone thoughtfully, then put it in his pocket.

16

'Are you going to tell me where we're going?'

'I could, but if I did I would have to kill you.'

Mowgley looked across at Ivo Georgiev to check he was joking. He decided on balance that he was, and it was the Slavic accent that made him sound as if he meant it.

They had checked out of the hotel earlier and Mowgley's miniature suitcase was on the back seat of the Skoda V6. The car had a well-used look, and, as Ivo Georgiev had said, it did not stand out in a crowd. But under the bonnet there was much more to it than you would think from its age and condition. A little, he had added, like his passenger, who he heard used a chair better than most lion tamers.

Mowgley had not responded, but almost smiled at the reference. He liked man-banter. Fighting men had used mock insults as a way of relieving tension since wars and battles began. But a week before he would not have imagined he would be indulging in badinage with a Bulgarian special forces operative on their way to a safe house to keep him from harm's way at the hands of the Bulgarian mafia.

They had left Ivo's father at the hotel with a forensic team going through Jen Cullan's room. Mowgley had told Inspector Georgiev about the call and given him the mobile phone he had found. The inspector had said he would check out the address book and join Mowgley and Ivo at their destination that evening. As Jack would find, it was a beautiful and very peaceful place.

In spite of himself, Mowgley let out a bleat of terror. Like nearly all the drivers they encountered on the coastal road from Varna to Burgas, Ivo Georgiev drove too fast; unlike most of the drivers he encountered, he drove very skilfully. But it was still not much fun being on the wrong side of the road with a petrol tanker fast approaching.

On the outskirts of Burgas, Ivo took the main road heading west towards Stara Zagora, which was, he explained, in the geographical centre of Bulgaria and one of the oldest continually populated towns in Europe.

'Bulgarians seem very proud of their history,' Mowgley observed, wincing as a motor bike ripped by, the helmet-less rider's long hair streaming behind him.

'That is because we have not so much else to be proud of,' said his driver. We have had nearly eight thousand years to get it right, and still we fuck it up.'

Unable to come up with a suitable response, Mowgley concentrated on ignoring the closest encounters and wishing he were allowed to smoke. The car was almost ankle-deep in food cartons, empty plastic bottles and other detritus, but the no-smoking rule was absolute and Ivo had said, another offence which was punishable by death. 'Of course,' he had observed, 'if you live that long you will die because of smoking anyway.' Mowgley had protested that Inspector Georgiev smoked a pipe, and Ivo said it did not count as his father did not inhale.

'Ah, you mean like Bill Clinton and cannabis?'

'What?'

'Never mind. He went on to use cigars anyway, as Monica Lewinsky could tell you.'

~

A couple of hours in to their journey and they had stopped to stretch their legs, take a comfort break and eat. Mowgley found his first cigarette for more than a hundred miles very comforting.

Ivo Georgiev had chosen a restaurant outside the gates of a massive gilt-and-gingerbread-styled monastery and suggested a walk in the grounds before they ate. His guide had remarked that such buildings were unique in the world, and Mowgley had refrained from observing that he could see why. To him, the architecture and presentation seemed a strange hybrid of sanctity and showbiz. The zebra-striped cloisters, garish paint jobs and adornments and the golden onion-domes looked like something a colour-blind TV game show set designer might come up with.

The building and its surroundings were, to be fair, scrupulously maintained; the whitewashed walls were whiter than white and the lawns so green they looked dyed.

On their way back to the main gate they passed a man sitting on a bench. He was wearing a severe expression, an Al Capone-style fedora hat and an ankle-length black robe. He was also wearing a beard which reached almost to his waist. He was, said Ivo, either a resident brother or a mad person.

The interior of the restaurant was far more restrained than the golden-icon laden chapel in the monastery, and Ivo led the way to a table in the far corner. Mowgley noted that he sat with his back to the wall and would have a clear view of the other tables and the entry point.

After inviting Ivo to choose what they ate as long as it did not involve a *Shopska* salad, Mowgley opted for a carafe of red wine, while Ivo took only bottled water.

'I see your body is your temple' Mowgley said as he took a swig.

'What do you mean?'

'I mean you like to keep in good shape.'

Ivo shrugged his broad shoulders and reached for the bowl of roasted sunflower seeds. 'I try to eat good and go to the gym.' He looked at Mowgley speculatively. 'You could give it a try, maybe?'

'Too late now, mate,' Mowgley said, frowning at the menu. 'Too late for me, mate. So are you going to tell me who you work for? Are you special forces, secret service or just a toned-up policeman? And before you say it, I know if you tell me you'll have to kill me.'

'It's no secret. I work for SANS.'

'And they or it are who?'

'The State Agency for National Security.'

'And what does that involve? Counter-terrorism?'

Another shrug. 'It could do. Or investigating money laundering or counterfeiting-or stealing and smuggling treasure out of the country. As the name suggests, our brief covers anything that threatens the nation's security. But there is a lot of corruption and that keeps us busy.'

Their meal arrived and when the waiter had left, Mowgley said: 'So it's all the serious stuff and lots of action, then?'

Ivo gave a thin smile. 'Not really. A lot of it is routine, but we do have some interesting times.'

'I bet you do. And do you always work with your father?'

'No, very rarely. This is a treat for me.' He picked up a knife.

'Any more questions before we eat?'

Mowgley looked down at his plate, 'Only if this is another national dish stolen from Bulgaria?'

'I don't think so' said Ivo Georgiev through a mouthful of melted cheese and anchovy, 'we call it a pizza and it comes, I believe, from Italy.'

~

The Rhodopes mountain range sits mostly in south-east Bulgaria and spills over the border and into Greece. Its highest peak is over 2000 metres and it is a place of dark forests, deep gorges and caverns.

Mowgley knew all this because Ivo Georgiev told him as they drove ever upwards on a mountain pass which corkscrewed it way through vast tracts of towering fir trees. Streams babbled and bubbled their way down rocky slopes and often across the road. Occasionally, they would pass parked cars, their owners filling plastic containers. Ivo explained that the water was free, very pure and said to be good for the health. Provided, he added dryly, that the collectors did not get too close to the road.

'It's a very beautiful place,' said Mowgley, stating the very obvious as a break in the treeline revealed distant peaks piercing an azure, cloudless sky. In the foreground a great waterfall cascaded over the edge of a plateau. Occasionally hidden by the smoke-like spray, two figures were working their way up the sheer rock face alongside it.

'Yes,' Ivo said. 'You will know of Orpheus?

'He was a Greek God, wasn't he?'

'No, he was not Greek or a god.' Ivo spoke with an irritated edge to his voice, which Mowgley suspected happened quite often. 'He was born here in this mountain, and his music was so beautiful that he could charm the animals and even make the rocks dance.'

'I did not know that - about him being Bulgarian, I mean. What happened to him?'

Ivo shook his head as if perplexed by Mowgley's lack of what should be common knowledge. 'He was not Bulgarian but Thracian. He was killed by people who did not like his music.'

'Ah,' said Mowgley, 'so there were critics even then.'

He saw the couple hanging from the cliff face were taking a rest, and one was using an arm to indicate and encompass what must have been a spectacular if perilous vantage point.

'I could never see why people would want to do that,' he said.

Ivo looked at where he was looking. 'Some people,' he said, 'like to take risks.'

~

The Skoda had left the road and was climbing a steep, winding trail. Mowgley did not know whether to be happy to be away from traffic or anxious about the challenges of the unfriendly terrain. The forest stretched endlessly on either side of the track, its tall trees reaching for the sky as biblical shafts of light picked out clearings and dense areas of waist-high fern.

'It is good cover,' said Ivo as he saw what Mowgley was looking at.

'I imagine there would be plenty of wildlife?'

'Yes. *Gligan* - boar - are everywhere and it is said there are still wolves and even bears in the more remote parts.'

'And what about humans? Do any people live here?'

Ivo leaned forward to turn on the windscreen wipers and dispel a shower of pine needles. 'Not usually,' he said, 'unless they are hunters or hermits or people who don't want to be found because they should not be here.'

As if on cue, they turned a bend and found the trail blocked. The blue SUV was side-on, its balloon tyres keeping the chassis high above the ground. On the roof was a slowly revolving blue light, and two men in uniforms and peaked caps stood by the bonnet. Mowgley saw that one had a hand resting on the holster on his left hip, while the other was cradling what looked like a short-nosed machine pistol.

Ivo Georgiev pulled up about ten paces short of the SUV and put the gear stick into neutral. Mowgley noticed he then put both hands on the wheel so they would be in clear view through the windscreen. The man with the machine pistol stayed where he was, while the other one started walking towards them. As he approached, Ivo reached down with one hand and slipped the gearstick into reverse. Then he pressed the button to wind his window down.

The man arrived at the driver's door and leaned down to look inside. He was bulkily-built with a swarthy complexion and a moustache which made Inspector Georgiev's growth look modest. He spoke tersely to Ivo, who replied, then slowly reached into the breast pocket of his shirt. He eased out a laminated card about the size and shape of an international driving licence and handed it over. The man looked at it carefully and it seemed to Mowgley that his eyes widened slightly. The next exchange was marked by a much more friendly and even respectful tone from the man. At one point, Ivo nodded towards Mowgley and said something which provoked a grunting laugh. Nodding in a friendly fashion, the man handed the card back and shouted to his companion, who climbed into the SUV and backed it off the track.

'So who were they?' asked Mowgley as they drove past the car and the man with the machine pistol waved. 'We have forest rangers, but they don't usually go around armed with machine guns.'

Ivo Georgiev gave his faintly irritated look. 'It was a submachine gun. They were Border Police. Their job is to stop illegal migrants coming in to Bulgaria.'

'From Greece? Don't you have an open border policy with the rest of the Union?'

'Of course,' Ivo navigated a sizeable log which occupied the centre of the trail. 'It is not the Greeks who are the problem, but people coming from Turkey. The border is nearly three hundred kilometres and we have built a wall along one hundred of them. The Turks did not like it, but now they are building a wall in the south to keep people from the Middle East and Africa out. People try and get across our border with Greece because it is an easy route.'

'What's the problem with new blood? I thought you were short of people.'

Ivo looked to see if he were joking. 'That doesn't mean we want people coming in illegally...or bad people. The EU law is that we have to look after anyone who gets through. Bulgaria is a poor country and hundreds try to get in every day; that's why the Militia is encouraged by the government.'

'The Militia?'

'Volunteers who help catch illegal immigrants. They say many of those trying to cross the border with Turkey and then here are ISIS terrorists in disguise.'

'And are the militiamen armed?'

'Some have knives and some have guns. One famous militiaman has his own tank. He appears on YouTube and is a hero to some people.'

'And what do they do with those they catch?'

'They hand them over to the Border Patrol. Or most do.'

'And the others?'

Ivo shrugged 'There are stories. People feel strongly.' He turned to look at Mowgley. You cannot understand. You live on an island and are very rich. We are surrounded by other countries and are very poor.'

Mowgley smiled. 'I think we still get more people trying to sneak in than you do.'

'That's because you are soft and pay out money for doing nothing.' Ivo dropped a gear as the trail got steeper. 'Are there any more questions for now? You are making my head hurt.'

'Only what you said to the man to make him laugh.'

'I told him you were an illegal immigrant from England and I was taking you deep in the woods to shoot you.'

~

'Can we stop for a pee and a fag?'

'No point,' said Ivo, 'we are nearly there and then you can piss and smoke whenever you like in the woods outside the house.'

The modified Skoda V6 had been happily bumping up the trail for nearly half an hour since their encounter with the Border Police. As they gained altitude, the forest was becoming less dense and the individual trees more stunted. Ivo had wound down both windows, and the air was decidedly cooler and fresher.

Then, around a bend, their way was again blocked. The steel goal post looked oddly out of place as it was the sort of height restrictor common to supermarket car parks. A horizontal swinging arm joined the uprights at waist level. On either side, gaps between thick-trunked pine trees were bridged by giant logs and concrete posts.

'You don't like unexpected visitors dropping in, then?' asked Mowgley as Ivo got out of the Skoda.

His minder looked back at him, sighed almost theatrically and shook his head 'I think,' he said, 'that's why it's called a safe house.'

17

The safe house looked very safe.

In its forest setting, Mowgley had expected some sort of hunting lodge or even a characterful log cabin. In fact, the squat brick and concrete building looked more like a particularly strongly-built nuclear bunker. It sat at the top of the trail on an obviously artificial hump, the ground dropping away steeply on all sides and the nearest trees more than a hundred metres distant.

There were small, square metal shutters at regular intervals at two levels and Mowgley assumed they covered windows. If so, he thought, they would provide all-round visibility as firing points as well as natural light. Concrete steps led up to a door-sized shutter in the centre of the ground floor of the front elevation. Like the window coverings, it was studded and painted blood-red. On the roof was a small structure which probably housed the water tank and air conditioning unit, and it looked as secure as the building it served.

Ivo parked the Skoda well away from the building and began to unload a number of boxes and bags from the boot. Mowgley took his suitcase from the back seat and looked up at the roof of the building. 'No vats for boiling oil, then?' he said.

Ivo looked up. 'What?'

'Never mind.' He started to walk towards the building, took in the array of aerials, masts and satellite dishes alongside the tank house, then said: 'Hope you've got Sky Sport Cricket Channel.'

~

If the exterior of the safe house was uncompromisingly functional, the inside was in comparison almost decadently indulgent. It was also a rather uncomfortable mix of transient fashion imperatives and the latest technological advances.

Opening up from a double-doored vestibule, the high-ceilinged main room was floored and walled with stripped pine planking. Animal skin and fur rugs lay scattered on the floor, and the walls were festooned with hunting trophies. One was the head of what must have been a sizeable boar. It wore a doleful and, Mowgley thought, sadly reproachful expression.

In between the rows of heads and horns and skulls, wooden racks carried a variety of firearms which ranged from antique muskets to shotguns and sleekly menacing automatic weapons. Standing against one wall was a leather-topped and tubular chrome-legged desk; on it was sitting a control board, large computer monitor and keyboard. Alongside, a huge screen was fixed to the wall. In contrast and nearby was an antique gaming table with a chessboard set up ready for use on the green baize top. Stripped pine doors led off from one wall, presumably to the kitchen and bathroom, and between them a wide staircase led up to a gallery which spanned the width of the building.

The main feature of the room was a sunken central area with a raised, square hearth laid with logs. Above it was a stainless steel hood, the ducting from it rising vertically to and through the ceiling. Three black leather sofas were arranged around the fireplace, and on the fourth side was a long pine table with eight chairs. This part of the room looked as if it had been modelled on any one of a host of seasonal Hollywood movies of the1960s, where the snowed-in lovers spent most of their time in each other's arms in front of the roaring log fire while the radiogram played lushly orchestrated Christmas carols.

Having taken the boxes and bags through one of the doors,

Ivo Georgiev walked over and flicked some switches on the control box on the desk. Almost immediately, the big screen on the wall came alive. It was split into six squares, each showing a view of the clearing from a different perspective.

'Very nice,' said Mowgley, but what happens if someone cuts the power cables?'

'They are underground,' replied Ivo, 'and there is a stand-by generator.'

'I'm impressed,' said Mowgley. When was it built, and for who?'

'It was built after the Communists came to power. It was supposed to be a secret communications centre. In fact, it was a retreat for high-up officials and somewhere to come with their women while their wives stayed at home.'

'Another example of privileges for the few rather than the good of the many, then?'

Ivo Georgiev shrugged. 'It's the same everywhere isn't it, even in long-time democratic countries like yours?'

Mowgley looked around and nodded. 'Yep, and sometimes especially so in long-time democratic countries like mine.'

~

Mowgley was studying a painting on the wall next to the big screen. It was executed in oils and showed a winter scene with a heavily wrapped-up hunter standing over the body of a stag with imposing antlers. He wondered if one of the skulls on the walls belonged to the unfortunate animal.

He looked up as the door to one of the ground floor rooms opened. 'What's this, sentry-go?'

'What?' Ivo Georgiev was wearing a camouflage jacket and trousers, tucked into the tops of shiny, calf-length boots. He was carrying a bolt-action rifle mounted with telescopic sights.

'Are you going on guard duty?'

'No', said Ivo, 'I'm going hunting.'

'For illegal immigrants?'

'No, for supper. But an illegal immigrant would be a bonus.'

Mowgley looked around the trophy-lined walls. 'Pity there's no space for another head up there.'

Ivo smiled darkly, 'I am sure we could make room.'

'Then you really are going to shoot something to eat?'

'That's the idea. But I've brought some frozen pizzas and tins in case.'

'And when do you reckon your dad will get here?'

Ivo looked at his watch. 'Anytime now. He phoned just now to say he was on the trail. You will see him arrive on the screen.' He walked towards the vestibule door, then looked back.

'There is no SKY Sport channel, but lots of Russian porn on the computer screen if that is your taste - and you can work out how to work the remote control...'

~

Inspector Georgiev arrived shortly after his son left, and Mowgley watched one of the panels on the big screen as the inspector eased himself out of his car and walked across to the steps up to the front door. Then his image disappeared, the inner door opened and he walked in, pipe in mouth and carrying a small holdall.

'Hello Jack,'

'Hello, Gosho. Did you find her?'

'No, but there is news. Where is my son?'

'He is out hunting illegal immigrants?'

'I am sorry?'

'Only joking. He is shooting our supper. Is he a good shot?'

'Very.'

'I thought he might be. So what about Jen?'

Georgiev held up a placatory hand. 'Please give me time to get through the door. For now, I am almost sure she is alive. I will tell you everything I know as soon as I have had a cup of coffee. Do you know where the kitchen is?'

'No, but I can find it.'

Georgiev put his bag on the table by the fireplace. 'On second thoughts,' he said, 'I will make it. I have noticed that people from the West like coffee too weak to get out of the pot.'

~

'So why do you think Jen is okay?'

Georgiev laid down his pipe and reached for the tall, ornamental metal coffee pot. They were sitting opposite each other at the pine table. 'I repeat,' he said, 'that I don't know that she is okay, but I do know she is not in the hands of the *mutri*.'

'How can you be sure?'

'I have been talking to a man who would know if she were.'

'What man?'

Georgiev stirred his coffee and began to fill his pipe.

'Once upon a time he was an influential figure in the Communist party.' He waved his pipe at their surroundings.

'He would have come here when it suited him. Then the party collapsed in 1990 and he was out of a job. So he joined the *mutri*.'

'Wait a minute. Call me over-anxious, but if he used to come here, he'll know that it's used as a safe house now, won't he?'

'Of course.'

'So you're keeping me safe in a safe house that the local mafia know about?'

Georgiev nodded. 'That's right. They will probably know you are here.'

'Is that to make it easy for them if they want to knock me off?'

The Inspector smiled. 'Be calm, Jack. They would have known or could find out where you were wherever we had taken you. From what I learned today, they are not interested in you.'

'That's nice to know. So this contact of yours is pretty high up the mafia ladder. Did he just apply to join?'

'He had something to bring with him. He had been a high-ranking officer in the army and had many contacts in the military and the Party. Some Party members managed to find good positions in the government after 1990, so his area of influence spread wide - and still does.'

Mowgley frowned. 'So how come you - a senior police officer - can phone up and have a chat with a top man in the Bulgarian Mafia? What are you doing on such chummy terms?'

Georgiev shrugged and blew out a cloud of pipe smoke before answering. 'It is how and what it is. I cannot change what happens here. We all have our places and have to fit in. If powerful people thought I was doing my job too well they could squash me like a fly. That is why I investigate individuals who are not directly connected with the *mutri* and try to achieve results by stealth. In the case of Mr Cullan, they are actually pleased that I was investigating him.'

'But I thought you said he was part of the mafia?'

'No, I said he had dealings with them, but then something happened which upset them very much.'

Mowgley looked at him for a moment, then lit a cigarette and said: 'I really don't get it. Are you telling me you work with the mafia rather than against them?'

Georgiev smiled sadly. 'How little westerners understand of what real life is like in this part of Europe. It is all a game, but a very dangerous one and it has its rules. Here, politicians can make millions if they play the game properly and don't tread on other people's toes. Corruption is everywhere and goes to the very top. Do you know what people call our prime minister? The Bulgarian Al Capone. If the players get it wrong or upset the wrong people, they may be exposed or worse. Every now and then someone in an influential position will be thrown to the wolves. As in Sicily and Russia, the mafia is a fact of life. There are more than a hundred organised crime groups in Bulgaria, and not a single major figure in any of them has ever been prosecuted. Since the fall of Communism there have been more than a hundred and fifty contract killings in Bulgaria. Do you know how many people have been arrested and convicted in that time?' Inspector Georgiev held up a single finger, 'just one.' He refilled his cup, re-lit his pipe and continued: 'I do my best to do my job and still survive. Sometimes I can achieve things by working with honest people. Sometimes I have to look away. Do you remember what I told you about the gang who were caught trying to sell millions of Euros worth of looted gold artefacts and how one of them was a SANS officer?'

Mowgley nodded.

'The undercover officer who set the deal up was my son. And the *mutri* had not been included in the deal so were pleased with the result.'

Mowgley frowned. 'Are you saying you have to have the permission of corrupt officials and organised crime gangs to do your job?'

'It is not as simple as that, Jack. I wish it were. As you must know, a too-honest man does not prosper in any profession or country. It is even more so in Bulgaria.'

Mowgley sat and looked at the inspector and thought what it would be like to try and remain uncorrupted in a sea of corruption. And stay alive.

'I'm sorry Gosho,' he said eventually. 'I did not know how bad it was here.'

Georgiev nodded as if in acceptance of Mowgley's apology. 'Not many people from outside do, Jack. To us, it is how it works, and you have to play within the rules or leave. If they let you.'

18

'But what about Jen? If it wasn't the mafia who took her, who did?'

Mowgley was standing by the table, a beer in his hand and his back to the log fire. Although nights were still warm and sticky on the coast, it grew cold after dark in the mountain reaches. He looked up at the big screen and saw that dusk was falling, and realised that Ivo had yet to return from his hunting trip.

'A good question,' said Inspector Georgiev.

'And do you know the answer?'

'No.'

'But you have an idea?'

Georgiev fiddled with his moustache. 'I am beginning to have an idea.'

'Well' said Mowgley shortly, 'why don't you share it?'

'Not yet. It would do no good.'

Mowgley let out a long sigh of frustration. 'Okay. And what about your mafia mate - did he have any ideas? Could it have been another branch of his firm?'

Georgiev smiled and sipped beer from his tall glass. 'The mafia doesn't have branches, Jack. There are other groups, but they have agreements and do not operate on each other's territory unless they want to start a war. My contact had heard about the kidnapping, and believes it to have been people working on their own.'

'What, you mean like freelancers?'

'Something like that.'

Mowgley sighed noisily again. 'But why?'

'That is what I don't know.'

'So what are you doing about finding Jen?'

'There is a nationwide alert for the van, but it is very unlikely the people who took her would still be using it. Mrs Cullan's description has also been circulated to every police station and agency site in the country.'

Mowgley put the empty beer bottle on the table and rubbed his hands on his face. 'But there must be something we can do? What about her phone?'

'Ah yes.' Inspector Georgiev fumbled in a pocket of his jacket, then produced Jen's mobile. 'I have started going through the contacts list.'

'Is there anything of interest?'

Georgiev frowned. 'It is too soon to tell. There were more than a hundred names and numbers on the list. I have someone checking her friends and relations in England and putting those who have no obvious relevance to one side.'

'And her sister has been told about the kidnapping?'

Georgiev toyed with the right side of his moustaches again, which Mowgley had learned was a sure tell that something was bothering or puzzling him. 'Curiously,' said the inspector, 'her contact number was not on the list, or appears not to be. She may be under a married name or a nickname of course. My man has instructions to let me know when and if he contacts her.'

'If? Surely Jen would have her sister's number in her phone?'

'Yes,' said Georgiev thoughtfully, 'I would have imagined so.'

'And what about the guy who was on the other end of the line when I took the call?'

'Ah yes. Professor Kirov.'

'The archaeologist bloke? What did he want?'

'I don't know. He has not answered my calls. Or those from my man. I will go and find him tomorrow.'

Mowgley paced alongside the fire and tried to stay calm. 'Do you find it suspicious that he should have Jen's number?'

'Not really. We know that he was an associate of Mr Cullan, providing provenance for the artefacts that he was offering for sale. But if Mrs Cullan was not involved in the business, it is perhaps unusual or curious the professor would have her number or want to call her. It is for the moment a small mystery.'

Georgiev knocked his pipe out in a large ornamental bowl in the middle of the table, pushed his chair back, stood up and stretched, then said: 'Are there any more questions for the moment, or can we make ready to eat supper?'

'Just a small but slightly important point from my perspectve. You said earlier that the mafia no longer wants to kill me, which is nice to know. Did your man say why they lost interest?'

'He said that when you arrived they thought you might be part of Mr Cullan's little team of helpers. They had you checked out and knew of your past association with Mr Cullan - and Mrs Cullan. They could see no reason why you would have come over after Mr Cullan disappeared unless it was to take over or help with the operation. But then they checked further and realised you had no connection with the business, and just wanted to help and support Mrs Cullan.'

'I guess you mean they couldn't understand that someone would fly sixteen hundred miles just to show support to an old friend in distress?'

'Precisely. And for a while neither could I.'

Georgiev reached into a pocket and took out his phone. 'Now, if you are happy, I will call my son and see how successful he has been - or not, and whether it is venison or pizza for supper.'

~

'I thought you said you liked to keep in shape and eat good food?'

Ivo shrugged. 'Pizzas are good food. It's not my fault there was nothing to shoot.'

He and Mowgley and Inspector Georgiev were sitting at a picnic table at the foot of the mound on which the safe house sat.

It was a beautiful night and the clearing was bathed in the light of an almost full moon. There was not a breath of wind to disturb the trees ringing the safe house, and Mowgley could not remember being anywhere so utterly silent. It was good to be outside the windowless confines of the safe house, but he felt more than a little exposed. He had questioned the wisdom of taking a mafia boss's word for it that they had no interest in killing him, but his companions seemed unconcerned. As Ivo had said while plating the pizzas and oven chips, it would take a really skilful assassin to get close enough to have a clean shot at Mowgley. And if he did, he would know nothing about it anyway.

'Well that's a positive way to look at it, I suppose,' said Mowgley, topping up their glasses from the bottle of rakia he had been given by Magda Abadjiev's father. 'He looked up at the night sky. 'It's what we call a smuggler's moon.'

'It's what we call a hunter's moon,' said Georgi Georgiev, 'but no help if there is nothing to hunt. Did you not see anything at all, my son?'

'Only a black squirrel, and I did not think our guest would be happy to see its poor little dead body, let alone eat it.'

'A black squirrel? Is this another Bulgarian tall tale?'

'Not at all,' said Georgiev. 'We have black squirrels and black herons as well as black bear and a Black Sea. There are many unusual creatures in the most remote parts of our country. I propose a toast to Bulgaria and those creatures of the night that are rarely seen.'

They clinked glasses, then Mowgley broke the silence. 'And you think the dodgy professor may be able to help find Jen?'

Georgiev reached for his pipe and toyed with it. 'Who can say? But he may have some information. I hope to find out tomorrow.'

'And he was involved in Den's business?' Mowgley emptied his glass and put it on the table. 'By the way, you have never properly explained how Den's business worked, and what he was doing that was illegal.'

As Georgiev opened his mouth to speak, his son got up from the bench. 'I have heard this and need a piss,' he said. 'Excuse me.' He walked off towards the ring of trees, and Mowgley noticed he took his hunting rifle with him.

'To understand Mr Cullan's business and what he did,' said

the inspector, 'you must first understand how things have changed. When Bulgaria was part of the Eastern Bloc, looting of artefacts was punished very heavily. The problem grew massively after the fall of Communism. In 2002, for example, one person shipped a ton of ancient coins from Bulgaria through Frankfurt and to the United States of America. The load was made up of more than 300,000 coins. In 2009 a new law was brought in with severe penalties for plundering archaeological sites, but it has had little effect. You have to realise that there is a huge worldwide market for antiquities, especially Thracian artefacts.'

'But Den was trading legally?'

'On the surface, yes.'

'And what makes an item legal?'

Georgiev smiled. 'Broadly, because the state doesn't want it.'

'And where does or did professor Kirov come into it?'

'This is a key question. Professor Kirov is known internationally as a remarkably successful finder of artefacts and ancient sites. Some would say he has been suspiciously successful. Apart from the golden death mask you saw him 'discovering' on You Tube, he has unearthed no less than three Thracian temples and many hundreds of precious items over the years. To be fair, he spends a lot of time on various sites, but still seems to be very lucky. He is known in some circles as the 'truffle hound' archaeologist.'

'And giving approval to the artefacts the government didn't want and Den was selling would give them a real seal of approval?'

Georgiev nodded. 'That is right.'

'But if the state didn't want them, they must have been pretty low-level finds?'

The Inspector nodded again. 'Exactly. Certainly not valuable enough to allow him to buy a luxury apartment block and invest in so many other businesses.'

'So, what do you think the pair were up to?'

Georgiev tapped the stem of his empty pipe against his teeth. 'Obviously, Kirov could have been finding more buried treasure than he declared and passing on the choicest finds to Mr Cullan.'

'And where would the mafia come in?'

'As you know, the *mutri* work with other organised crime

gangs around the world. They would have located and set up wealthy collectors. The Varna group would probably have organised the smuggling of the items out of the country. Mr Cullan and the professor would get a cut.'

'So, what went wrong? Wouldn't getting rid of Den be a bit like killing the goose that laid the golden eggs?'

'Very much so.'

'Was Den doing deals elsewhere - or did the mafia want to cut out the middle man and work directly with the professor?'

Georgiev slowly re-filled his pipe, teased out the tobacco strands, tamped them down and applied a match. 'It could be, but I think it is more than that.'

'More?'

'Whatever Mr Cullan was doing, it made his business partners very angry. I think they lost face, which is the worst thing which can happen to any mafia group.

That would explain why they did not simply shoot Mr Cullan in the head but left him to drown in despair. It would also explain the theatrical way they killed Magda Abadjiev. As I said before, it would guarantee maximum publicity around the world and send the signal out that they were not to be trifled with.'

'And what do you think Den did to so upset them?'

Georgiev looked at his empty glass thoughtfully. 'I think they thought he had made them look, as you I think would say, like mugs.'

'Yes, but how?'

Georgiev shrugged. 'I think Mr Cullan was selling more artefacts through the *mutri* than the professor was finding.'

Before Mowgley could ask the obvious question, a shot rang out.

Both men looked at each other, and Mowgley struggled to swing his injured leg over the bench seat. Before he could disentangle himself there was a shout and a figure broke cover from the ring of trees and walked towards them. It was Ivo Georgiev, and he was struggling to drag a body across the grass.

As he drew nearer, Mowgley saw that it was a huge and obviously dead wild boar.

Its conqueror arrived at the bench and Mowgley saw that it had been shot in the head, and bore a similarly bemused and reproachful expression as the head on the trophy wall in the safe house.

Clearly elated and his eyes shining in the moonlight, Ivo waited to regain his breath, then smiled at his father. 'You were right, papa. It is a hunter's moon.' Turning to Mowgley, he nudged the body with a booted foot. 'Better than pizza, eh?'

Mowgley tried to think of a suitable riposte, then said: 'Poor thing. Did you shoot it while it was tucked up in bed?'

Inspector Georgiev knelt down and looked into the dead eyes. 'He does his business at night, Jack. Boars are nocturnal, like many dangerous animals.'

As the inspector got to his feet, his phone rang. Reaching inside, he held it to his ear. Someone at the other end began to talk very fast, his voice audible in the surrounding silence.

Georgiev listened intently, interrupting the flow with questions. Finally, he took the phone from his hear and looked at it with a frown.

'Who was it?' asked Mowgley. Was it your man who's checking out Jen's contacts list?'

'Yes,' said Georgiev heavily,' but he was not calling about the list. He wanted me to know that the van which was used to abduct Mrs Cullan has been found.'

'Empty?' Mowgley asked quickly.

'No.' said the inspector slowly. 'There were three bodies in it. Two men and a woman.' He saw Mowgley's face change and quickly said: 'It was the woman who was with the gang. There was no sign of Mrs Cullan.'

19

To some of her neighbours in Winsor Close, Rowena Skase was a sad but harmless curtain-twitcher. Others saw her as a nosey, interfering old cow. In truth she was just a lonely old lady who had been soured by time and circumstance.

She had lived in the house for more than half a century, the first forty of them with her husband Tom. He had died the most lingering and undignified of deaths, losing his mind in small pieces across a decade. At first it was little things like an old friend's name, then he began to forget his own. Towards the end he stopped remembering who she was, and that was the hardest blow of all.

Now, all she had to do all day was think about the past and look out of her window at her neighbours, registering the small triumphs and tragedies in their lives. Sometimes she would catalogue their comings and goings and indiscretions in an old notepad. It was not a malicious act; it just made her feel part of the world beyond her garden gate.

This morning she felt a frisson of anticipation as she shuffled to the front door and saw the silhouette through the rippled glass panel. Had perhaps something dramatic happened in the Close - perhaps even a bloody murder?

'Hello. Sorry to bother you.'

The policewoman was small, pretty and impossibly young.

Rowena smiled and wished she had put her teeth in. 'It's not a bother. Would you like to come in for a cup of tea?'

She saw the indecision, and opened the door wider.

The WPC smiled and reached up to take off her hat. 'That's kind of you.'

Rowena led the way down the passage and into the kitchen, faintly embarrassed that the smell of cabbage from lunch still lingered. She reached across the sink and opened the window a little, then pointed at a chair.

'Thanks.'

'Do you really need to wear one of these things?'

The officer looked down at her anti-stab vest.

'I'm afraid it's standard issue.'

'Yes, it's a dreadful world now, isn't it?'

Not expecting an answer, Rowena turned away and busied herself with kettle, tea caddy and pot. 'I like a proper cup of tea,' she said. 'Are you the same?'

'Um, yes. It's nice.' The young officer reached up and took her notebook out as a signal it was time for business.

Rowena saw what she was doing and decided to go on the offensive. 'I suppose someone's been complaining about me? Number 37, perhaps?'

The WPC gave her a puzzled look. 'No.'

'Well, that makes a change.'

'Okay. No thanks.' The policewoman held a palm-out hand up to the plate of custard creams, almost in the way she had been trained to calm an escalating situation. 'I -we - just wanted to know if you've seen your neighbour lately.'

Rowena put the plate of biscuits back on the table, warmed the pot then began to spoon loose tea into it. 'Which one?'

WPC Russell opened and looked at her notebook although she did not need to. 'It's, um, number 26. Mrs Cullan. She's not in and the lady at 24 said she hasn't seen her for weeks.'

The answer was dismissive. 'Oh, her. She's never there.'

'Oh? What do you mean by that?'

'She's always away,' said Rowena, pleased that she knew something of value to someone else. I see her coming and going with her posh matching luggage and taxis arriving at all hours. Why do you want to know? Has something happened?'

'No, not particularly. It's just we need to see that she's

169

alright.'

'Alright?' The old lady mentally sniffed the air. 'Why wouldn't she be? Do you think something's happened to her?'

WPC Russell tried to look authoritative. 'No, not necessarily. When did you last see her?'

'It must be three weeks ago. The taxi arrived just after Coronation Street ended.'

The new officer nodded and made a self-conscious note. 'Okay. Thank you. And do you know which school she's a teacher at?'

'School?' Rowena put a tray on the table next to the WPC, ensuring the handle of the cup was pointing in the right direction. 'Help yourself to milk and sugar. What school?'

'Our information is that she's a teacher.'

'Not for a dozen years or more. She's been a real lady of leisure since her husband ran off.'

'Okay.' WPC Russell poured a little milk into the delicate porcelain cup, then looked at her notes. 'And do you possibly know where her sister lives? It would be great if you knew her name.'

'Rowena Skase paused with the cup midway to her mouth. Sister? What sister?'

The young police officer looked puzzled. 'We were told that Mrs Cullan's son was staying with her sister.'

The old lady licked her lips as if savouring the knowledge that she knew something that the Metropolitan Police Force did not.

'I've lived in this house since 1966, and I see her front door every day. I've never seen or heard of her having a sister, and I'm even more sure she hasn't got a son.'

~

Mowgley stretched and yawned as he luxuriated in the king-size bed. Despite the tongue-and-groove pine boards on walls and ceiling making it feel like an oversized sauna, it was a pleasant enough room. No window, natural light or view, but that was fair enough because it was a safe house. He yawned again. It was also pleasant to know that, if Gosho Georgiev's inside information was correct, nobody wanted to kill him at the moment.

He lay there and thought what a beautiful and mad and sometimes bad country Bulgaria seemed to be. It was certainly not a good place to be on your own and in trouble.

Jen was somewhere out there, alone and frightened - he did not like to think of the alternative - and all he had to do now was find her.

~

'How do you like your eggs?'

Mowgley looked up to where Ivo was standing in the open doorway of the kitchen. He was holding a frying pan and wearing a frilly, pink apron over his olive-green military-issue vest. The apron did not go well with the vest, nor his hairy chest and bulging biceps.

'Nice and runny, with toasted soldiers if you have any sliced bread, please.'

'We don't have any eggs,' said Ivo. 'I just wondered how you would have liked them.'

'You must forgive my son,' said Georgi Georgiev, 'he has an unusual type of humour.'

'It is not at all unusual in the UK,' said Mowgley. We call it taking the piss.'

They were sitting at the long pine table by the fire, which had been re-made but not lit.

Outside it was still dark, but floodlights covering the area around the house made it seem lighter than day on the big TV screen.

Mowgley made a face of displeasure, put down the tiny cup of acrid coffee which even three spoons of sugar did not render palatable, then lit his first cigarette of the day. There were no ashtrays on view so he assumed it was officially a smoke-free safe house. He had refrained from lighting up in his room, but Gosho had been puffing away at his pipe when Mowgley came down the stairs. The night before he had said that as the fire smoked, he could see no reason why they should not do the same in that part of the house.

'So, what happens today?' asked Mowgley. 'Do you have any more information or ideas where Jen may be?'

'Nothing more about Mrs Cullan than I told you yesterday,' said Georgiev. 'I know it is hard but you must also know how it is from your time with the Special Branch. If someone is missing and there are no leads and you have done all you can, there's not much else to do except wait.' He watched the smoke drifting towards the chimney cowl and ducting. 'But I have a feeling that it might be helpful to our search if we talk to Professor Kirov.'

'You think he may have something to do with her disappearance?'

'I should not imagine so, but he did try and call her when you were searching the hotel room. That shows a closer connection than I had suspected.'

'Suspected?'

Georgiev raised a hand. 'Perhaps not the best choice of words. What I meant was that I did not know the two knew each other. I had been led to believe that Mrs Cullan had nothing to do with her husband's business.'

'Having his number in her contact list doesn't mean she did have anything to do with what Den was up to.' Mowgley spoke a little more sharply than he had intended. 'She might have met him or passed on or taken messages between them. Don't forget she speaks fluent Bulgarian. Did Den?'

The Inspector lifted one eyebrow. 'I believe he did, though probably not as well as his wife. But if they were acquainted, it is a little curious to me that Professor Kirov did not come over and offer his condolences to Mrs Cullan at her husband's funeral.'

Mowgley tapped his cigarette against the rim of the bowl they were using as an ashtray. 'Perhaps you made him nervous, being a policeman who investigates looting from archaeological sites.'

'Hmm.' Georgiev smiled. 'That is a possibility but then you saw him talking to and shaking hands with my superior, Commissar Dragov, so he is clearly not afraid of some policemen. And there is another curious thing.'

'Go on then,' said Mowgley, 'don't keep me in suspense.'

'You must have seen that when they spoke together at the funeral, it appeared that my boss and Mrs Cullan were strangers.'

'So?'

'So -' the inspector laid down his pipe and began to fiddle with his moustache. '-If that is so, why is his number also on Mrs Cullan's contact list?'

~

'If not boiled eggs I was at least expecting boar for breakfast.'

Ivo shrugged. 'It is hanging in the kitchen and I will take it home when we leave. This is much better for you.'

Mowgley looked dubiously at the glass and plate Georgiev's son had placed in front of him. The glass contained a thick, brownish liquid, while the stack of round, puffed-up flatbreads on the plate looked like a cross between naan bread and over-thick poppadums.

'This is *boza*', said Georgiev, nodding at the glass. 'It is a very traditional breakfast drink, made of fermented barley or sometimes another cereal. It is slightly alcoholic and very popular, but the word *boza* is also slang for something which is bland or boring.'

'A bit like a boring boar,' said Mowgley.

'What?' said Ivo.

His father said something to him in Bulgarian at machine-gun speed, but Ivo still looked puzzled as he returned to the kitchen.

'Cheer up,' said Georgiev, saluting Mowgley with his glass, 'you will like the *mekitsas*. They are a sort of fried bread made with eggs and flour and yoghurt, and you eat them with jam or cheese.'

'Not sure about the jam or cheese, but fried bread sounds good. But I thought Ivo said there were no eggs?'

'I expect he is right. These would have come from the freezer, ready-made.'

'Okay,' said Mowgley. 'Now what about your boss being on Jen's contact list? Are you sure it was his number?'

Georgiev tasted the *boza* and licked his lips appreciatively.

'Oh yes. It is a private number that he keeps for very special calls, and nobody is supposed to know of it.'

'So how do you know about it?'

The inspector reached out towards the plate. 'Will you pass the jam, please?' He concentrated on spreading a thick layer

173

on his *mekitsa*, then smiled. 'I know a lot of things I am not supposed to know.' He took a bite, then wiped his moustaches with a handkerchief he had pulled from the top pocket of his jacket. 'I find it helps me, as you might say, stay ahead of the game. As someone else said, a little knowledge can be a powerful thing.'

As Mowgley picked up and bit into one of the *mekitsas*, the kitchen door swung open. Ivo was holding a phone to his ear and called out something to his father.

The inspector looked at his watch and replied, and Ivo ducked back into the kitchen.

'We had better eat up,' Jack,' said Georgiev. 'The helicopter will be here in half an hour.'

'The what?'

'There is something I did not tell you about a telephone call I had after you went to bed.'

'About Jen?'

'No. It was from Professor Kirov.'

'He called you? I thought you said he had disappeared?'

'He had. Police went to his home near Stara Zagora and found him gone, if you see what I mean.'

'He's been kidnapped as well?'

'No. The apartment was orderly and his computer and other things had been taken. A neighbour said she saw him leave with a suitcase yesterday morning. He was alone and she thought he did not look his usual …ebullient self.'

'But if he wanted to disappear, why would he call you?'

'He is a very frightened man, and wants protection.'

'Who from?'

Georgiev shrugged. 'From whoever he is frightened of.'

'And did he tell you where he is?'

'Yes. He is on an island in the Black Sea. It is the home of an ancient temple to Apollo.' Georgiev smiled wryly. 'But from what he said, I think it should be re-named Treasure Island.'

20

The helicopter hovered high above them like a giant and very noisy bird of prey considering whether they were worth swooping on. The three men were standing by the landing pad which lay behind the safe house in a separate clearing ringed with arc lights.

'Is this a regular event?' shouted Mowgley.

'It used to be,' replied Georgiev. 'The party members liked to travel in style to and from their dirty weekends.'

'And how come you can summon it up?'

Georgiev smiled. 'It's no good having a little influence if you can't use it. It will save a lot of time. Someone will take our cars the slow way back.'

Georgiev looked up at the helicopter as it began its descent. Leaning closer, he shouted: 'You know I could get the driver to take you to the airport at Varna? But I think you want to see this thing through?'

Mowgley looked up at the underside of the helicopter and thought about the offer, then bellowed: 'Yeah. I'd rather see it through. I think.'

Georgiev cupped his hand and shouted: 'To the end?'

'Yeah,' replied Mowgley, speaking more to himself than the inspector. 'To the bloody end.'

~

It was the first time Mowgley had taken a ride in a helicopter, and within moments of clambering aboard he hoped it would be his last.

It was almost unbelievably noisy in spite of the padded headphones and the din rose to a screaming crescendo just before they took off. By the time he had opened his eyes they were high above the treetops.

He took a deep breath and tried to think about the nice things in his life, but gave up when he couldn't think of any.

'Cheer up.' Georgiev's voice crackled in his ear. 'You could be risking your life down there.'

Mowgley steeled himself and snatched a look at the road far below.

'Statistically,' continued the inspector, 'flying is a hundred times safer than driving. In Bulgaria it is much more so.'

'That's all very well,' said Mowgley after fiddling with the microphone attached to his headset, 'but if you have an accident up here it's likely to be your last one.' He looked round at the interior of the ageing Westland WAH-64. 'So where did you borrow this from - the Varna museum of aviation?'

'Don't let the pilot hear you say that - he will be very hurt. It was bought to patrol the borders some years ago when Bulgaria joined the EU.'

'That would explain the bullet holes in the bottom, then.'

'Not at all,' replied Georgiev. 'They come from an earlier time. This one has been grounded for the past year and it's the first time it has flown since then.'

'Oh,' said Mowgley, reluctant to ask the question in case the answer was not what he wanted to hear. 'Why's that?'

'There was a problem with the insurance,' said Geogiev.

~

As their flight got under way, Mowgley found the advantage of helicopter travel diminishing his fear level and was almost beginning to enjoy the experience. In a passenger plane the view was limited to what you could see through a small window and clouds seen from above look much the same. The comparatively panoramic view from the Westland made him see that it could be fun being above and beyond the restraints of gravity and almost as free as a bird.

The journey which would have taken three hours by car lasted less than one. As they approached the coast, Inspector Georgiev explained that they would be landing at an historic port.

'Nessebar has three thousand years of chequered history, and was known as the pearl of the Black Sea', he said. 'Nowadays it is a major seaside resort,'

'You sound disapproving,' said Mowgley.

'Not really. Times change. But I am a little sad that it is so full of history and yet most visitors lay on the beach or go to the bars.'

Mowgley looked down as the helicopter descended over red roofs, yellow beaches and lines of moored boats. Used to the limitations of fixed wing flying, it looked to him as though the pilot would overshoot the town. 'Am I missing something,' he said in a strained voice, 'or are there floats as well as wheels on this thing?'

'It's okay,' said Georgiev, reaching over and pointing past him. 'There's the landing pad.'

Mowgley looked to where the inspector was pointing and saw a circle enclosing a large 'H'. It did not comfort him that the circle was almost as wide as the narrow concrete jetty on which it had been painted. Moored nearby was a blue and white police launch, which began to bob and swing in the downdraft from the clattering blades as the helicopter descended. Then the Westland touched down with hardly a judder, and Mowgley resisted the urge to applaud the pilot.

Freeing themselves from harnesses and headsets, the passengers climbed down to the jetty and Inspector Georgiev led the way towards the launch.

'Aren't we supposed to be bending down and running?' asked Mowgley.

'I have always wondered why they do that in films,' said Georgiev, looking up as he patted his jacket pockets to locate his tobacco pouch. 'I think you would need to be a giraffe to be in peril from the rotor blades.'

~

The sharp-prowed police launch cut through the water, spray regularly cascading over the wheelhouse where Mowgley and Georgiev were taking shelter.

Ivo had refused a life jacket and was standing in his summer uniform of soaked tee-shirt and combat trousers at the stern. He had his legs braced and arms folded as he regarded the foam-topped wake from the launch's turbo-thruster. Two tough-looking men in blue ballcaps, blousons and trousers tucked in to Doc Marten-style knee-length boots were leaning against the starboard rail. Both wore heavy belts carrying pouches and holsters, and one was cradling what Mowgley now knew to be a Bulgarian police-issue submachine gun. Perhaps, he thought, their presence was why Ivo had chosen not to wear a life jacket and to stand so obviously exposing himself to the elements. He had noticed that many Bulgarian men liked to indulge in a bit of willy-waving.

He saw Georgiev looking thoughtfully at the two policemen, and asked: 'Are you expecting trouble?'

'Trouble? Ah, you mean our bodyguards? I did not ask for them, but someone senior obviously thought we would need taking care of.'

~

'What are they up to – diving for sunken treasure?

'I think that may be exactly what they are doing.'

Nessebar had dropped below the horizon and the launch was powering down as it approached a sturdy-looking craft sitting at anchor next to a large, yellow buoy.

Flying above the wheelhouse was a blue and white pennant which Mowgley knew to be the international warning that a diver was working below.

To Mowgley, the boat looked like a larger version of the one from which Den Cullan had fallen or been thrown. Unlike the Treasure Seeker, this one had a swim platform, sitting at the rear no more than few inches above the water.

A crackle of static filled the wheelhouse and the pilot spoke

---

178

rapidly into a hand set hanging above his head. Another burst of noise, then a response came from the loudspeaker by the wheel.

Mowgley looked enquiringly at Georgiev, who nodded towards the dive boat. 'Our pilot is asking their business, and the man at the other end says they are on an official exploration.'

The inspector gave the man at the wheel a look of enquiry and words were exchanged. The patrol launch picked up speed, rose up out of the water and came on the plane, and Mowgley saw a figure on the dive boat wave. The officer with the submachine gun straightened up and returned the wave as the launch sped away. It was, Mowgley thought, a rather contrived gesture. The man with the gun did not look the sort of person who went in for waves.

Mowgley looked back as a wet-suited diver broke water and heaved a wire cage on to the dive platform. The man who had waved at them hurried to the stern, reached over and dragged the wire cage inboard. From that distance it seemed to be filled with nothing more exciting than a few rocks.

Mowgley watched and then turned to Georgiev. 'That was all a bit casual, wasn't it?'

The inspector frowned. 'What was casual, Jack?'

'Taking the bloke's word for it that they were on an official dive.'

The inspector shrugged. 'We have urgent business elsewhere, and I know the pilot knows the boat and its captain. They are archaeologists, not looters. I do not think even the mafia would go fishing for sunken treasure in the daylight so close to shore. Anyway, they don't like to do the dirty work; they prefer other people to find the treasure for them.'

'Like Den, perhaps?'

Georgiev nodded. 'Perhaps. Or perhaps not. I think Mr Cullan got his loot from above the waves.'

Mowgley stepped from the wheel house and looked out across the water. 'Is there much down there, do you think?'

Georgiev joined him at the rail and smiled as he reached for his tobacco pouch.

'You could say that,' he said dryly. 'You must remember that for thousands of years this was one of the most important and busy trading junctions in the world. East met West here, and ships came from all over the world to buy and sell. But there was a cost. This has always been a place of dangerous waters, and the Greeks called it the 'Hostile Sea'.

Mowgley looked at the surface of the placid waters and thought about the secrets it held and how close yet far away its treasures were. 'So, lots of shipwrecks and their cargoes down there?'

Georgiev pointed with his pipe to the eastern horizon. 'Many here and probably more out there. There is what they call a 'dead zone', where the water is much deeper and richer. Below 150 metres it is so cold that the shipwrecks are in a very good condition. Nobody knows how many wrecks from across the ages lie down there, but there will be hundreds. Last month the oldest shipwreck in the world was discovered in these waters.'

'Yes,' said Mowgley thoughtfully, 'I heard about that.'

There was a shout from the stern and the two men looked to where Ivo was leaning over the rail and pointing at the bubbling wake. The two men stared at the water, then the inspector took the pipe from his mouth and said 'There!'

Mowgley moved along the rail and saw the torpedo-like shape pursuing the boat, twisting and turning in the wake.

'Is it a shark?' Mowgley asked.

Ivo looked to see if he were joking, then said: 'No, it is a dolphin. They like the extra oxygen from the wake. In Bulgaria the sharks are mostly to be found on land.'

~

'He must have been kept busy.'

For all its history, the island looked an unremarkable place to Mowgley. Once, Georgiev had said as they approached the small and mostly featureless piece of rock, it had been the site of a temple to the Greek god Apollo. As a son of Zeus, he was one of the most important deities and a god of music, poetry and healing as well as plague and sun and light and the truth.

More recently, the island had been home to a community of monks, and the ruins of their 5th-century monastery were the only thing breaking the skyline of the flat, treeless place. This enhanced its air of desolation and, Mowgley thought, added a hint of menace. Once-inhabited but now empty places often made him feel like that; especially if they were sitting alone in the sea and far from the mainland.

'Who?' asked Georgiev. He and Mowgley were leaning on the rail and looking at the island across a hundred or so metres of calm sea as Ivo and the pilot worked on lowering a sleek-looking craft from a pair of davits on the stern. Mowgley knew it was a R.I.B. or Rigid Inflatable Boat, which was in effect a permanently blown-up and solidly braced dinghy. This one had a large outboard motor on the wooden transom across the stern.

'Apollo. And wasn't he a messenger for the gods as well?'

'No. That was Mercury, He was a Roman god. In his spare time he looked after shopkeepers, travellers, thieves and tricksters.'

'Of course.'

A curt shout drew their attention to the activity at the stern. The R.I.B. was dangling close to the surface, and Ivo had climbed on board. He was obviously calling for assistance, and after a moment one of the police guards left the rail and walked across to the davits. Mowgley noticed that, rather than move the harness to leave his hands free, he was still cradling the squat PM9 submachine gun.

~

The R.I.B. crossed the short distance to the shore in a couple of minutes, and Ivo did not bother to use more than a fraction of the power of the giant Mercury outboard engine. Georgiev and Mowgley were sitting on the bench seat directly behind the wheel position, and the two bodyguards were in the bows.

Georgiev turned and waved his pipe as the boat skidded up the beach, and Mowgley saw that the pilot was standing at the rail, watching them.

'Seems a nice bloke,' said Mowgley, 'is he a friend of yours?'

'Yes,' said the inspector, 'you could say that.'

~

After the brief but bumpy ride, they had left the R.I.B. aground on the narrow, sandy strip between the sea and the more elevated part of the island.

Beyond the beach was a mixture of rock and scrub, and only the ruins of what Mowgley took to be the old monastery broke the skyline. Ivo, Georgiev and Mowgley were walking abreast, followed closely by their bodyguards. Mowgley was in shirt-sleeves, but Georgiev had chosen to keep his tweedy jacket on. Although it was warmer than on the launch, Ivo was wearing his camouflaged, military-style body-warmer and forage cap.

'So where are we meeting the professor?' asked Mowgley, favouring his stiff leg as they mounted the rise.

Georgiev raised his hands in a small 'who knows?' gesture. 'He said he would be at the ruins.'

'I didn't see a boat?'

Georgiev repeated the gesture. 'Perhaps it is on the other side of the island or hidden somewhere. Remember he is a very frightened man.'

Mowgley looked at the grim, grey ruins and desolate surroundings.

'He must be to hide out here,' he said.

As they neared the remains of the monastery, Georgiev stopped and said something to his son, and Mowgley thought he seemed to speak more loudly than necessary. Ivo made an exasperated gesture, replied, turned and walked back towards the shore, pushing irritably between the guards.

'What did you say to upset him?' Mowgley asked.

'I asked if he had brought his sidearm, and he said he had forgotten it. He is going back to the launch to get it,'

'Aren't those two weaponised enough?' said Mowgley, nodding towards the two police officers. 'Are you expecting trouble?'

Inspector Georgiev had begun to answer when several events occurred in quick succession.

Mowgley had not previously heard a submachine gun being cocked, but knew instantly what it was as the man holding the MP9 swung round and away from them. Beyond the policeman, Ivo was standing with legs braced, holding a pistol in both hands. In his grip, it looked small. As Mowgley tried to take in what was happening, the barrel jerked and there were two sharp reports, followed by the yatter-yatter of the submachine gun. Mowgley watched in slack-jawed shock as the man who had pulled the trigger crumpled and fell slowly to the ground, the rounds he had let off drilling harmlessly into the scrub. Still numb and not yet grasping what was happening, Mowgley looked at Georgiev and saw that, pipe still clenched between his teeth, he had reached into an inside pocket of his jacket. He was struggling and grunting and whatever he was trying to pull out had obviously snagged on the lining.

Feeling as if he were watching something happening somewhere else, Mowgley looked back to where the shot man was laying on his side, curled up in a foetal position and cradling the submachine gun. A thin trickle of blood was running from beneath his chest. The other policeman was fumbling with his holster as Ivo moved his stance to point his pistol at him. Without thinking why, Mowgley took a step forward and threw himself at the back of the guard. The man grunted and pitched forward and Mowgley fell awkwardly on top of him as another shot sounded.

The policeman was younger and obviously fitter than Mowgley and threw him off with ease before getting to his knees and pulled a pistol from the now-opened holster. Mowgley was still spread-eagled on his back and for some reason recalled reading that turtles on their backs cannot right themselves.

He stared up with fascinated horror as the man pointed the pistol at his face. It was, Mowgley thought almost dispassionately, the second time it had happened in a few days. Two shots cracked out, and Mowgley winced and shut his eyes as he felt wetness spatter his face. Then he opened his eyes and saw that the blood was coming from the head of the man kneeling over him. His face assumed a bemused expression as he looked down at Mowgley and then towards where Ivo was standing. Then he gave a slight and almost deferential cough as he fell forward on top of the prostrate private detective.

It then became quiet and still, and Mowgley made no attempt to move until a figure loomed above him and hauled the body of the dead man aside.

'You prick,' said Ivo Georgiev, shaking his head as he offered Mowgley a helping hand. 'I wanted him alive.'

21

'Are you feeling a little better now?'

'Better than what?'

Mowgley shook his head in disbelief. 'Thank you for your solicitous enquiry and I'm sorry if I seem a bit out of sorts, but it's not every day I see two men killed and someone tries to blow my fucking head off. And that's the second time this week, I would add.'

It was only half an hour after the blood and death and drama and all was still. The sun was overhead and Mowgley and Georgiev were sitting in the shade of one of the remaining walls of the old monastery.

Georgiev patted Mowgley's arm. 'You are probably in shock. It is understandable.' The Inspector reached into an inside pocket of his jacket, saw Mowgley flinch and very slowly and deliberately brought out a small, metal container. 'It's okay.' he said, 'it's Scottish whisky, not rakia.'

Mowgley took a long pull and handed the flask back. Georgiev looked at the curved surfaces reflectively. 'It took me some time to realise they called them hip flasks because that was where they were meant to be kept.'

Mowgley did not reply and Georgiev offered him the flask again. 'I know how you must feel,' he said, 'but you will understand it really was them or us. They meant to kill us. And I am not much more used to seeing people killed than you are. Or,' he said thoughtfully, 'having someone try to kill me.'

Mowgley took the flask and drank deeply. 'I thought you said the mafia were not interested in me?'

'I don't think they are,' said Georgiev. I think those men wanted me dead. Ivo and you would have been no more than…collateral damage.'

The whisky was making Mowgley feel a little steadier. 'So, who wants to kill you – do you know?'

Georgiev frowned and pulled at his moustache. 'I am still not sure, but I have a good idea. Two days ago I told my man to let it be known that Commissar Dragov's name was on the contacts list in Mrs Cullan's phone. The call from Kirov came the next day.'

Mowgley pulled a packet of cigarettes from a trouser pocket, but found his hands were shaking too much to open it.

'Please.' Georgiev reached over for the packet, took out a cigarette and put it between Mowgley's lips. He lit it and Mowgley sucked in a lungful of smoke then leaned back against the wall.

After a moment, he looked directly at Georgiev 'You knew what was going to happen, didn't you? Otherwise why are you so calm?'

The Inspector shook his head and a look of irritation crossed his face. 'No, of course not I did not know. Do you think that a gun battle is a normal part of my working day? It is Ivo's job, but not mine. Believe it or not and except for when I drive, it is the first time someone has tried to kill me - as far as I am aware.'

He patted Mowgley's arm again to show he was not angry.

'I thought it strange that Kirov should want a meeting here, but I could not miss the chance that he might be genuine. It is said that the island is a staging post for looted treasure and I know he has done some digging here in the past on the temple site. When we got to Nessebar it made Ivo uneasy that the usual crew had reported in sick, and that the armed guards were unknown to us. He checked but he could find no record of the men being detailed to join us. That could just have been the usual breakdown in communications, but as it proved they had been sent to kill us.'

Mowgley looked up as a seagull wheeled and screeched overhead and thought how close it had come to the end of everything. He took another long pull on his cigarette and held out a hand for the flask. 'What will you do now? Are you going to keep looking for Kirov - and Jen?'

'Of course. What else can I do? And I have some more information of where the professor may be found.'

'Where?'

'I will show you when we are safely away from here.'

Mowgley eased his back against the wall and looked at the hand holding the cigarette. It was still shaking, but less than before the first dose from the hip flask. 'But what do we do now?' he asked. 'Who will you tell about the dead men? And what about the man on the launch?'

'He is on our side.'

'"On our side?" Are you sure?'

Georgiev smiled. 'I hope so, he is Ivo's brother, my youngest son - Aleksander.'

'And where is Ivo?'

'He has gone back to the launch to get a spade.'

Mowgley sat up straight and stared at the inspector. 'You're not telling me you're leaving the bodies here?'

Georgiev shrugged and tapped his pipe against the wall. 'What do you think we should do? If we took them back and reported the incident there would be an enquiry and it could take weeks. And whoever sent them would know what happened. This way we have a little time on our side. And remember there is no record that they were with us.'

Mowgley shook his head, laughed without humour and reached out for the hip flask.

'What's the matter,' asked Georgiev, 'what is it that is amusing you?'

Mowgley began to unscrew the lid of the flask. 'I just can't believe I'm sitting on an island in the Black Sea, having a drink with someone whose son is busily burying a couple of hired assassins he just knocked off.'

Georgiev smiled sadly and reached for the flask. 'Welcome to Bulgaria, Jack,' he said, 'but please believe it is not always like this in my country.'

~

The sun was falling into the sea and the last of the summer visitors were getting their money's worth on the beach or wandering around the old town. Others were exploring the seafront bars and restaurants, while a surprising number were queuing at the cemetery to see the last resting place of the Vampire of Sozopol.

Mowgley and Inspector Georgiev were sitting on the balcony of an hotel overlooking the bay. On the table between them was a bottle, two glasses, an ashtray and an Apple laptop.

The hotel, Georgiev had explained, specialised in cheap package holidays and was popular with people from elsewhere in Europe looking for guaranteed sun and the lowest of prices. It was probably not the sort of safe refuge most people would have chosen to spend a night after an attempt on their lives, but as Georgiev had said, it was as good a place as any to hide in plain sight. It was also probably safer than most of the other hotels as it was owned by a local division of the Bulgarian Mafia.

'Won't your wives want to know where you are?'

It was, Mowgley realised, a completely vacuous question, but his mind was still occupying another place.

'My sons are not married, and my wife their mother left us five years ago.' Georgiev pulled at his moustache and looked out across the bay as if thinking of past times.

'It happens to a lot of policemen where I come from,' said Mowgley. 'Mine buggered off with a Frenchman.'

Georgiev turned to look at him. 'I am sorry to hear that, Jack. But my wife did not leave me in that way. She died of cancer. Of the breast.'

'Ah. Sorry.'

Georgiev shrugged. 'You could not know. We had twenty-five happy years together. Not many couples can say that, I think. Not even in the United Kingdom.'

There was silence as they looked out over the bay, where a line of characterful fishing boats bobbing appealingly along the jetty. 'I wonder,' said Georgiev absently, 'if they ever go out to sea or have just been put there to please the eye of visitors.'

With hands that still shook, Mowgley lit a cigarette from the glowing stub of the current one. 'What happens now, then? Do we sit here and hope not to be mullered?'

'Mullered?'

'Killed.'

'Ah. As I said, I do not think that is likely' Georgiev spoke phlegmatically. 'The two men on the island were not from the mafia. They were, like the people who took Mrs Cullan, working alone. They had been recruited.'

'How do you know that? And who 'recruited' them?'

'Ivo has been making calls. It still astonishes me what can be done with a mobile phone camera and the Internet and a list of useful contacts.'

Mowgley thought of the SANS man calmly taking snapshots of the dead men and shuddered. 'But you think the men were working for Dragov?'

The inspector raised an eyebrow. 'Perhaps. Or perhaps someone even higher up the ladder.'

Mowgley shook his head. 'My God. Is the whole of your police force rotten?'

Georgiev looked mildly offended. 'Not all of it. There are many honest and good men. It is like your curate's egg, and good in parts, I would say.'

Mowgley shook his head again. 'What a country.'

Georgiev re-lit his pipe. When he next spoke, it seemed to Mowgley that his mask of imperturbability had slipped a little.

'Yes, I know what people from more civilised parts of Europe think of us. But we have had good teachers. And do you think it does not exist where you come from? The European Union is a monument to greed and the corruption greed leads to. It is just that people In the West are less open in the way they go about their dark practices and are better at hiding what they do. I think anyone who has studied the history of the British Empire would see what self-interest in the name of nationalism, greed and hypocrisy can achieve.'

Mowgley smiled sourly. You won't get any argument from me. But we weren't the only ones. But what'll happen now? If it was your boss who tried to have you killed, won't he try again?'

A bubble of laughter rose from the street as Georgiev puffed reflectively on his pipe. 'I don't think so. Or I hope not. My sons have been busy talking with contacts throughout the law enforcement agencies. People that they can trust. They have let it be known in the right places that I have made a detailed account of all I have learned about complicity in the sale of looted treasures abroad, and I have given examples and names. If I die suddenly, the report will be made public. That would worry a lot of people in high office.'

'And how high up the ladder are these people?'

Georgiev pointed a finger towards the sky. 'Right to the top, it is said. I do not make it my business to enquire too closely and cause too many ripples in the pond, but let me say that some people call our Prime Minister the Al Capone of Bulgaria.'

'Bloody Hell.' Mowgley reached for the bottle of single malt and poured a generous measure into each glass. He raised his glass and Georgiev followed suit.

'And what is your next question, my ever-curious friend?' asked the inspector.

Mowgley sipped at the Glenfiddich. 'That is good. Why the fuck do you do it?'

Georgiev savoured the aroma, then drank delicately, put the glass down and patted his moustache. 'Yes, I do believe that it is genuine malt.' He swirled the whisky round in his glass and looked at it reflectively. 'Why do I do what I do? I wonder every day, and especially when bad things like today happen.'

'You mean people get killed around you often?'

'No,' said Georgiev thoughtfully, 'as I said before, not that often. As to why I carry on, who can say? Why do you do what you do? I started off thinking I could make a difference, but soon realised I could not. Then my wife died and I thought about joining her, but I knew that would not be fair to the boys. So here I am. Sitting on the balcony of a cheap hotel, drinking expensive whisky with a new friend. I don't know how you felt when you were - forgive me - a 'proper' policeman, but like you I have a curious mind and I am not content until I have reached the end of any trail. Of course, my scrabbling around will make no difference and things will go on as they were. But if I can get to the end of all this I will feel I have won a small victory. I was determined to bring your friend to some sort of justice, but then someone took away that possibility. Dennis Cullan's death also left a mystery, and I cannot bear an unsolved mystery.'

'But you know that he - Den - was trading in looted treasure?'

Georgiev scratched his head with the stem of his pipe. 'I think your friend was part of something very big which involved organised crime gangs, anti-corruption authorities and even the archaeological establishment. Then it went wrong, which is why Mr Cullan and Magda Abadjiev died. I am sure Professor Kirov is the key.'

'And you know where he is?'

Georgiev put his glass down, stood up and walked to the balcony, then said: 'I know where he has been.' After looking out to sea for a moment, he walked back, sat down then reached over and lifted the lid of the laptop. After a moment he touched a button and an image of a woman appeared on the screen. She was young and pretty in a vacuous way and was holding a microphone like a badge of attainment. Her lips were set in full pout mode and her face in the falsest of smiles. In the bottom corner of the screen was a TV channel logo. Georgiev touched another button and the reporter came to life. She spoke rapidly, then the point-of-view moved to a woman standing next to her.

She was larger and older than the reporter, wore no make-up and her face was framed by an extravagant shock of red hair, but Mowgley found her by far the more interesting and attractive of the two. While the TV reporter exampled perfectly how many women thought they should look nowadays, the interviewee evoked the unselfconscious and fulsome sensuality of a Rubens painting.

The woman answered the reporter's question in English, then her voice faded and a line of Cyrillic script appeared and moved across the bottom of the screen. As she spoke, there were frequent cutaways to what looked like the sort of village where Magda Abadjiev's parents lived. The difference was that the houses featured had no death notices on the gates and were well-maintained. One had a Native American dream-catcher hanging from the porchway, and wind chimes were much in evidence. Above one home fluttered a flag showing the Welsh dragon.

The piece ended with a shot of the two women, standing in the village square. It had obviously been set up by the producer and looked more like a Montmartre bistro in the Sixties than a Bulgarian village. In front of the brightly-painted cuboid Communist-era shop an assortment of chairs and tables and brightly coloured umbrellas had been laid out. The tables were occupied by middle-aged and older people of what Mowgley would have categorised as arty-crafty. One was a man with a goatee beard, Breton cap and paint-spattered smock. Obviously acting under direction, he was showing a woman a small painting, while she reciprocated with a wooden carving of what could be a wild boar or a large dog or a small giraffe.

At another table a portly man with a full-set beard and waxed moustaches was strumming at a guitar and entertaining a trio of women in caftans with a plaintive folk song. Mowgley snorted his irritation. It was the sort of tragic ballad composed by, for and about working people in harder times, and now beloved by middle class people who had never done a real day's work in their lives.

The scene was allegedly being captured by an elderly man sitting at an easel and canvas and he was working in the shadow of a massive sculpture. It was made of some sort of dark stone and of an ovoid shape with a hole in it. Beyond the statue an elderly local sat on a donkey cart, watching the scene. The camera zoomed in and showed he was wearing an expression of complete bewilderment.

As the camera returned to the presenter and the Rubenesque woman, Georgiev hit the pause button. Mowgley replicated the expression on the face of the man in the donkey cart.

'Was that for real?'

Georgiev nodded. 'Very much so. It is something happening in a village at the other end of the country.'

'And why are you showing it to me?'

In answer, the inspector re-started the video, spooled back and froze it on the shot of the man in the donkey cart.

He pointed at the screen with his pipe. 'You see that?

'The mystified local'?

'No, beyond him. 'The vintage car. And the man getting out of it.'

Mowgley leaned forward and narrowed his eyes. 'Yes, okay. So what?'

Inspector Georgiev sat back, reached for his glass and spoke with quiet satisfaction.

'It is Professor Kirov's car. And that, minus his famous beard, is the great man himself.'

22

Their journey from the Black Sea to the western extremes of Bulgaria was made by car. Inspector Georgiev said it would not be easy and perhaps not wise to ask for the use of the helicopter. People would then know where they were going if not why. Mowgley was unsure whether to be glad or unhappy that they were travelling on the roads rather than in the air. On balance he was glad the former option had been chosen.

The long journey from the eastern coast to the border with Serbia also gave Mowgley more than an impression of a sometimes breathtakingly beautiful country.

All the long day they sped through dark forest, deep valleys and over winding mountain passes. There were gorges with soaring cliff faces riddled with caverns, and lofty waterfalls cascaded down to join wide and serene rivers crossing vast green plains.

Despite his fears, Mowgley was able to enjoy the parade of nature's works more than he had expected. This was because he was in the middle vehicle of a three-car convoy and protected from the everyday insanities of other road users. The two unremarkable-looking but souped-up protection cars came courtesy of the State Agency for National Security. The Skoda VG in the lead was driven by Aleksander Georgiev, while his brother Ivo was at the wheel of the tail car. Their father was driving the middle car, hemmed in by his sons he was protected from his own excesses as well as those of other road users.

'We do have modern railways; that one is put on for the tourists. So, what do you think of our little country now you have seen more of it?'

Mowgley looked away from where a steam train was keeping pace with them as they passed through a verdant valley dotted with villages clinging to its steep upper slopes.

'It really is a beautiful place,' he said. 'It makes it worse that the people running it are so bent.'

'Not all of them,' said Georgiev, waving his pipe cheerily at the train 'Just some.'

Mowgley looked back at the train. 'How deep and wide do you think the corruption goes?'

Georgiev put his pipe back in his mouth, puffed on it for a moment then placed it on the dashboard. 'Nobody knows. Ivo tells me there was said to be a report by SANS claiming a sort of parallel government exists alongside the official one.'

'Parallel government?'

'Yes. The report claimed that the body is made up of influential figures in business, the media, state institutions and organised criminal groups. They all work together so that, whichever government is in place, they would still be in control.'

'Do you think it's true?'

Georgiev shrugged and picked up his pipe. 'Could be. Or not.'

'But surely it'll be huge news when it comes out?'

Georgiev waved goodbye to the train. 'It won't. The report went missing and there are no copies. Allegedly.'

~

Montana is the most westerly of the four provinces of Bulgaria. It is also the poorest part of the poorest country in the European Union.

In contrast to the well-heeled Black Sea coastal resorts, the towns they now sped past or struggled through looked decidedly down on their luck. As Georgiev said, Montana had been the most enthusiastic supporter of Communism. Whether this was what made or kept the region so depressed was open to opinion.

After eight hours on the road the mini-convoy pulled up in a town close by the border with Serbia. It sat in the shadow of the first peaks of the Balkan mountain range and had an air of having seen better days and suspecting it would not see them again. The hotels ringing the centre looked as if they would rather be elsewhere and the shop windows were wide and tall but mostly empty.

The central square was very formal and angular, and some of the walls of the surrounding box-like buildings bore reminders of the Communist era. One giant mural showed an avuncular Lenin looking fondly down on ranks of contented workers saluting the Father of the Revolution.

It was market day, and the older citizens who would remember and benefitted or suffered from the fruits of the great man's vision were wandering past stalls or sitting outside the bars and cafes.

Georgiev led the way to a bar opposite the market; Mowgley noticed that Ivo and Aleksander took separate tables, sitting so that between them they had an all-round view.

A pretty waitress came and went, and Georgiev eased stiff shoulders and took a long, deep breath before patting his pockets with increasing urgency. After a moment he cursed. 'I left my pipe and pouch in the car. May I have a cigarette?'

Mowgley pushed his packet across the table top. 'If - I mean when - we get out of this, I'm going to buy you a Persian slipper to keep your tobacco in.'

Georgiev nodded gravely. 'I am flattered that you compare me with the great Sherlock Holmes.'

He lit a cigarette, sat back and took another deep breath. 'Do you notice how good the air is? Because of the altitude, wrestlers would come to train here in the old days.'

Mowgley looked at two overweight men in bomber jackets and trainers outside a kebab shop. 'I suppose that would explain the number of men with no necks.'

The inspector smiled. 'In fact, you are correct. Wrestling and building their bodies are still a popular activity.'

Mowgley sipped his beer and looked across the square to

where a Roma gypsy sat on a pony cart. He was holding the reins loosely and watching an old lady who could have been his mother. She was wearing traditional costume, with headscarf, wide-sleeved and heavily embroidered blouse and a long, full skirt. She was sitting on a kerbstone at the entrance to the market, surrounded by small candles. One was lit and Mowgley assumed the rest were for sale. People occasionally stopped to look at the display, but most walked past as if she were not there. Even at that distance Mowgley could see that she must once have been very beautiful. Near her, a mangy-looking dog lay stretched out in the sun and a Roma child sat beside it, pulling its ear.

Georgiev saw Mowgley watching the people visiting the market. 'You may not believe me,' he said, 'but it was once proposed that this should be a destination for the jet-set.'

'You're right,' said Mowgley, 'I don't believe you.'

'It is true. When it was made public that Bulgaria was to join the European Union, it was planned to make the town a leading winter sports resort.' He nodded towards the looming skyline of the Balkan range. 'Sofia airport is only sixty kilometres away, and it was even proposed that a tunnel be blasted through the mountains to make the journey quicker.' He reached over and took another cigarette from the packet on the table. 'Investors rushed to buy land and build hotels, and it was like a gold rush town.'

'So, what happened?'

Georgiev lit his cigarette. 'Nothing. The tunnel was never built and many people got their fingers burned. Of course, many people made a lot of money.'

Mowgley reached for his beer, then sat up as a giant figure crossed the square towards them. He was walking determinedly, and Mowgley saw he had a large knife in a sheath on his hip. The man was tall, but so wide he looked stocky. He had the standard Bulgarian buzz-cut and his head seemed too small in comparison with his massive shoulders. A khaki-coloured tee-shirt strained to contain his deep chest and prodigious paunch. As he came closer, Mowgley saw that three fingers were missing from his right hand, and a tattoo of a snarling black beast wound around his forearm.

Georgiev turned to see what had caught Mowgley's attention, then smiled. 'Don't worry; it is only Panther.'

Mowgley frowned. 'I don't know about 'only.' He's a big unit. I wouldn't want to upset him.'

'You would be right not to' said Georgiev as the man walked past them and, after nodding respectfully to the inspector, stopped at the table where Ivo was sitting. Georgiev's youngest son stood and the two men embraced.

'Panther was in the army with Ivo,' said Georgiev. 'They saw some action together and became close friends.'

'Is that where he lost the fingers? In action, I mean?'

'No.' Georgiev smiled. 'He is a butcher and, as he says, he sliced the wrong piece of meat after too much brandy. Or at least that is what he claims. Some think he came off worse in a knife fight but would rather say it was an accident.'

'And he's a local?'

'He has a sheep farm in the hills close to the village where the mad English woman lives and Kirov's car was seen. He owns a butcher's shop here and is also the enforcer for the family money-lending business.'

Mowgley looked across at the giant figure.

'You are kidding?'

Georgiev shook his head. 'You must know that many Bulgarians are addicted to gambling. They see it as a way to escape poverty, when of course the opposite is true. If they borrow and do not repay their debts, they get a visit from Panther.' He looked to where the two men were deep in conversation. 'Since the professor was seen in the television feature Ivo has been talking to him about the mad Englishwoman and her commune.'

'So remind me what that's all about, and why would Kirov be there?'

'Excuse me.' Georgiev raised a finger, pointed at the giant butcher and then at their glasses. The girl nodded and hurried to the bar and Georgiev continued. 'The woman is a teacher in art, or was. She and her husband bought a holiday home there and decided to start an arts and crafts community to save the village from dying. As she said in the interview, the peace and pure air of the mountains is a good place to find inspiration.' He smiled. 'You can also buy a home there for the price of an expensive bicycle elsewhere in Europe, which might be a part of the attraction.'

'And why do you think Kirov was there? You don't think he's

a keen amateur painter or sculptor?'

Georgiev smiled. 'Not as far as I know. But we knew from Ivo's conversation with Panther that the professor is a regular visitor. That is why we came here.'

Mowgley frowned. 'Okay, but why would he come here regularly?'

Georgiev gave his signature shrug. 'He must have his reasons, and I think they will not be legitimate ones. That is why we are here.'

'I understand. But if he is on the run it was a bit silly of him to appear on national TV, was it not?'

'I don't think he meant to, and if he did see the camera pointing at him there was not much he could do about it. As the picture showed, he has shaved off his beard so is clearly trying to avoid recognition,'

'Then it was a bit silly to keep such a distinctive car, wasn't it?'

Georgiev nodded. 'You are right. But I have learned in life that there is no limit to vanity. The professor obviously likes to drive such an unusual and expensive car because it gets him noticed. You saw how much he loved the camera in the You Tube film. It is like those people who wear dark glasses because they want people to look at them.'

Georgiev looked at his watch, 'So any more questions, detective Mowgley?'

'Lots. But for starters, how come you know so much about the area?

The Inspector shrugged. 'Montana is where I come from. Other people leave Bulgaria to live in a more prosperous country. I moved to a more prosperous location. As I said when we first met, Varna is a treasure trove for those interested in archaeology. He nodded towards the mountain range. 'But there is much gold and treasure here if you know where to look. There were gold mines here, worked by slaves of the Romans, and there are several forts at the highest points. They say it is a looter's paradise, and that may be a reason the professor is a regular visitor.'

He emptied his glass, wiped his moustaches with the back of his hand and then signalled to the waitress. Now, if you are ready we shall make our way to what I hope will be the end of our journey.'

Mowgley looked at the distant hills and the mountain range beyond. 'I'm not sure I like the way you put that. Before we go, be honest and tell me how much danger you think we're in.'

'I always try to be honest, Jack,' said Georgiev as he reached for his wallet. 'If we are being watched by the *mutri*, that would be bad. If we are being watched by corrupt police, that would also be bad. If we are being watched by both, that could be very bad...'

23

'Look at that. Is this not a beautiful land?'

'Yes, but I'd rather you look at the road than the scenery.'

Mowgley resisted the urge to grab the wheel as the car swerved towards what appeared to be a sheer drop into the vast valley. His fear was the greater because Ivo and Aleksander were not there to curb their father's driving excesses. They had stayed in town, Georgiev had said, so as not to alarm the villagers -or Kirov- by arriving in force. And anyway, he and Mowgley were not likely to be in danger in a ghost village peopled by elderly locals and artistic foreigners.

Practicing his deep breathing technique, Mowgley tried to ignore the fact that there were no crash barriers between the car and the void and concentrated on the beauty of his surroundings.

Far below, a sparkling river ran through the lush and greenest of valleys, and beyond it lay a deep, dark forest. Alongside the river was an old shepherd's hut. It sat on high iron wheels and had a curved tin roof with a satisfyingly crooked stove pipe emerging from it. It would, he thought, be prized almost beyond rubies in any London auction rooms.

Near to the mobile hut a gaggle of sheep grazed the river bank, and further on a handful of cows moved slowly through the unfenced pastureland. The valley was so peaceful and the air so clear that Mowgley could hear the tinkling of cow bells.

At the far end of the valley he could see a huddle of habitation. Distance lent the scene enchantment and the homes looked quaint rather than decrepit. Vegetable plots stretched down the slope from the backs of the houses to the river, some with lines of brightly coloured boxes in their gardens.

'Bee hives,' said Georgiev. 'Making honey is what you would call a cottage industry in Bulgaria. People sell it by the roadside and it is used as medicine as well as food. Because of the herbs and climate, Bulgaria makes the best honey in the world.'

'Naturally,' said Mowgley dryly. 'There's smoke coming from one of the houses. Surely it's too hot for a fire?'

Georgiev grunted his amusement. 'Like your upper-class country ladies with their Aga stoves, our peasants cook on wood fires. The difference is that our peasants have no choice. It could also be that they are heating water for a wash. Or, though it is the wrong time of year someone could be making a batch of rakia.'

Suddenly the tranquillity was shattered by a harsh screech and Mowgley's heart lurched as a fleeting shadow passed across the windscreen. He converted his gasp into a cough, then leaned forward and looked up to where a giant bird was wheeling above the car.

'It is just an eagle,' said Georgiev, enjoying Mowgley's discomfiture. 'It was warning us away from its home - or perhaps he wanted to see if we were edible.'

Around the next bend they came upon a huge vineyard. Thousands of vines had been planted with military precision, and row after row marched up the slope to the skyline. A wiry-looking man in bib and brace overalls was pushing a plough uphill between two rows and urging on the donkey pulling it. As they passed, the man stopped, looked down at them, wiped his brow with a bare forearm and raised a hand.

Mowgley instinctively returned the wave. 'That looks hard work,' he said. 'Wouldn't he be better off with a tractor?'

'Perhaps he would. But they like the traditional ways here. And there is another reason.'

'What's that?'

'Even an old tractor would cost years of his income. The donkey is free, and it is good company. You cannot talk to even the most expensive and advanced tractor.'

~

On the outskirts, Krasiva looked much like the ghost village in which Magda Abadjiev's parents lived. Most of the houses were in a parlous state, some with death notices on rusty gates held together by a padlocked chain.

As they approached the heart of the village, they found the occasional property in much better condition, and he recognised some from the television feature. In between the tumbledown cottages would be the occasional smartly-renovated property with a new roof and even plastic double-glazed replacement windows. The result looked very odd, Mowgley thought, like a man with a mouthful of rotten teeth interspersed with gleaming white implants. It was not something you would see in a Home Counties village where the value put on one cottage would outstrip that of the hundred or so in this one.

They bumped on along the track where the only signs of life were a handful of chickens scratching in a front garden and a donkey chained to a gate, its ears twitching in a vain attempt to deter the squadron of flies buzzing around its head. After solemnly regarding the passing car the donkey returned its attention to an elderly man on the other side of the track. He was short and stout and very red-faced, and was pitch-forking grass on to the roof of a corrugated lean-to with practiced ease. He looked up as they passed, but showed less interest than the donkey before turning back to his work. Mowgley assumed that since the formation of the arts and crafts community the man was accustomed to passing strangers in smart cars.

The track masquerading as a road ended at the square with the giant abstract sculpture at its centre. The umbrellas, chairs and tables were still in place outside the shop/café, but the only occupants were a very fat man with a stylised goatee beard, and a painfully thin short man who appeared to be sharpening a hunting knife. The fat man was reading a book, wore a straw hat and looked like a foreigner trying to look like a local, while the small man looked like a local trying to look like a Red Army officer. He was wearing a Russian Army officer's peaked cap and a much-buttoned and distressed greatcoat with red epaulettes, but the effect was spoiled by his shoulder-length hair, wild beard and even wilder eyes.

Elsewhere a donkey cart stood by the steps up to the shop/café, and two cars were parked outside houses on the far side of the square. One was a battered Lada and the other a shiny Range Rover. There was no sign of Kirov's vintage Soviet Zhiguli.

Georgiev made a U-turn and parked, and the two men had almost reached the row of tables when a chugging sound drew their attention to a track leading from the far side of the square. The source was a bright red sit-on rotovator, towing a trailer piled high with logs. In the saddle of vehicle was the Rubenesque woman who had appeared in the television feature. Today she was wearing an off-the-shoulder peasant-style blouse over a voluminous, heavily-embroidered skirt, and a pair of goggles kept the sides of her shock of red hair in check. As she approached them, her generous cleavage rose and fell with each pothole traversed.

'Blimey,' said Mowgley.

'A rotavator is a status symbol in poor villages,' said Georgiev. 'You can use it to work the land and go for the shopping. I think Madame likes to identify with the locals.'

The machine arrived and the rider dismounted, adjusting her blouse and removing her goggles as she approached.

'It's the flies,' she said, holding up the goggles. 'they get everywhere at this time of year. They like the donkeys, you know.'

Georgiev nodded gravely. 'Inspector Georgiev,' he said with a polite nod, 'and this is my colleague Inspector Mowgley. It is good of you to see us.'

'I was intrigued by your call,' she replied.

Hands were shaken and Mowgley noticed how strong the woman's grip was. She saw his reaction and said: 'I'm sorry. My husband says I don't know my own strength. It's spending so much time with a mallet and chisel in my hand, I think.'

Georgiev led them to the table furthest from the two men and pulled back a seat.

'All will be explained about our visit,' he said. 'Before then can I offer you a drink, Madame Parkinson?'

The woman looked up at the sky, then smiled at him. 'It is a little early, but a glass of wine would be nice. Madame Andonov will know what I like.'

~

The shadows began to stretch across the square and they were on their second bottle of red wine.

'So how long is it,' asked Inspector Georgiev, 'since you founded the commune?'

'We're coming up for our first anniversary.' Emily Parkinson shook her head to Georgiev's offer of a cigarette but emptied her glass pointedly. Mowgley noted she put it down on the table close to the bottle.

The inspector re-filled her glass. 'And are you happy with the way things are going?'

'Very happy. It will obviously take time, but we're getting enquiries from all over Europe and - as you know - attracting a lot of media attention.'

Georgiev nodded. 'And the intention was to save the village by building a community of people interested in arts and crafts?'

'Exactly that.' She waved a much-bangled arm in the direction of the valley. 'We bought a place here five years ago and loved the surroundings and the peace and the people. We restored our cottage and bought another as a studio, but were saddened by the way the village was literally dying. I found the environment perfect for anyone with a creative mind, and it occurred to us there might be a unique way to rescue Krasiva. That was by setting up the commune.'

'So how does it work?' asked Mowgley, 'people apply to join?'
'That's right.'
'And what qualifications do they need?'
She laughed and put her empty glass on the table. '"Qualifications?" It's not an art college, Inspector. All people need is an interest in the arts and crafts and to afford to be able to spend some time here.'

It was Georgiev's turn to recharge their glasses. 'And do they have to buy and restore a property?'

'Not if they don't want to.' Emily Parkinson lifted her glass and waved to a man passing through the square on a donkey cart. 'If they want to own a house here, we can find one and arrange the restoration. That gives work to local people, of course. If they don't, they can rent one of the properties we have fixed up.' She paused, took a draft of wine and then looked directly at both the men. 'I wouldn't like anyone to think of this as some sort of pie-in-the sky idea doomed to failure. We just want to bring the village back to life, and that takes money and purpose. In spite of the price of property and the weather here, I don't think we'd attract too many of the sort of people who buy holiday homes in Spain.'

She smiled at them and raised her glass. 'I hope you will be able to stay in one of our guest houses tonight. They're for prospective members of the community and there's a meeting in the square this evening. We'll have some music and folk dancing and some classic Bulgarian dishes. Have you tried *Shopska* Salad, Mr Mowgley?'

'Yes,' said Mowgley. 'I have. And how many members are there?'

'So far, more than a dozen. I know it's not enough, but it's a start.

'Most admirable,' said Georgiev. Are they all artists?

'No, we have different pursuits and disciplines…and interests. As you can see, I work with local stone -' she gestured towards the massive sculpture in the middle of the square '- and we have several painters, a very talented guitarist, a composer, a resident poet and even a creative cook who wants to promote traditional Bulgarian cuisine around the world. Next year we're hoping to stage a major exhibition and attract visitors from across Europe, and perhaps beyond. Hopefully it will be launched and attended by a number of celebrated Bulgarians with an interest in the history and ancient culture of the country.'

'I wish you much success.' Georgiev lifted his glass. 'And will Professor Kirov be one of those celebrities?'

'It would be wonderful if he were able to come along.'

'Does he visit often?' asked the inspector. 'I noticed he appeared in the report which was shown on Nov TV?'

She thought about his question, then nodded and adjusted

her bangles. 'He comes here regularly, at least once a month.'

'And he's a member of the community?'

'No, he comes to see Jerome Varden.'

'But Mr Varden is a member of your community?'

'Yes, he was one of the earliest joiners.' She pointed across the square. 'He lives and works there.'

Mowgley and Georgiev looked at the house. It faced on to the square, looked in good repair and had a new or recent roof. The forecourt was enclosed in an ornamental metal fence with high gates. Unlike all the other properties in the square, it had roller shutters on windows and doors, and they were down.

Georgiev tugged at his moustache. 'I take it Mr Varden is away?'

'Yes. We have not seen him since the day the television programme was filmed. He is often away for a few days or more. I think he delivers orders to a wholesaler in Sofia. Or I think that's what he said.'

'Ah,' said Georgiev, 'and Professor Kirov is a friend?'

She nodded and looked meaningfully at her empty glass.

'Yes, I suppose so, but I think his main interest is in Jerome's work.'

'And what would that be? Is he a painter perhaps, or a musician?'

'Oh no,' said Emily Parkinson, smiling. 'Jerome makes the most wonderful jewellery. As you may know, ancient Thrace was famed for its production of gold artefacts and beautiful jewellery. You could say Jerome is following in their footsteps and keeping a great tradition alive.'

24

It was well past the witching hour and Mowgley could hear the silence.

The gathering in the square had been more bearable than he had expected, which was probably partly due to his involvement as a judge in the flavoured rakia competition.

There had also been, as promised, copious amounts of food and entertainment.

The entertainment had begun with a very Welsh poet comparing the mountains of his native and new lands, and concluded with a retired banker from Surrey singing what he claimed to be traditional Bulgarian folk songs. He had accompanied himself on a ukulele and watched approvingly as his wife performed what she claimed to be traditional Bulgarian folk dances.

To his surprise, Mowgley had found the food as good as the entertainment bad. Emily Parkinson had baked a mountain of delicious and tooth-rottingly sweet cakes and pastries, and the 'culture-fusion' cottage pie and mish-mash made by the commune's creative cook was very much to his taste. Most of the original villagers had turned up, but Mowgley thought that was probably for the free food and drink. All had departed before the entertainment began. The chairwoman had said the villagers liked to take to their beds at a very early hour; Mowgley suspected they had known what was coming from the banker and his wife.

Now he and Inspector Georgiev were taking a nightcap on the balcony of one of the Parkinsons' guest homes for potential commune members. The renovation and furnishing had been done mostly by Emily Parkinson and her husband Roger. He was as quiet and reserved as his wife was forthcoming, and obviously enjoyed turning tumbledown properties into homes the original owners could hardly have imagined.

Like the fusion cottage pie, the house was a meeting of Bulgarian and middle-class British tastes and styles. It occupied the side of the square overlooking the valley and the distant but looming mountains, and enjoyed a spectacular view. As with most autumnal nights in the foothills of the Balkan range, the sky was crystal clear and light pollution was not an issue. The great valley was in almost total darkness and the twinkling lights of the far-away town made a poor reflection of the star-suffused sky.

'Well,' asked Mowgley as he lit what he had promised himself would be a last cigarette before bed, 'What's next? I saw your reaction when the Rubens lady said they had a retired jewellery-maker in the commune. Do you think he's the final link in whatever's been going on?'

'Yes, I do, Jack.'

'Why?'

'Why? You simply have to ask yourself for what reason Professor Kirov would make regular visits to a remote village to see someone who is, as Mrs Parkinson says, so skilled at working with gold and jewellery.' He looked at Mowgley shrewdly.' And I think you have already guessed what I think is the solution.'

Mowgley put his glass on the balcony rail, frowned and scratched a stubbly cheek. 'Do you know, in spite of the rakia I do think I get it. You reckon this bloke is making fake stuff to order for Kirov, don't you?'

Georgiev nodded. 'I do.'

Why would Kirov want it?' I thought you thought he was digging up real treasure, giving some to the authorities to keep 'them happy and passing the undeclared stuff on to Den to sell.'

The inspector smiled. 'That is what I thought was happening until recently. Now I don't believe Kirov was digging up any genuine artefacts. I think the operation worked so well that the professor would not have been able to keep up with the demand if he was selling only genuine artefacts. I think that all the allegedly ancient treasures he came up with were fakes.'

'You mean he was even surrendering fakes to the museums as if they were the genuine articles?'

Georgiev shrugged. 'Of course, why would he not? Going by the fakes buried with Magda Abedjiev, the quality of work and 'distressing' processes were near perfect.'

'Good enough to fool experienced museum curators as well as the mafia and their customers?'

'Exactly. Donating his 'finds' to the state kept his name in the headlines and gave validity to the fakes he sold through your friend Dennis Cullan. Kirov was the rubber stamp that they were genuine.'

'So, Kirov was faking the discoveries to give the forgeries what-do-you-call it.'

'Provenance? Yes, that is it exactly.' Georgiev tapped his pipe on the balcony rail and patted his pockets. 'What better guarantee of authenticity could there be than the artefacts being unearthed in a noted archaeological site by the eminent archaeologist who discovered the mask of Thetes and so many other ancient treasures?'

'And Jerome Varden was making them based on Kirov's knowledge of what the stuff should look like?'

'That's the really clever part. All Kirov had to do was instruct the forger to make things that would look like the genuine articles but not exactly the same as existing items. As long as he stuck to objects similar to those which had already been unearthed, why would anyone think they were not genuine?'

'Okay. Mowgley held a hand up in mock-surrender. 'So far so good. But would it be that easy to fool the experts?'

Georgiev shrugged. 'Why not? What else would give the game away? The thing that makes gold so desirable is its rarity and malleability and immutability. There is a limited amount on earth and it cannot be changed in state or manufactured, although alchemists have been trying for many centuries.' The inspector took a drink and pointed over the balcony with his pipe.

'Out there somewhere in the world, a beautiful woman will be wearing a pair of earrings made from gold mined by Roman slaves in these hills two thousand years ago. Even the tiny amount of gold in your mobile phone could once have been part of a headdress made for Cleopatra.'

'So where does or did gold come from?'

Georgiev pointed up at the night sky. 'It is thought to have been formed by colliding stars - and was in the dust that made up the universe.'

Mowgley looked upwards and shook his head. 'Wow. And they won't be making any more?'

'That is right. Nobody knows how much gold is still to be discovered, but the best guess is around 50,000 tonnes. That is quite a lot when you think that there are fewer than two hundred tonnes above the ground and in circulation.' He smiled. 'It is also a small irony that so much that came from the ground and became coins or precious ornaments is now below the surface waiting to be rediscovered.'

If he could have whistled, Mowgley would have done so.

'Wow again. So the gold our man has been forging ancient artefacts from would be the same gold the real things are or were made of?'

'Exactly. If you forge an old painting, someone may point out that the paint did not exist at that time, or that the canvas or its frame are not of the right date. Not so with fakes of pure gold. All it needs is for people to believe they are real.'

'And nobody is going to question the provenance of artefacts dug up by the celebrated archaeologist.'

'Precisely.'

Mowgley frowned. 'But if it was all going so well, why were Den and Magda killed, and why is Kirov in fear of his life? And why was Jen kidnapped?'

Georgiev fiddled with his pipe, filled the bowl, tamped down the tobacco and lit it.

'I believe someone discovered what was going on, and that would make those who sold on the allegedly priceless artefacts very angry.'

'You mean the mafia?'

Georgiev nodded.

'Okay, nobody likes being taken for mug, but why would the mafia care if the stuff was real or not? They were still getting the money and there was a virtually endless supply. Why would they kill the golden goose?'

Georgiev puffed at his pipe reflectively, then said: 'You must understand how these things work, Jack. No matter how bizarre it sounds and like any mafia organisation, the *mutri* prize their so-called honour and reputation. To have been seen to have been made fools of in this would be unthinkable. Especially as it would cost them a fortune in compensation if the secret came out.'

He looked at his glass of rakia ruminatively, then continued: 'Therefore they got rid of Dennis Cullan in what could have been an accident, but made an example of Magda so that it would seem she had been discovered co-operating with the police. Cutting or tearing a tongue out - before or after death - is a favourite way of showing that the victim had been talking to the wrong people.'

'So it was all a big cover-up?'

Georgiev nodded. 'Exactly. The death of Mr Cullan and the dramatic circumstances of the discovery of Magda Abadjiev dressed at a Thracian princess and entombed at an ancient burial site would have sent the message out to all interested parties. That message was not that the victims had been trading in fakes, but that they had been talking to the authorities.'

Mowgley sat back and looked out into the velvety darkness.

'Okay, I think I get it all now. The *mutri* are now on the trail of the professor and whoever has been making the faked artefacts. But why was Jan taken?' He lowered his head and took a steadying breath before asking the question he did not want answered. 'If they thought she was involved, why has she not been found...dead? Where do you think she is? And what about her sister and son? Have you told them she is missing?'

Georgiev sipped his rakia and took another tug at the left side of his moustache, which Mowgley had learned was a 'tell' that he had something difficult to announce. 'I do not know where she is but I do not think Mrs Cullan is dead. And I have not told her sister and son about the kidnapping.'

Mowgley sat up straight and stared at the inspector. 'Why not?'

'Because they do not exist.'

~

They heard the sound of the car long before it reached the square.

As the engine died, Georgiev and Mowgley exchanged looks, then the inspector stood up and walked to the end of the balcony. After a moment, Mowgley put down his glass and joined him.

Leaning over the wrought iron railing they could just see the house Emily Parkinson had said was home and workshop to the commune's resident jeweller and goldsmith. They could also see that the car parked outside was the classic Soviet Zhiguli which had made a fleeting appearance in the TV feature.

The two men looked at each other again, then the inspector shrugged and held his hands up in a 'what else can we do?' gesture.

Mowgley looked back at the car and then Georgiev before speaking in a stage whisper. 'Have we not got time to phone your sons?'

'No,' said Georgiev, patting his jacket pocket.

'Are you carrying?' asked Mowgley.

Georgiev frowned. 'Carrying?'

'Have you got a gun?

'Ah. No, I am just making sure I've got my pipe.'

Mowgley groaned. 'I suppose you could always throw it at him - or them,' He looked round then picked up a piece of wood from the pile by the door to the sitting room. He weighed it in his hand, then looked at Georgiev as if in search of a reprieve. 'Are you sure about this?'

'No,' said the inspector mildly, 'but we can't let him - or them - get away, can we?'

'You could phone your boys and get them to set up a roadblock or something.'

Georgiev thought about it and then shook his head. 'If it is to be only a short visit the car could be gone before my sons left the town. And there are many navigable tracks across the hills. They would not be able to watch them all. I will phone Ivo now, but I think we must be prepared to stop whoever is in the house from leaving.'

'I thought you said earlier that Plan 'A' was to break into Varden's house and see what we found there?'

Georgiev shrugged. 'It would not have been easy with all those defences. And now someone has opened the house for us. I think we must see who it is and what is in there.'

'Or who they are. They could be mob-handed, remember.'

He waited for a response but one came.

'Okay. Have it your way.' Mowgley sighed and handed the length of wood to Georgiev, then started to walk back towards the door to the sitting-room.

'Aren't you coming?' Georgiev called after him.

'I suppose so.'

'Are you getting your cigarettes?'

'Yeah. How could I go anywhere without my fags? And I think I saw a hand axe next to the stove.'

~

The steel blind had been rolled up, and the light coming through the open door stretched across the square and made the chrome brightwork on the classic car sparkle.

The two men were standing by the line of tables outside the café/shop, fifty metres from the Zhiguli and the open gates of Jerome Varden's house.

'The professor's obviously not going to be long,' whispered Mowgley.

Georgiev frowned. 'How do you know it's Kirov?'

'Well it's his bloody car, isn't it?'

'That doesn't mean it was he who drove it here, Jack.'

Mowgley blew his cheeks out in frustration. 'For fuck's sake. Okay, what's the new Plan 'A', Monsieur Poirot?'

'I beg your pardon?'

'Never mind. What do you want to do now?'

Georgiev pulled at his moustache, then looked at the lump of wood in his hand. 'I think we must go in and detain whoever is inside. Have you any alternative suggestions?'

'How about going back to the house and waiting for the heavy mob?'

Georgiev smiled faintly. 'It is tempting, but as I said, what if they get here too late?'

Mowgley shook his head. 'Is this the bit where you say 'Do you want to live forever" and lead the charge?'

'I'm sorry?'

'Never mind. How about my Plan 'A'?'

'What is that?'

'Mowgley nodded at the car. 'We let the tyres down and scarper back to the house and keep obbo - observation - on the car. Whoever's in the house won't get far on foot, and they can hardly make their getaway by hijacking a donkey cart.'

Georgiev looked almost regretfully at the piece of wood in his hand. 'I did not understand all you said, but I suppose that would be the safest thing to do. Shall we go?'

He nodded towards the car and Mowgley sighed deeply and then nodded back.

'You're bloody enjoying this, aren't you?'

'It is just that - as I think I said when we met - I hate mysteries.'

His teeth white and eyes sparkling in the moonlight, Georgiev smiled and waved his piece of firewood like a conductor calling the orchestra to order. Then he turned and led the way across the square.

They came within a dozen yards of the gleaming Zhiguli when night became day.

To Mowgley, it seemed as if some heavenly hand had turned the light up and the sound off. His last memory was of the house coming apart and the car rolling over and towards him as if casually tossed aside by a giant hand.

25

Sofia airport was having a quiet day.

Bored taxi drivers smoked in their cars outside the main terminal or lurked in Arrivals like predators at a waterhole. Near the roped-off entrance to the check-in desks a smattering of passengers looked bemusedly at the information boards or stared with rapt attention at their phones and tablets. Baggage handlers in orange overalls loitered on the tarmac apron, looking somehow disgruntled that they would have a limited selection of items to lose, damage or pilfer from.

It was the end of the season, and the hordes of summer visitors to the Black Sea coast would be flying from Varna or Burgas. Most of Mowgley's fellow travellers at this end of the country would be British expats and holiday home owners, or young Bulgarians returning to their new lives after reminding themselves of what they'd left behind. Some would be sad to leave, others glad.

Mowgley and Georgiev were sitting at a table in a bar in the Transit lounge, and the inspector's status had ensured that Mowgley had been whisked through Check-in and Security like a foreign dignitary or international rock star.

To passers-by, the two men would look as if they had been involved in an accident or violent incident, and most averted their eyes as they hurried by. Had they been bold enough to take a lingering look, they would have seen that Georgiev's left hand was bandaged mitten-style and three fingers of the other were strapped together with tape. One eye was closed by a cartoon-ish purple bruise and he wore a large piece of sticking plaster across his forehead. His walking stick was propped against the table.

As he had been directly behind Georgiev when the house exploded, Mowgley had escaped relatively lightly. Adding to the powder burns from the kidnapping incident at Varna was a nasty facial rash resulting from contact with a gravel patch in the middle of the square. His black eye was almost as impressive as Georgiev's, and a line of surgical clips were holding together the lips of a gash which ran down his left cheek from eye to upper lip. Three days on from the explosion, both men were speaking over-loudly as their hearing had not returned to normal levels.

Whilst they had come through the incident with relatively minor injuries, Jerome Varden's house had been almost completely destroyed. A forensic team from Sofia was sifting through the rubble but at this stage there was not much to report. No probable or possible cause of the explosion had been established, or even how many people had been inside the house when it disintegrated. Human remains had been found, but it would take time, as the head of the forensics team had said with grim relish, to go through, identify and count the bits before they could come up with a definitive head count. If the explosion were found to be malicious, someone had done a very good job. Clearly, had the inspector and his foreign colleague been a few steps closer to the source of the explosion the team would now be engaged in scraping their remains off the village square. They had been extraordinarily lucky that the Zhiguli had shielded them from the blast, and that it had been built when they knew how to make cars that lasted.

As Mowgley had pointed out to Georgiev, it had been he who delayed their approach to the house and suggested they let the tyres down rather than charge onto the premises. If looked at in that way, it could be claimed that he had saved his friend's life.

After watching Georgiev struggle with a packet of biscuits,

Mowgley took and opened it and put a biscuit in Georgiev's less - damaged hand.

'Thank you, Jack,' said the inspector.

'Not a problem,' said Mowgley, 'as long as you don't ask me to help when you need to go to the toilet.'

Georgiev smiled. 'I can manage...big things; it is just the more delicate operations I have problems with.'

He chewed and swallowed, then said: 'I hope that the events of the last week have not sullied your impression of our country?'

'What, you mean because of a couple of near-death experiences and ending up with a face like a tomato pizza? Perish the thought.' He lifted a hand and touched the wound on his face 'So, are we going to have a wash-up before I go?'

'Wash-up?' Georgiev looked at his bandaged hands and then back at Mowgley.'

'I mean,' said Mowgley, 'aren't you going to fill in all the blanks about what's been going on? It's what Poirot always does when a case is solved.'

'I understand. But I would not say it is solved - just closed. Apparently. And where would you like me to start?'

Mowgley took another biscuit from the packet. 'Well, to begin with and working backwards, why would Kirov want to blow the house up? Was he setting a booby trap for Varden, or did he set one off? Or was he planning to destroy the evidence? It seems a bit of a heavy-handed way of going about it.'

Georgiev put his coffee cup carefully back on its saucer. 'As I said before, we do not know it was the professor just because it was his car outside. We will hopefully know who it was or they were when the body parts have been identified.'

'But what's your gut opinion?'

Georgiev looked down at his ample stomach and smiled. 'My guts tell me it is time for breakfast. Beyond that, we shall have to wait and see who was in the house and why the bomb was set. If it was indeed a bomb. If you want to make me make a guess, I think it could have been the *mutri*. The explosion would make sure the evidence of the fraud was destroyed. And perhaps the people who took part in it.'

'And Kirov or Varden or both set it off when he or they went in the house?'

Georgiev tried to tug at his moustache but gave up. 'Perhaps.

It could have been on a delay setting to give the intended victim time to get inside. Or perhaps he or they were setting the bomb and it went off too early. Or It could be that the person or people in the house were already dead when the bomb went off. As you must know, things are rarely as simple as they may seem.'

Mowgley nodded gloomily and dipped his biscuit into his coffee. 'Tell me about it. But what if when they piece the bits together it turns out there was only one body in the house?'

Georgiev shrugged. 'Then the DNA will tell us whose body it is.'

'And you're not worried who it belonged to?'

'Not really. If it is not Kirov the *mutri* will find him. If it is Kirov and the faker is still alive, he will have to, as you might say, make himself scarce.'

'But aren't you worried about either of them getting away with it? Don't you want to clear the case up? Don't you find it frustrating that you haven't arrested anyone for the murders?'

Georgiev pursed his lips. 'What more can I do? If Kirov is alive and turns up, I will go after him, and the same with Mr Varden. If because of finding them I can get anything on Dragov I will try to prove his complicity. But only if the odds are good that I could get a conviction and live to see him go to prison.'

He noted Mowgley's expression and smiled ruefully. 'You must know that in any country truth and justice do not always prevail. It is or can be especialy so in Bulgaria. As I said when we first met, I do what I can even though I know it won't make any real difference. Things will go on as they were whatever I do. It is all a big game. At least this one has come to an end.'

'I think I understand.' Mowgley fished a piece of soggy biscuit from his coffee then patted the breast pocket of his new jacket. 'God, I could do with a fag.'

'I know how you feel,' said Georgiev, 'but even I can't change the rules here. Anyway,' he added plaintively, 'it is very hard to fill a pipe with one hand.'

'It's a bugger, isn't it?' Mowgley looked out through the glass wall to the tarmac, where the garishly painted airplane he would soon be boarding was taxiing slowly towards the terminal building.

'So, has your man found out any more about Kirov's tame

forger?'

'A little. Surprisingly, Varden is or was his real name. I suppose he thought that working and living in a remote village in a foreign land meant there was no need to go to the trouble of changing his identity,'

'And was he known to the UK authorities?'

'Very much so. He was quite renowned in criminal circles in Britain. He is a forger acknowledged to be of the very best, specialising in ancient treasures. His main claim to fame in criminal circles was helping disguise some of the proceeds of the Brink's Mat gold bullion robbery.'

Mowgley tried to raise his eyebrows to demonstrate surprise and interest and immediately regretted it. He winced and stroked the closed eye as if in appeasement. 'Sounds interesting. How?'

'By converting gold bullion into what was claimed to be undeclared treasure trove from the discovery in Sutton Hoo. It would have been even more valuable in that form. He was eventually caught making fake Roman gold coins in 2001, and sentenced to ten years in Maidstone Prison. You may guess who the arresting officer was.'

Mowgley's eyes widened. 'Not Chief Inspector Dennis Cullan?'

Georgiev nodded. 'Quite so. And according to the records your old friend and colleague was a fairly regular visitor to Mr Varden during his five-year spell in the prison.'

'Blimey.'

'Indeed,' said Georgiev dryly. 'Blimey.'

Mowgley sat back and raised a hand in salute. 'You've got it all sorted, then, Gosho? Dirty Den saw a business opportunity and roped Varden in to making fake treasure for selling to collectors through the mafia.'

'That's right.'

'Case solved, then?'

'Not quite Jack. I think you have been avoiding mentioning what I think you would call the elephant in the room.'

'Eh? What elephant? What room?'

'I speak of the actions of your friend, Mrs Jenifer Cullan.'

Mowgley looked down and fiddled with his coffee cup. 'We have had other stuff on our minds, but I have been thinking about her.' He looked up at Georgiev. 'Do you know any more than you told me yesterday?'

'Not really.'

'But you think she was involved in what Den was up to?'

'I know she was. In fact, I have reasons to believe she was the key player in the operation.'

'Jen?' Mowgley looked across the table for a moment, then took his packet of *Gauloises* from his inside pocket, shook it and spilled several on the table. Picking one up he put it in his mouth and lit it. He gave a deeply contented sigh, then caught Georgiev's eye and shrugged.

'What are they going to do, deport me?'

'I was not looking at you in censure, Jack; I was hoping you would light one for me.'

Mowgley did and Georgiev drew deeply on the cigarette before letting the smoke dribble from his mouth, 'To begin with we know that Madame Cullan had another passport and was visiting Bulgaria very often.'

'How do you know?'

'Because I had her followed to Sofia airport on several occasions.'

'Well, okay. But that doesn't make her the leader of the gang.'

'No, but I think the fact that she owned the block of luxury apartments that her husband lived in showed she had more than a little influence on him.'

Mowgley's eyes widened and he winced again. 'Okay. But lots of dodgy businessmen put the business in their wife's name.'

'Only if they really trust her - or have no choice.'

'And what about Magda?'

'What about her?' Georgiev sucked on his cigarette, then took it from his mouth and looked at it appreciatively. 'I do not believe Mrs Cullan was jealous, and poor Magda kept her allegedly ex-husband occupied and happy while she got on with the business. I do not think your friend loved her husband, but he was a good front man for the business. This is after all Bulgaria and a man's world.' Georgiev paused, then said: 'And she too had her dalliances.'

'Oh?' Mowgely tried to look disinterested. 'Who, for instance?'

'At least one member of the Varna *mutri*...and she may indeed have had an affair with Commissar Dragov.'

'My God. Wasn't that a bit dangerous, having lovers on each

side?'

'As you know, I am not sure Dragov is on the other side from the *mutri*. But it was a dangerous game, and that is why I think she made plans to get out of it when her customers began to suspect the artefacts she and her husband were selling were not real.'

Mowgley reached for another cigarette. 'You don't think she was involved in Den's killing, do you?'

'No, not at all. His death would have shown her that the game was up and she had to get away. Quickly.'

'So why not just jump on a plane?'

'She had unfinished business here. The apartment block was being sold and there must have been a large amount of money to be moved in cash as well as various accounts in other names.'

'But why get me involved?'

Georgiev held his hands up, palms out. 'That's one of the things you cannot know for sure, and nor can I. But there are several possibilities. As you told me, when Mrs Cullan called your old office she thought you were still in Special Branch. She would probably have thought you could use your contacts and influence to put some pressure on the police here to investigate her husband's disappearance properly. Knowing what she knew, she suspected something bad might have happened to him. And that she might be next. Also, she was all alone and in trouble and I think she thought of you.'

'But what good could I do her here?'

Georgiev smiled. 'Remember, she did not ask you to rush to her side. When you insisted on coming to her aid, she had to think of how best to take advantage of your protective instinct. She was all alone and I think she thought you would be a good escort until she was free to go. I have to say that she may also have wanted it to look as if you were a business associate, not an old friend.'

Mowgley sat back and thought about what Georgiev had said.

'So I was being set up? She thought the mafia might think I was part of or even the key player in the fake ring and knock me off instead of her?'

Georgiev looked uncomfortable. 'The truth is I don't know. Perhaps she was still fond of you and just wanted some support.'

'You don't sound convinced. And what about the kidnapping?'

She would have arranged that in the hope that the *mutri* and I and you would think she had been killed. She had time to start to put things in place before you arrived, or perhaps she had planned it already as a good way to disappear She would have known some suitable freelance criminals, or been able to find them.'

'But surely she didn't have the phoney kidnappers killed?'

Georgiev shook his head. 'I don't think so. I think they were found and made an example of by the people who were after Mrs Cullan.'

'So where do you think she is now? And what about 'John'?'

Georgiev shrugged. 'She could be anywhere in the world. She may even have prepared a place to escape to long before things started to go wrong.'

'And why invent a son?'

Georgiev examined his bandaged fingers, then said: 'Perhaps she thought it would make her seem more vulnerable. Perhaps she thought you might think the boy was yours.'

'Mine?'

'If you think of the age she said he was, it could be possible.'

Mowgley thought about the possibilities, then said: 'And now?'

'Now? Mrs Cullan could be anywhere in the world. She will certainly have enough money to retire and have a good life far away from Bulgaria.'

Mowgley sat back and looked out at the Easyjet plane. An overladen baggage train was snaking across the tarmac, and passengers were filing down the stairs at the front and rear. It always surprised Mowgley that such a big lump of metal so filled with people and things could actually get off the ground.

He turned back and saw that Georgiev was looking at him with sympathetic concern.

'I am sorry to have been the one to tell you that Mrs Cullan was not who you thought she was.'

Mowgley held up one hand as if to nullify the apology. 'No problem,' he said, 'Just think how I would have felt if she had been telling the truth and the mafia had got her.'

~

The announcement echoed around the complex of bars and shops, the sharp-edged female voice bouncing off the hard surfaces of floors, walls and ceilings.

The passengers standing, sitting and laying around Gate 14 got to their feet and hefted their haversacks or got to grips with their on-board bags and cases. Those who had been queuing looked warily around and shifted and shuffled to close ranks to make sure their lines were not breached.

Georgiev and Mowgley stood and looked at each other across the table.

'I hope you have a peaceful flight,' said the inspector. 'It has been a busy time for you.'

'You could say that.' Mowgley picked up his bag and followed Georgiev towards the gate. As they neared the queue a voice called out and the two men stopped and looked back.

It was Ivo Georgiev. He was wearing his para-uniform of tight olive-coloured tee-shirt and camouflage trousers, and carrying a parcel about the size and shape of a pizza delivery box.

Ivo handed it to his father, then held his hand out towards Mowgley. It was the first time he had seen Georgiev's son smile, and, he thought, probably the last.

He took Ivo's hand and tried not to wince. 'I reckon you'll be glad to see the back of me?'

Ivo Georgiev shrugged. 'It has been interesting to see how British policemen react when the going gets hot.'

Mowgley drew himself up and lifted his heels a fraction to look down on the young man. 'You forget I am a former policemen, matey... and an old one. A few years ago I might have been of more help when things got, as you say, hot.'

Inspector Georgiev said something to his son in a tone which indicated a mild rebuke, then handed the parcel to Mowgley.

'It is a souvenir,' he said. 'Not for you, but for one of your lady friends, perhaps.'

'I think that would be 'the' lady friend, Gosho. And she's engaged to someone else. What with one thing and another I seem to have been a bit careless with female friends.'

Georgiev smiled sadly and lifted his shoulders a little. 'It is how things turn out', he said, looking briefly into his own past.

'Some of us are lucky with their relationships, and some not so.'

The two men stood facing each other for a moment, then embraced. It was another first for Mowgley.

'I am sorry you have had such a bad experience of my country,' Georgiev said softly. 'I hope you may feel able to come back some day.'

'Somehow I think I will, Gosho,' Mowgley replied, 'Going by the last week I don't think I could ever get bored here.'

~

'It's a gift. From a Bulgarian friend. A police officer.'

The return flight had been much more peaceful than the outward journey. Even the long hike from plane to Arrivals had been largely jostle-free. All had gone smoothly till Mowgley had taken the option to join the shorter queue for those travellers with biometric passports. For a man who had never managed to cope with getting a loaf of bread through a supermarket self-checkout, it had been an optimistic move and one which was bound to draw attention to himself.

After three failed attempts he was helped through the barrier by a fairly tolerant Border Force Officer. The officer who stepped forward as Mowgley walked through the Blue channel had not been at all tolerant.

'So you're saying your police officer friend gave you this as a present just before you boarded?'

They were sitting in a harshly-lit cubicle beyond the Blue nothing-to-declare channel, and on the desk between them was the box Mowgley had been carrying under his arm. The paper wrapping had been removed and the lid of the plain wooden box was open. Alongside it lay a necklace, bracelet and pair of earrings. The metal had the dull but warm gleam of gold. The earrings were large loops from which were suspended tiny but intricately-detailed pitchers, complete with handles. The necklace was made up of three ropes of intricately articulated gold. The bracelet was a wide and finely chased hoop, studded with green stones.

The officer looked down at the jewellery and then up at Mowgley. 'And he didn't say what was in the box or why he gave it to you?'

'He said it was a souvenir of Bulgaria, and a lady friend might like it.'

The man shook his head and half-smiled as if to convey that he thought Mowgley could have come up with a better story. 'Okay, let me get this right. A friend in a foreign country gave you a present for another friend and you didn't bother to take a peep inside?'

'No.'

'I see.' The man scratched the top of his bald head, then looked at his fingernails. 'Do you have any idea how much ancient gold jewellery is looted and smuggled out of Bulgaria each year?'

'Yes,' said Mowgley levelly, 'I do.' He nodded at the desk. 'But that's not looted treasure, it's a copy and quite legal. Do you think I'd try and smuggle looted treasure through Customs in an old cigar box tucked under my arm?'

The man gave a full smile. 'You'd be surprised at how many people try to get things through without burying them in their baggage. It's called hiding in plain sight.'

He used a pencil to prod the necklace. 'Lovely thing, isn't it? As it's a copy you'll have a receipt of course?'

'No. Had I known what was in there I would have assumed it would be in the box.'

'Ah. So your friend forgot to put it in there?'

'I think his son chose not to put it in there.'

'And why would he do that?'

'As a joke. In case this happened.'

'Some joke eh? Funny sense of humour these Bulgarians must have, eh?'

'Yes,' said Mowgley, 'they do like a bit of fun and games.'

Epilogue

'Are you sure you did not bring them back for me? As a surprise?'

To the best of his recollection it was the first time a woman had pouted plaintively at him, and he could see that Mimi was an expert. It was probably, he thought, something to do with her being French.

'Did I bring what back for you? My dirty washing?' He moved away a little and tried to avoid staring down her cleavage as she leaned over his desk and tapped one of the top drawers.

'The jewels. They are very... tasteful. Did you choose them?' She sounded doubtful and looked at him as if confident what his answer would be.

'No, they were a present from a friend. And hang on a minute. How did you know what was in the drawer? I locked it.'

She repeated the pout. 'I have a spare key. Do you want me to tell you what else you keep in there?'

'No, you're alright.'

'So, if they are not for me, who are they for?'

'A friend.'

'But am I not your friend?'

Mimi leaned over further and he could smell what would undoubtedly be a very expensive perfume.

'Yes, of course, but this is a very old friend.'

'You mean the woman who was your assistant when you were a policeman?'

'Yes, that's right.'

'Hmmm.' Mimi stood up and frowned and shook her head.

'What's the matter. Don't you think she'll like them?'

'Perhaps. But I think they would not suit her. I don't think she is the sort of person who should or would wish to wear gold. And is she not anyway with Colonel Degas?'

Mowgley nodded. 'Yes, but she is still my friend. Can't a man be just friends with a woman?'

She looked at him as if genuinely puzzled. 'Of course not.'

She walked back to her desk and Mowgley was sure she was swinging her hips more than usual.

He opened the drawer, took the box out, lifted the lid and looked at the contents.

After a long wait involving several phone calls to Inspector Georgiev's office and a flood of e-mailed credentials and verifications, Mowgley and the cigar box had been allowed to leave by the openly disappointed official. Since his return, Mowgley had taken the jewellery from the drawer a dozen times. He had moved it around under the desk lamp and run the cool metal of the necklace through his hands. As he had reminded the Customs officer at Gatwick, making replicas of ancient Thracian artefacts was legal. Curiously, the only proviso was that the copies differed from the originals in appearance by at least ten percent. And of course, that they be declared to be copies. Made of real gold and precious stones the copies would be hugely expensive, but still only a tiny fraction of the going rate for the real thing.

He cradled the satisfyingly heavy weight of the necklace in his cupped hand and thought about how much it must be worth and why Georgi Georgiev would give him such an obviously eye-wateringly valuable gift. The obvious assumption was that it was an example of the work of Jerome Varden, perhaps an illegal copy which Gosho had acquired in the course of his investigations. If that were so, by rights it would be the property of the Bulgarian authorities, but it would be typical of Inspector Georgiev to divert it to someone he would feel more deserving. Otherwise, he supposed, it would have been locked away somewhere or end up adorning the wife or mistress of a Bulgarian politician or gangster. Georgiev would see it as small compensation for and a suitable reminder of Mowgley's short but eventful stay in his beautiful but troubled country.

There was also a further possibility. It would be the ultimate irony that, after busting a scam involving fake artefacts masquerading as the real thing, the jewellery on the desk was the real thing masquerading as a fake.

That was so unlikely as not to be worth considering, he thought.

Mowgley put the items back in the cigar box and pushed the thought from his mind as the phone on Mimi's desk purred discreetly.

He saw that she had been watching him toying with the bracelet, and with another reproving pout in his direction she picked up the slimline receiver. '*Bonjour. Ici Services d'Enquêtes Privés Cornec. Puit-je vous aider?* '

After listening for a moment, she said '*Ne quittez pas*,' then pressed a button on the mini-PX system.

'It's for you,' she said, still looking as if she had not forgiven Mowgley for his sin of omission in not presenting the jewellery to her.

'Who is it? What's it about?'

Mimi shrugged. 'I don't know. She says she is a friend and you will take her call.'

Grudgingly, she added 'She speaks good French but is English.'

'Ah. Is it my former colleague? I can tell her you think she should not wear gold.'

The pout returned. 'No, it is not her.

'So, who is it? Did she give a name?'

'Yes. She says her name is Jen.'

~

'Hello Jack'

'Hello Jen.'

Her voice was warm and her tone intimate and light as if her dramatic departure had never happened. 'So how are you, Mog?'

'Still alive, no thanks to you. That's one up on the three people in the van.'

'I had nothing to do with that.'

Mowgley grunted derisively. 'Oh really? That's not what I heard.'

At the other end of the office Mimi stood up, adjusted her skirt, patted her hair and walked towards the door to the street. As she passed she picked up his packet of *Gauloises*, then used two fingers to draw on an imaginary cigarette and blow the smoke his way. He nodded, waited until the door closed

228

behind her and then asked: 'Where are you?'

She giggled almost girlishly. 'Somewhere a long way away. It's nice and warm and the beaches are very sandy.'

'Not the Black Sea coast, though?'

'No.'

He reached for the cigarette packet that wasn't there and tried to keep the pitch of his voice level. 'So how's our son?'

'I never meant you to think that, Jack.'

'So why drop the heavy hints?'

A pause and he could hear her lighting a cigarette and drawing on it and it made him want one even more. She gave a little cough, then said: 'I honestly don't know. It was just a way of getting you to stay, and to care about what happened to me... and us. I panicked.'

'So why did you want me to stay? And can you tell the truth just for once - if you remember what it is.'

'Ouch. The honest truth is that I was alone and frightened.'

'So why not get yourself a bodyguard? You could afford it.'

'I wanted you, Jack. Don't you remember what we had together?'

He groaned theatrically, 'Oh pleeaaase. Is that the best you can do?'

'Alright, I get it. Any more questions you won't believe the answers to?'

'Only a couple. To start with, why are you calling me? And are you pissed?'

Another giggle, then: 'Not really, but it is nearly midnight here. There's a clue for you.' There was a pause and he could hear her taking a drink. 'And the Pisco Sours are excellent. Whoops, there's another clue.'

He didn't respond, and after a pause she said: 'I called because I wanted to speak to you. To try and explain. I thought you might even want to meet up again.'

'Depends where you are.'

'Why are you asking? Would you like to come and see me?'

'No. But I know someone who would.'

The tone of her voice got sharper. 'Ah, the good inspector. Your bromance partner. Tell me, why do you think he would want to know where I am?'

'So he could at least try and get you extradited.'

She sighed breathily. 'You really don't know about Georgiev, do you?'

'What don't I know?'

'The real reason Georgiev wanted to find me. It was to kill me, not rescue me.'

Another pause, then: 'You still don't get it, do you? The inspector was part of it. And his sons. They knew what was going on and like everyone else in the chain they were getting their share. Your seeker after truth and justice was part of it and as dirty as the others...and anyone who threatened the set-up had to go. '

'I don't believe you.'

Another sip and draw on her cigarette, then she said: 'I know you don't. You really can be naïve for someone who's had so much experience of the darker side of human nature, can't you? And do you want to know the real reason I just left without telling you?'

Mowgley shrugged. 'Because you didn't want me tagging along?'

'No, I wanted you to come. But I couldn't trust you.'

'Couldn't trust me?'

'The truth is I thought you might be in on it with Georgiev. After a while in Bulgaria you learn not to take anyone at face value, no matter how convincing they seem.'

Again, Mowgley made no response, and after a long pause she sighed and spoke in a soft, regretful tone like someone who has been wronged but forgives the offender. 'Okay. I can see I'm wasting my time. I suppose that's it, then.'

He nodded at the mouthpiece. 'Yep.'

'Goodbye then. I would say take care of yourself, but you'd think I didn't mean it.' 'You'd be right.'

He waited till he was sure she had broken the connection, then put the phone back on the cradle. He saw that his hand was trembling, and shook his head. Then he reached down, opened the drawer and took out the cigar box. Putting it on the desk, he lifted the lid and looked at the contents and thought of what might have been.

He had just closed the lid when Mimi returned and put his cigarette packet on the desk. 'Are you okay? Who was that? What did she want?'

He reached for the cigarette packet. 'I'm good. It was just someone I used to know.'

She laid a hand on his shoulder. 'It's another half hour to the midi, but we could start early. You look like you need to eat some good food. And perhaps drink a glass of good wine.'

He nodded. 'That's a good idea, mate.'

Mowgley put a cigarette in his mouth and stood up. Mimi looked down at the box and said: 'You should put that somewhere safe and lock it up. The things inside could be worth a lot of money. If they are real.'

He smiled. 'What do you mean "If they're real?"'

She reached down again and stroked the box before picking it up, weighing it in her hand then offering it to him. 'Don't forget I have seen them. They look and feel like gold and are heavy like gold, but there are no markings to say they are. Do you think they are the real thing or a fakery?'

Mowgley shrugged as he took the box and dropped it into the open drawer before offering her his arm in a parody of old-style courtesy. 'Who can say?' he said, 'It's hard to tell what's real and what's fake with a lot of things, isn't it?'

Author's footnote

As far as 'everyday' crime is concerned, Bulgaria is statistically a much safer place to live in than the United Kingdom. Organised crime groups tend not to bother ordinary folk unless they get in the way. However, major criminality and corruption is not unknown, as indicated by these recent media reports:

Seven people have been detained for attempting to sell and buy looted buried treasure. The operation was a 'sting' which was a joint initiative between the DCOC (the Directorate for Combatting Organised Crime) and the State Agency for National Security (SANS). The treasure, which was put on show at a press conference and guarded by heavily-armed and masked police officers, included a solid gold crown for which the asking price alone was a million Euros. The buyers and sellers were Bulgarian, and the meeting was arranged by an undercover SANS officer. It is believed one of the detainees is also a member of SANS.

Authorities in the Bulgarian town of Stara Zagora have seized more than 700 ancient artefacts and arrested two suspects, the country's Ministry of the Interior said in a statement on Thursday. During the operation against illegal seekers and traders of archaeological artefacts on Wednesday, police arrested a 57-year-old man and found in his home some 600 ancient objects of various ages, 25 ancient coins, a metal detector, and a long-range locator for precious metals, the statement said. The second suspect, a 42-year-old man, was arrested on the same day after police officers found in his home four Roman antique objects and 96 identical metal ornaments, probably from a medieval belt. Also found were a metal detector and a long-range locator for precious metals. The investigation is ongoing.

Bulgaria, located on the Balkan Peninsula at the crossroad of different civilizations, has one of the richest archaeological heritages in Europe.

A raid on an hotel outside the town of Varna has exposed a counterfeit printing press and 'bank'. The raid followed the discovery of fake notes in locations around Bulgaria. The total face value of the haul of large-denomination notes was more than eleven million Euros and nearly two million US Dollars. The going rate to customers was six percent of the face value of the Euros, and twenty percent of the face value of the Dollars. The printing press was in action when police arrived and two men were arrested. They are both thought to have connections with organised crime bodies.

Police stopped a SUV carrying more than half a million Bulgarian Leva in cash near Varna yesterday. It is believed that the money may be connected with a VAT fraud run by an organised crime group. So far, more than ten million Leva have been seized.

Senior state officials and at least one government minister and one deputy prime minster are said to be involved in a corruption scheme for acquiring Bulgarian citizenship. Under the scheme, more than 100 people wanted by Interpol paid up to 3000 Euros for the false documentation. Said former Director of Bulgarian Citizenship Katya Mateva: 'This traffic is hidden at the highest level of the State.' Ms Mateva said she had sent 'signals' of the illegal scheme to the Chief Prosecutor, Intelligence bosses and even the Prime Minister Boyko Borisov. No one, she said, reacted.

About the Author

 Whilst seeking a vocation to suit his talents, George East occupied himself as a pipe fitter, welder and plumber, private detective, film and TV extra, club bouncer and DJ, demolition engineer, labourer, bread and lemonade roundsman, brewer's drayman, magazine editor, pickled onion manufacturer, snooker club and hotel manager, publican, failed rock god, TV and radio presenter, PR and marketing honcho, seamstress... and the world's first and probably only professional bed tester. He gained his early knowledge of police procedure and attitudes as a result of a number of encounters with the Law in his extreme youth.

In the 1980s, he gained more of an understanding of and a definite affinity for plain clothes policemen while running an inner-city pub which acted as a local (and once as a murder room) for a whole police station's-worth of CID officers.

Printed in Great Britain
by Amazon